Praise for *The Peculiar Miracles of Antoinette Martin*

"*The Peculiar Miracles of Antoinette Martin* is the kind of book that invites you home, sits you down at the kitchen table, and feeds you something delicious and homemade. You will want to stay in this world, where new relationships bloom out of broken ones, sisters find one another again, and miracles really do occur. *Antoinette* will stick in your head like a beautiful song."
—Tiffany Baker, bestselling author
of *The Little Giant of Aberdeen County*

"The little girl at the center of Stephanie Knipper's magical new novel, *The Peculiar Miracles of Antoinette Martin*, is afflicted with the gift of differences. As she moves with silent grace through daily life on a flower farm, she proves to be the point around which all of her family's troubles reconverge . . . Antoinette's internal dialogues prove to be [the novel's] loveliest passages, as she seeks the music in the word around her and reaches out to smooth the particular tunes of the people she loves most."
—*Foreword Reviews*

"From her lifelong reading appetite and education, Stephanie Knipper quickly grasped a literary fundamental: Write what you know. To bring about her first novel, Knipper blended familiar elements—Kentucky, flowers, motherhood and life with children with physical and mental challenges. But then she added a touch of magic and produced *The Peculiar Miracles of Antoinette Martin*, a story that explores the depths of compassion and love."
—*The Cincinnati Enquirer*

"*The Peculiar Miracles of Antoinette Martin* is a lovely story of family and love, with a few miracles mixed in . . . Stephanie Knipper might be writing about one autistic miracle worker, but there is an underlying message that Rose's answer might just apply to everyone."   —*New York Journal of Books*

"This fast-paced story of sisterhood with a hint of magic (and a hint of romance) will appeal to fans of Sarah Addison Allen."
        —*Booklist*

"*The Peculiar Miracles of Antoinette Martin* transports the reader to the beautiful Eden Farms and into the lives of sisters, Rose and Lily, as they grapple with life's biggest challenges: love and death. Stephanie Knipper's rich prose moves us through Rose, Lily, and Rose's daughter, Antoinette's, points of view to weave this beautiful portrait of a family as they grow through life's difficult moments."   —*The Huffington Post*

"A haunting and beautiful story."   —*The Oklahoman*

The Peculiar Miracles of Antoinette Martin

The

Peculiar
Miracles
of
Antoinette
Martin

A NOVEL

Stephanie Knipper

ALGONQUIN BOOKS OF
CHAPEL HILL
2017

Published by
ALGONQUIN BOOKS OF CHAPEL HILL
Post Office Box 2225
Chapel Hill, North Carolina 27515-2225

a division of
WORKMAN PUBLISHING
225 Varick Street
New York, New York 10014

LIBRARY OF CONGRESS CATALOGING-IN-PUBLICATION DATA
Names: Knipper, Stephanie, author.
Title: The peculiar miracles of Antoinette Martin /
a novel by Stephanie Knipper.
Description: First edition. | Chapel Hill, North Carolina :
Algonquin Books of Chapel Hill, 2016. | "Published simultaneously
in Canada by Thomas Allen & Son Limited."
Identifiers: LCCN 2016006236 | ISBN 9781616204181 (HC)
Subjects: LCSH: Autistic children—Fiction. | Gifted children—
Fiction. | Healers—Fiction. | Sisters—Fiction.
Classification: LCC PS3611.N5744 P43 2016 | DDC 813/.6—dc23
LC record available at http://lccn.loc.gov/2016006236

ISBN 9781616207359 (PB)

10 9 8 7 6 5 4 3 2 1
First Paperback Edition

For my daughter, Grace.

People always say you're lucky to have us as parents, but I know the truth. We're the lucky ones, because we have you.

Hug. Tap, tap, tap.

I love you too.

The Peculiar Miracles of Antoinette Martin

ROSE'S JOURNAL
April 2013

———+———

MY DAUGHTER, ANTOINETTE, whispers in her sleep. Real words. Tonight when I hear her voice, I rush upstairs, but I'm too late. She is quiet. And the sounds could have been anything. The wind. An owl. Crickets.

She lies on her side. Her right hand stretches toward the doorway, toward me, as if even in sleep I'm the sun she rotates around.

I reach for her too. But I don't enter her room.

When she sleeps, I can pretend I don't notice her eyes, a finger's breadth too far apart. Her arms are relaxed, not held tight against her shoulders as they are much of the day. Her white-blonde hair, still newborn fine, fans out behind her like a dandelion puff, or as if she were running and the wind caught it.

The window is open, and a breeze flutters the sheer white curtains. It's the first week of April, but already the air is so warm the tulips are sprouting. Kentucky is like that. Unpredictable. Tonight is dark, but here in the country, street lights don't obscure the stars.

I close my eyes and summon a dream. In it, Antoinette sprints through the farm, fingers brushing the daffodils and tulips. Her legs are strong, pounding the dirt like any other ten-year-old girl. But this image ignores the child she is. In a more accurate vision I see her walking toward me, marionette-like, arms cocked, hands curled toward her chest, knees bending and popping with each step.

I move into the past, pulling up memories of us sleeping curled into each other as if still sharing the same body. Swaying in time to field sparrow songs. Dancing under a shower of lavender petals in the drying barn.

She shifts, turning toward the window. Outside I envision the fields bursting with white tulip buds. It's too early for them, but stranger things have happened.

My sister, Lily, used to be fascinated by the Victorian language of flowers, memorizing the meanings for each plant we grew on the farm. It was a game to us. She scattered bouquets around the house, and I tried to guess her message. Daffodils represented new beginnings. Coneflowers were for strength and health.

And white tulips were for forgiveness and remembrance.

My heart stutters, and a familiar pressure builds in my chest. I breathe deeply, counting each beat. When my body calms, I look at my daughter.

A strand of hair sticks to her cheek. I walk into the room to free it, but she turns away from me and curls into a ball. I stop, unwilling to wake her, letting her linger a bit longer in dreams, safe in a place where I can't hurt her.

That will come soon enough.

Chapter One

Antoinette Martin stood in the kitchen, staring at the alarm above the back door. The red light was not on, which meant it wouldn't scream and wake her mother if she opened the door. She could walk in the garden.

Pops of joy burst through her body. She bounced on her toes, bare feet slapping against the old oak floor. The smooth wood felt like creek water in July. A happy thought. She bounced again.

When her body calmed, she reached for the doorknob, then hesitated. She and her mother lived on a commercial flower farm in Redbud, Kentucky. Though most of their fifty acres were cleared and given over to flower fields, thick woods rimmed the back edge of their property. Antoinette was not supposed to go outside alone. It was easy to get hurt on a farm.

She mashed her nose against the cool glass of the kitchen door window. Outside, she didn't need music or art to block the white noise that engulfed her. The groan of the refrigerator; the swish, swish of the washer; the hum of the air conditioner. Outside, the land sang, and that was better than the Mozart and Handel compositions their neighbor Seth Hastings played on his violin.

At night, Antoinette would sit on the back porch of their farmhouse listening while Seth played the violin, or she would page through her mother's art books. She could name Bochmann's *Lark Ascending* from the first trill of the violin. She could close her eyes and re-create the crooked grin of Leonardo da Vinci's *Mona Lisa* or the slope of the hill in Wyeth's *Christina's World*, brushstroke by brushstroke in her mind.

Unusual for a ten-year-old, but then very little was usual for Antoinette.

The sunlight shining through the door was sharp. Tears filled her eyes, and she screwed them shut. She felt tied up inside, as if her muscles were too tight. The sun still glowed red behind her eyelids, but the hurt was gone and that helped her decide. She needed music to calm down.

With her mind emptied of everything else, she forced her arm outward until her fingertips brushed the flaked paint on the door. It felt sharp against her skin, and she almost recoiled. But when would the alarm be off again?

Summoning control, she flapped with one hand and pushed the door with the other.

The door opened with a sigh, and the light fell harder on her face. With her eyes closed she leaned into the sun, wishing it could draw her outside. Controlling her body was sometimes difficult, but that morning she moved like a ballerina, swiveling her hips and sliding through the door like a ribbon of silk.

On the porch she threw her arms open, ready to fly to the sun. Then she listened. The land sang to those who stood still long enough to hear it.

People had songs too, but Antoinette needed to touch them to hear their music. Sometimes she grabbed her mother's hand,

and the low, sweet sound of a pan flute filled her body. When that happened, Antoinette felt like she could do anything. Even speak.

Today the outside world sounded mournful, like the oboe's part in *Peter and the Wolf*. Antoinette wiggled. She almost opened her eyes, but she thought better of it; if she did, she would be lost. Her brain would lock on to the blades of grass, and she would start counting. One, two, three . . . four hundred, four hundred one, four hundred two. The counting would trap her for hours.

She kept her eyes closed as she climbed down from the porch. A breeze snaked around her ankles, making her nightgown dance. She laughed a high-pitched giggle that bubbled up from her throat. If she raised her arms, she might be light enough to fly. She lifted her hands, then brought them down hard enough to clap her thighs.

The flagstone path would lead her to the flower fields, but today she wanted more than the feel of stone beneath her feet. She left the path and pushed her toes into the soil. The ground buzzed, a tingle of electricity that vibrated up her legs, calming her muscles so that on the way to the garden she didn't bounce or flap, so that her legs didn't fly out from under her.

She walked until her feet bumped against a ridge of soil that marked the start of the daffodil field. From her bedroom window she could see the bright yellow heads nodding in the sunlight, but out here she could *feel* them.

She squatted and pushed her hands into the loamy soil. It slid from her fingers, coating her nails and the creases of her small hands. She inhaled, filling her lungs with the scents of the garden: soil, compost, and new green grass.

With her hands in the dirt, the music was louder. A chorus of woodwinds flooded her body: clarinets, flutes, and bassoons. But the tempo was too slow and some of the notes were off. Sharp in one place, flat in another. Her heart pounded in her ears, and her arms tensed. She needed to flap, but she forced herself to stay still while a picture formed in her mind, a picture of a bulb bound by clay soil, and a plant weakened by root bores.

Antoinette hummed, increasing the tempo and correcting the notes. When everything was right, she stopped. Her body was calm now, but she slumped to the ground, exhausted. Bits of mulch pricked her cheek, but she didn't move. She breathed deep, listening to the robins calling from the nearby woods.

"Antoinette?"

At first she didn't hear her name; she was lost in the sensations around her. Then a rough hand fell against her neck. The touch sent a jolt through her body, and she fell back, her eyes wide with fear.

"Sorry. Sorry," a man said as he snatched his hand away.

She tried to sit up, but her muscles weren't working yet.

"Antoinette." The man was calm. "Antoinette. What's wrong? It's Seth. Look at me. Are you okay?"

He touched her cheek and turned her head toward him. When she leaned into his calloused hand, her heart stopped racing and she relaxed. Seth was as much a constant in her life as her mother. Like her, he understood that speaking wasn't the only way to communicate.

He crouched in front of her, the tips of his long dark hair tickling her cheek. "Can you tell me what's wrong?" he asked.

Her arm felt heavy, but she pointed over his shoulder, back home where the blue clapboard farmhouse rose beyond the sea of daffodils.

"Home?" he asked. "You want to go home?"

She pointed and opened her mouth. *Home.* That's what she wanted to say. The word would be whisper light if she could get it out.

Seth slid his arms under her body. She picked a daffodil before he lifted her. The commercial fields weren't for home flower picking, but the yellow daffodil would make her mother happy.

Seth cradled her as he walked back to the house, and she melted into him. He smelled like green grass and tobacco. Through his thin T-shirt, she felt the steady thump of his heart, which was its own form of music.

THE KITCHEN DOOR popped open with a thud. Antoinette raised her head from Seth's arms and saw that the room was empty. Her mother was probably still asleep.

"Rose?" Seth called. There was no answer. The air inside the house was heavy and quiet. He started down the long hallway that led to the bedrooms.

Through an open door, Antoinette saw her mother, sitting in one of the two blue chairs by the window overlooking the back field, her journal open on her lap. She turned when Seth knocked on the doorframe.

Focusing on faces was difficult for Antoinette; they changed every second, tiny muscles shifting with each smile or frown. One person could wear hundreds of faces. But Antoinette forced herself to study her mother's face. Her lips were rimmed with blue, and deep circles sat under her eyes. Her short blonde hair stuck out in all directions and shadows highlighted her gaunt face.

"I found her outside in the daffodil field," Seth said.

Her mother closed the journal and stood. "She's been wanting to go outside, but I've been so tired." She leaned over Antoinette who was still snug in Seth's arms. "You always were persistent."

Antoinette held out the daffodil.

Her mother smiled when she took it. "Daffodils symbolize new beginnings," she said to Seth. "From Lily's flower book. I can't believe I remember."

Antoinette felt Seth flinch. "Hard to forget." His rough voice was tinged with something that sounded like regret. "She carried that book everywhere."

Antoinette was sandwiched between the two of them. *Content.* The word floated up from somewhere inside her. Her entire body felt warm. She stretched toward her mother, wanting to hear her song.

Her mother drew back. "You need to sleep," she said, her lips forming a sad smile.

"She was lying among the daffodils," Seth said. "Last night, I noticed some of them had browned around the edges. I planned to harvest them today, but then this morning they were fresh when I got there. Antoinette was half asleep in the middle of them. She didn't hear me until I was right next to her." He spoke slowly and his voice was heavy with meaning, but Antoinette was too tired to figure out what he was trying to say.

He sat in one of the chairs and shifted Antoinette so that his arm was behind the crook in her neck.

"She's so tiny," her mother said as she sat across from Seth. "It still surprises me how heavy she gets after a while."

Seth laughed. Antoinette liked the sound. She closed her eyes and let the noise wash over her. She was too tired to flap her hands, but she twitched her fingers against Seth's arm. *Happy.*

She usually was happy around Seth. He could be abrupt with others, but he was always kind to Antoinette and her mother.

Once, some boys at the farmers' market had giggled at Antoinette as she stretched up on her toes and walked in circles under the Eden Farms tent. When Seth heard them, he stopped unloading flats of impatiens, walked over to Antoinette, and put a hand on her shoulder. In his presence, the tension left her body, allowing her to stop walking and stand still.

Seth didn't say a word. He just glared at the boys until they started fidgeting. Then one by one, they apologized.

"They're kids," he said after they scattered. "They don't know what they're doing, but it hurts anyway."

He had been right. It did hurt. Every time someone stared at Antoinette a little too long or crossed the street to avoid her, a small, bruised feeling bloomed in her chest.

Knowing that Seth, along with her mother, understood how she felt eased the hurt a little.

Thinking of her mother, Antoinette cracked her eyes open, and watched the slow rise and fall of her mother's chest. Despite her fatigue, she struggled toward her mother. If she could hold her mother's hand, everything would be all right. She imagined her mother's song—the notes of a pan flute, smooth and round as river rocks.

"Not now, Antoinette," her mother said.

Antoinette didn't stop trying. As she struggled to sit up, she stared at her mother's tapered fingers. At the green-and-purple bruise on the back of her mother's hand. It was from the IV she had in the emergency room last week.

Seth wrapped her tight in his arms and leaned back. Now she was even farther from her mother. "Your mom needs some rest."

Antoinette shook her head hard, making her hair lash against her cheek. *Mommy!* If she could say the word, she was sure her mother would respond.

"She can't do this much longer," her mother said, her voice cracking. "And I . . . well, it's not like I'm going to get better."

Seth sighed. After several long seconds he said, "It's time to call Lily. You can't keep avoiding her, Rose."

Antoinette strained against his arms, but he was too strong. The exhaustion that stole through her body trapped her, making her eyes shut as if tiny weights were attached to her eyelashes. She was tired. So tired.

"I don't know," her mother said. She sounded small and scared. "It's been six years. Antoinette was too much for Lily as a four-year-old. It's not like things have improved. And the way I left things with Lily . . . what if she won't come?"

Antoinette fought to open her eyes but couldn't. Her body grew heavier and heavier.

She heard Seth: "The three of us aren't kids anymore, Rose. Lily's your sister. The girl I know will come if you ask."

Antoinette couldn't fight it any longer. She sank into Seth's arms as sleep overtook her.

Chapter Two

L ily Martin lived a cautious life. She looked to numbers. Math was consistent: two plus two equaled four. Always. There was no way to make it something else. Rearrange the numbers, write the problem horizontally or vertically, and the answer was always the same. Four. Equations had solutions, and their predictability made her feel calm, settled.

Except today.

She had spent most of the day reformatting death tables for the life insurance company she worked for. They weren't really called death tables. *Life expectancy table* was the correct term, but what else did you call a collection of data that predicted when someone would die?

Lily headed the actuary department, and it was her responsibility to know when someone was likely to die. A healthy, male, nonsmoker could expect to live 76.2 years, whereas a smoker's life expectancy was reduced by 13.2 years. A thirty-two-year-old woman with congestive heart failure—well, she was uninsurable.

The death tables fed the rating engine that supplied price quotes for insurance policies. Over the weekend, the rates for smokers and nonsmokers had been switched until someone in the

IT department realized that a worm had slipped through their firewall and flipped the data.

Lily came in to work that Monday and spent the morning fielding calls from the CEO and the head of IT. At noon, after death had been restored to its rightful position in the insurance world, she grabbed her laptop and left, planning to finish working from home.

Upon arriving there, she opened the door to her study and set her computer on the desk. Sunlight filtered through the two large windows. While she waited for the laptop to boot up, she opened the windows. A yellow finch sang in the redbud tree outside. From her childhood study of the Victorian language of flowers, she knew redbuds symbolized new life, perfect for a tree that bloomed in spring.

She stared out the window, and for just a moment she was not in her house on the south side of the Ohio River; she was back at Eden Farms, in Redbud, Kentucky, where she grew up. April was her favorite time there. The land was waking, and the air tasted like hope.

Covington, where Lily now lived, was in northern Kentucky, on the banks of the Ohio River. The land there was steep hills and deep valleys, not mountainous like Appalachia in eastern Kentucky but different enough from the town where she grew up that she often felt she had moved across country instead of only two hours north.

Redbud was in central Kentucky, just south of Lexington. The land there was draped in Kentucky bluegrass and rolled like soft ocean waves, much of it decorated with white-plank fences that surrounded the area's sedate Thoroughbred farms. Nestled among them, Eden Farms was a burst of color. In summer, the fields behind their farmhouse were a crazy quilt of purple, pink, yellow, white, and red. For Lily, it was a wonderland, and she and her sister, Rose, used to pretend they were fairies, the fields their kingdom.

Outside her house a car honked, and Lily came back to the present. She pressed her fingers hard against the windowsill. Nothing good came of dwelling on lost things. She bit her lip as she turned from the window. Covington was nowhere near New York or Chicago in size, but it was a far cry from the country, where everyone lived acres apart. In Covington, if she stood in her side yard and stretched out her arms, she could touch her house with one hand and her neighbor's with the other.

She lived in the city's historic district, and her house was two hundred years old. The floors sloped in places and the yard was postage stamp size, but she had transformed the ramshackle place into a warm, inviting home. Here in the study, the walls were the color of sun-warmed soil, and three Kentucky landscapes hung above her desk. Her sister had painted them at age fifteen. The colors were too bright and the proportions were off, but Lily liked their slight awkwardness. It reminded her of Rose at that age, lanky but beautiful, child and adult at the same time.

A purple potted orchid and a small framed picture decorated Lily's desk. In the photograph, Rose and Lily stood with their arms wrapped around each other, holding on as if they'd never let go. Their cheeks were pressed together and their hair—Rose's light blonde and Lily's deep brown—twirled over their shoulders. Seth Hastings had snapped the picture right before Rose left for college.

At the thought of Seth, Lily clenched her jaw and quickly looked away. Losing him shouldn't hurt after all these years, but it did.

Focus on work, she thought. She sat in front of her laptop, and her stomach grumbled.

"If you'd let me take you to lunch like a normal person, you wouldn't make such awful noises." The voice startled her, sending her heart to her throat.

Her neighbor, Will Grayson, leaned against the doorframe. He slumped into the wall as if he couldn't hold himself up, reminding Lily of how he had looked when he'd been taking morphine. Almost a year had passed since his last chemo treatment, but from his appearance today she guessed he still had some pills left.

Automatically, her mind went to the death tables. A thirty-four-year-old male in remission from lung cancer had a five-year life expectancy of 13.4 percent.

Thankfully, Will stood solidly among that 13.4 percent.

Several months ago, she had accompanied him to his oncologist's office for a follow-up visit. The doctor smiled at them. "I don't get to say this often enough," he said. "Your CT scan is clear. We got it all."

Lily thought she might slide to the floor in relief, but Will was nonplussed. He nodded once and stood. "Cancer's got nothing on me," he said. That's what she liked about him—he made his total self-interest charming.

Now she looked up at him and smiled. "I thought you were finished with that stuff," she said, referring to the powerful pain pills he had taken when he was ill.

His dark hair shot up in surprising directions and smile lines feathered out around his blue eyes. He was an emergency room doctor at St. Elizabeth Hospital. She knew that before his illness he'd had the habit of spending an hour each day in front of the mirror, even on his days off. She'd once asked why he dressed like a member of the Young Republicans club.

Postcancer Will still wore khakis and button-down shirts, but on his days off he didn't tuck in his shirttails, and he no longer smoothed every hair into place. Sometimes Lily caught him taking deep breaths as if testing his lung capacity. When he finished, he'd close his eyes and smile, seemingly content in a way she'd never seen before.

He tugged his shirt cuffs over his still-thin wrists. "I'm not working, and it's too good to waste. Want some?" He fished the prescription bottle from his pocket and tossed it to her.

She tried to catch it but missed. The bottle smacked into her nose. "No," she said, leaning over to pick it up.

He shrugged as he took the bottle. "Suit yourself, but you're missing out. How about lunch? I'm starving."

She shook her head. "I have to work."

"Aw, come on. What's a guy got to do to impress you?"

They went through this routine at least once a week. Will wasn't specifically interested in *her*; he was interested in anything female. Since she fell into that category, he occasionally slipped into Romeo mode with her until she reminded him that she wasn't interested. Which was true. Most of the time, anyway. Sometimes her heart sped when his dark hair flopped into his eyes. Then she forced herself to count the girls she had seen leaving his house that month. Six in March.

"When are you going back to work?" she asked.

A month ago, Will had taken a leave of absence. "To focus on the things in life that really matter," he had said.

Now he crossed the room and spun her chair around till she faced him. Then he leaned down, putting his hands on the armrests. He was so close she felt his breath against her lips. "As soon as you agree to go out with me," he said.

She saw flecks of lilac in his blue eyes and felt her cheeks flush. "Did you get the coffee grounds I left on your stoop?" she asked.

"Thanks. Worked wonders for the azaleas." He pointed at her computer, which now sported the blue screen of death, warning her that a data loss was in process. "I think you've got a problem."

"Shit!" She turned away and jabbed the power-down button then waited for the screen to black out. "What do you want, Will? The key's for emergencies, not your daily drop in." He flinched slightly, and she immediately wished she could take back her words.

"Ah, cut to the quick. You're cruel, Lily Martin. Did anyone ever tell you that?"

She glanced at the picture on her desk then looked away, hoping he didn't notice. She had more photos, but this was the only one she displayed. Under her bed, she had eight boxes of snapshots. On nights when missing Rose made her head ache, Lily stared at the pictures until she fell asleep, surrounded by pieces of the life she used to lead.

She also had baby pictures of her niece, Antoinette. Sometimes Lily tried to imagine what the little girl might look like now, but she never could. As a baby, Antoinette had been different. Trying to picture her as a ten-year-old was impossible.

Will caught her glance at the picture. He snatched it up.

"Give it to me, Will." She held her hand out, but he jumped back.

"You were cute then, but I like you better now," he said. "Even that little wrinkle you get in your forehead when you're mad."

"I don't have a wrinkle." She raised a hand to her forehead and pressed.

"Yes, you do. Right here." He removed her hand and smoothed his fingers over her skin. "There. All gone now."

His fingers were soft, and she relaxed under his touch. He put the picture back on the desk. "Your sister doesn't have anything on you."

That was a lie. Rose was the beautiful one.

"Don't get me wrong," he said. "She's pretty in an obvious way. But who'd want a blonde, blue-eyed Barbie doll when they could have a girl with green eyes and skin like porcelain? Don't sell yourself short."

Lily looked up at Will. His eyes were the blue of the cornflowers that grew wild in the fields back home. No wonder he never had trouble finding women.

"Not funny, Will. Why are you here?" She didn't like being teased.

He grinned, flashing his perfect teeth. "It's an emergency. I'm out of coffee."

"There's a Starbucks down the street," she said as she turned around and shut her laptop.

"But then I wouldn't get to spend the day with you." He rested his chin on her shoulder. "Well? Do you have any?"

"It's in the kitchen, where it usually is."

He kissed her cheek then walked into the kitchen, looking for the coffee she kept on the counter next to the coffeemaker.

Will made her heart flutter and her palms sweat. She had often imagined his lips pressed against hers. Part of her wanted to leap head first into a relationship with him. But Lily never jumped into a pool without first testing the water. That part of her—the cautious side—told her to wait. Will was her best friend, and she didn't want to risk losing him.

She dropped her head to the desk and slowed her breaths, counting each one. The counting had started when she was a child. It grounded her when she was anxious: ceiling tiles, picture frames, flower petals. She counted them all.

When she was younger, and hadn't yet learned to count under her breath, kids at school christened her "the Count." Every day on the way into school, Lily counted the dirty white tiles between the entrance and the library. Her classmates would strike mock Dracula poses, pretend cloaks across their faces, and they'd yell out random numbers.

The teasing continued until one day when Lily was in fifth grade. After school ended for the day, some students encircled her while she waited for the bus. They shouted numbers at her, laughing when tears accumulated in her eyes, until her friend, and neighbor, Seth Hastings, shoved through the crowd. Seth grabbed the ringleader, threw him to the ground, and punched the boy in the gut. Then Seth hooked his arm through Lily's and walked her to the bus. When the stress of the situation made Lily start counting, Seth added his voice to hers. After that, Seth walked her to the bus every day, and no one called her "the Count" again.

Lily had since learned to count silently, but she hadn't been able to stop the habit. She had reached the number seven when Will called from the kitchen. "I can't find the coffee."

She closed her eyes and murmured, "Eight,"—she never stopped on an odd number—before answering. "It's on the counter."

"Lils! It's not out here."

His words were long and rounded, but if she didn't know him, she wouldn't realize he was high. She wondered if he ever went into work at the hospital that way. She pictured him in a white lab coat, sneaking into a supply closet and shaking a few pills into his hand. Maybe thinking you were invincible was a trait all doctors shared. Or maybe it was just Will.

"It's not here!" he said again.

She pushed back from her desk. Today wasn't a good day for work anyway. Every year, as spring beat back the winter gray, a sense of depression stole over her. Redbuds bloomed and daffodils poked their heads from beds that lined the streets. It was beautiful but felt somehow artificial, and it made her miss the farm.

Rounding the corner to the kitchen, she nearly ran into an open cabinet. All twelve doors were open. "I can't find it," he said.

She crossed the room, closing doors as she went, and picked up the bag next to the coffeemaker.

"Thanks." He measured out even scoops. "You want some?"

She nodded and grabbed tomatoes and cheese from the refrigerator. Since she couldn't work, now was as good a time as any for lunch.

As she put the meal together, she glanced out the window. Off of the kitchen was a small wooden deck with rickety stairs leading to a brick patio that filled what passed for her backyard. It was surrounded by a high stone wall. In late spring and early summer, white clematis and New Dawn roses scrambled up the wrought iron lattices covering the wall. It was beautiful and practical at the same time, providing a small barrier between herself and her neighbors. On one side was Will and, on the other, an artist who made kinetic sculptures out of Campbell's soup cans. While she loved her old brick house, living so close to other people was difficult for her, even after six years.

Everything was crowded here. The sidewalks were cracked and not quite wide enough. When passing someone, she had to twist sideways to avoid touching them. Birds fought to be heard over the constant rumble of cars and buses. Plants jumbled together, vying for the little pockets of soil that served as yards around the houses.

Lily carried the plates outside to the bistro table on the deck. Will brought their coffee. He placed her cup next to her plate, but he didn't sit. He paced, sipping his coffee and shading his eyes. There was a slight breeze, but the sun warmed the last of the winter air. Aside from the squeak of a rotating sculpture in the artist's yard and the street traffic, the day was quiet.

"How can you stand it out here? It's so bright," he said as he shoved a piece of cheese into his mouth.

She shrugged and held her face to the wind, feeling the coolness on her cheeks, drawing memories of her younger self to mind.

"That's right, you were a farm girl." Will laughed. "I wish I had seen that. Bet you were cute with your brown hair in braids and pig slop on your feet."

"It was a flower farm. There weren't any pigs." She closed

her eyes and concentrated on the red glow of the sun behind her eyelids.

"I can see you now. Barefoot in the dirt. A chicken in each hand."

With her eyes still closed, she said, "I told you, it was a flower farm. No chickens. No pigs." Her mind, though, was on the numbers of Eden Farms: the percentage she once owned (half), the percentage she now owned after signing her share over to Rose when their parents died (zero), the number of years that had passed since she had been home (over six), and the number of years since she'd last spoken to her sister (also over six).

Being apart from home, and from Rose, was like missing a limb, but going back would be like trying to sew an arm back on.

"Why won't you tell me about it? And when was the last time you went back?" Will asked, pushing her deeper into memories. "It's home. You know, that place where if you show up, they have to take you in?"

No, Lily thought. *They don't. And most likely, they wouldn't.*

Will was still talking. "It's half yours isn't it? Just because your sister's crazy doesn't mean you have to stay away."

"She's not crazy. She's mad at me." It wasn't half hers anymore either. Lily pushed her plate back and stood. She and Rose once had been sisters in every sense of the word, when they were young and naive enough to believe that something like blood could tie you together forever. What they didn't know then was that it could just as easily push you apart.

"Which in my book makes her crazy. How could anyone be mad at you? Come on. It's not far. Let's hop in the car and surprise her."

There was a pile of terra-cotta pots and concrete urns under the deck Lily had been meaning to go through. Most were cracked or broken in some way, but she hoped some could be salvaged. As Will prattled on about the farm, she stood and walked down the stairs to the patio.

After a moment, Will followed. The deck boards creaked under his feet. "You know I don't mean anything." He ducked under the deck. "I bet you were cute then. Barefoot in the dirt."

She reached into the jumble of pots and picked up a blue ceramic container. A thin crack slashed across its surface. She turned the pot over: the crack went all the way through. She put it aside. The next pot she removed from the pile had a thin coat of green mold on the outside but no cracks. Definitely salvageable. Inside the house, the phone rang, but she made no move to answer it.

Will took the pot from her and set it aside. He captured her hands and said, "I'm sorry. I promise I'll be good this time. Now come on back up and sit with me." In the sunlight she could see how dilated his pupils were. They squeezed out most of the blue in his eyes.

"Come on, Lils. It's a beautiful day. We'll sit on the deck, and I won't mention your crazy sister at all." Lily struggled not to smile, but he saw it anyway. "That's the Lily I know." This time when he tugged her hand, she let him lead her back up the stairs.

He guided her to the far edge of the deck and leaned against the rail. "See," he said, "I can be good."

"There's a first for everything," Lily said with a smile.

Will bumped his shoulder against hers. The gesture was friendly and intimate at the same time. "I just want you to be happy."

Lily looked out across her small backyard. The roses had

started to leaf out, but it would be a month or more before they bloomed. "I am happy," she said.

"I know you better than that. I see it every spring—you miss home."

He was right, but Lily didn't acknowledge it. Instead, she said, "Why does it matter so much to you?"

He twined his fingers through hers. "You should know the answer to that. You matter to me. What's important to you is important to me."

Her hand grew hot under his.

"Plus," he said, "I've got a thing for farm girls. You in a pair of cutoffs with your hair in braids." He grinned. "I'd die a happy man."

Lily's heart quickened. She was leaning into him when the phone rang again. Startled, she disentangled her hand from his and ran inside to answer the phone. She needed to get away before she did something she'd regret.

"Hello?" she said, out of breath.

Silence. Then, in a voice so soft it didn't sound real, "Lily?"

At first she thought she was imagining things.

"Hello, Lily? Are you there?" Rose's voice was the same, but beneath her soft Kentucky accent was an undercurrent of fatigue.

The surprise of hearing her sister's voice was so great, Lily's knees wobbled. Her response came out like a question. "I'm here?"

AFTER THE CONVERSATION ended, Lily remained seated on the cold tile floor, holding the phone, until a robotic operator voice said that if she would like to make a call, she should hang up and dial again.

Will was still on the deck when she went outside, but he seemed far away somehow. She felt odd, like she stood in a bubble. Everything was distorted.

"You okay?" he asked, surprising her with his concern. "What is it?" He closed the space between them and put his hands on her shoulders.

She closed her eyes, wishing she could hide from what she had to say. "That was Rose, my sister?" Again, it came out like a question. "She has congestive heart failure. She developed peripartum cardiomyopathy when she was pregnant. Most women recover from it. She didn't. I had assumed she'd be okay. She's not."

Rose had already outlived the statistics Lily knew.

Will brushed his hand across her cheek. "A transplant—"

Lily shook her head. "She has pulmonary hypertension. She doesn't qualify."

Blinking hard against the tears that stung her eyes, Lily said, "My sister is dying." The words suddenly made it real, and she began to cry. Will reached out to hug her; this time, she didn't pull away. She buried her face in his shoulder, her tears darkening his rough shirt. She could still hear Rose's voice: "I need you to come home."

ROSE'S JOURNAL
March 2003

———✦———

FEAR HAS A taste.

I'm sitting at our scarred kitchen table, tulip and daffodil bulbs lined up in front of me. I should be working on my senior portfolio. It's spring break, and I graduate in seven weeks. Instead, I'm writing in my journal and gulping lemonade, trying to wash the taste of copper pennies from my mouth.

My baby is due in late May.

My. Baby. I picture myself sailing across the stage at graduation, my black gown billowing like a circus tent around my belly.

Yesterday, when we arrived home, Lily dropped our bags by the kitchen door, then ran outside and clambered down the porch steps.

"Not going to give your mom a hug?" our mom asked. She stood in the kitchen waiting for us. It was March, but already her skin was dark from working in the fields. Her nails were bright red. Years of pushing seeds into the ground and ripping out weeds left them permanently stained. She always wore nail polish.

Lily glanced over her shoulder. The wind lifted her long brown hair. She looked like something that sprang from the ground. "In a minute. I've got to check something in the green-house first."

She returned holding a bouquet of herbs. One plant had airy, fernlike leaves, the other, small scalloped leaves. "Fennel and coriander," she said as she presented them to me. "Strength and hidden worth." She smiled as if I were someone worth looking up to, instead of a pregnant college girl abandoned by her baby's father.

Now I pick up a daffodil bulb and run my fingers over its smooth white flesh. The kitchen is the best place to work. In early morning, light fills the room. I can pretend I'm in an art studio on campus, my stomach still flat, my plans to travel to Italy after graduation intact. In those moments, I'm not returning home to work on the farm to support my daughter—I am an artist.

Briefly, my stomach muscles contract, and I can't breathe. "False contractions. They're called Braxton Hicks," my obstetrician had said at my last visit. He claimed they didn't hurt. He was wrong.

When my muscles unclench, the taste of copper pennies returns. I take a drink of lemonade, but it doesn't help.

I try to focus on the daffodil bulb I'm supposed to be sketching for my portfolio. Earlier, I slipped one of Dad's garden knives through the bulb's brown papery outer layer. I undressed it, removing the paper scales. Then I cut it in half, exposing the flower bud.

Most people don't realize that a tiny plant lies inside of the bulb, already germinating. I plan to create a series of drawings that capture flowers in various stages of germination.

The flower bud is folded over on itself. I set down the bulb and hold my arm out with my thumb up. I squint, aligning the tip of my thumb with the top of the first leaf. I measure the stem against the base of my thumb. The plant is a green so pale it's almost white.

I start drawing. I make my strokes thin and sparse. I concentrate on my arm moving in great swoops over the paper, on the feel of the bumpy cloth canvas under my charcoal.

I'm not afraid when I draw.

The charcoal makes a soft *phft, phft* across the page. I study the bulb and trace the bend of the stem, the pleat in the first leaf. As I work, I try to be the person Lily thinks I am, full of strength and hidden worth. I sit straighter, ignoring the slight pressure in my chest that developed when I hit the six-month mark and never left.

Lost in thought, I jump when Mom puts her hands on my shoulders. She's silent for a moment. Then she bends down and kisses the top of my head. The end of her long blonde braid tickles my cheek. "You're still an artist. Coming home doesn't change that."

When I don't answer, she turns to the kitchen counter. "Do you like the crib?" she asks. Her back is to me as she pours a cup of coffee, but I catch the slight stiffening of her shoulders that says my answer matters. She was disappointed when I told her I was pregnant, but after the shock wore off she and Dad began a campaign to get me to move home after graduation.

"It's beautiful," I say because it's true. My father, Wade, made the white crib that now sits at the foot of my twin bed. I see his hand in the precise curve of the spindles and the solid feel of the wood.

The thought comes before I can stop it. *If Lily made furniture, it would look like this. Solid. Beautiful. Something that will last.*

"I'm glad," Mom says. She looks younger when she smiles, and I wish she would do it more often.

Another pain grabs me. I groan and hunch forward. "Braxton Hicks," I say between clenched teeth. I clutch the stick of willow charcoal so hard it snaps in two.

I hear Mom's coffee cup clatter into the sink. "That's not Braxton Hicks," she says. "We need to go to the hospital."

My arms are heavy, and I can't open my eyes.

"Rose?" My mother's voice. "Can you hear me?"

I try to turn toward her voice, but I can't move. I can only flutter my eyes. Wherever I am, everything is dim. I don't know whether the light is off or if I slept all day and it's night now.

"Is she awake?" My father's voice. He sounds tired.

"Almost," Mom says. "Rose? Can you hear me?"

Yes, I want to say, *I can hear you.* Something is blocking my throat. I try to lift my hand to my face, but my arm is weighed down by sleep.

"Rose?" Mom says. She sounds far away.

I can't speak, and I am so, so tired.

I try to move again, but I'm trapped. I struggle, shaking my head. The pillow crinkles.

"Rose?" Mom touches my cheek.

When she does, I force my eyes open and try to take a deep breath, but something is clogging my throat. *I can't breathe!* I panic and slap my face. A plastic tube fills my mouth.

"Don't," Mom says. She grabs my hands. "Stop. You're in the ICU on a ventilator." Fear is etched across her face and deep lines furrow her brow. Her nail polish is chipped and hair pokes out of her messy braid.

"You gave us a scare," Dad says. Dark circles ring his eyes.

My brain is fuzzy. Ventilator? ICU?

Mom sinks into a chair next to me and drops her head to my bed rail. "You're okay," she says. The words come out in a rush.

I'm not okay. I'm empty. I drop my hand to my stomach.

It's flat.

Baby? I mouth around the tube.

Mom doesn't notice.

Where is she? The familiar taste of copper pennies fills my mouth. I wrench myself upright, and yank at the tube. *Where is my baby!*

"Stop," Mom says. She stands over me, cradling my hands in hers. "Wade, help me."

Dad grabs my arms and pulls them down. "Be still, Rose, calm down." His green eyes are rimmed with red.

Baby, I mouth again. *Baby!*

Mom, at last, understands. "Your baby's fine," she says, but I don't believe her. Her eyes are so wide the white swallows the blue, and her lips are thin with the effort of smiling. She doesn't let go of my hands.

I can't breathe. Something is crushing my chest.

"She's fine," Mom repeats. "Lily's with her. She hasn't left her side."

"She's little," Dad says. "No bigger than my hand. But she's fine." He holds out his hand, palm up, and smiles.

What? I mouth. My mind is white fog. I remember sitting at the kitchen table, drawing. Pain ripping through my abdomen. Then . . . nothing.

What? I mouth again. This time, Mom understands I mean: *What happened?*

She looks at the ceiling. "When we got to the ER, your blood pressure spiked. They had to deliver the baby. You had a heart attack on the table." Her voice wavers.

I shake my head. She's wrong. I'm twenty-two. Heart attacks happen to old people.

Dad takes over. "It's called peripartum cardiomyopathy. The pregnancy caused your heart to enlarge, and the muscle was badly damaged."

If Mom weren't holding my hands, I'd clap them over my ears. I am a child again. *La, la, la. I'm not listening.*

Her last words are small, and I almost miss them. "You're still here," she says as if to convince herself. "I didn't lose you." Then she drops her head to my chest and closes her eyes.

THE NEXT DAY, a doctor I've never met removes the vent tube. His long fingers curve around it, then he yanks like he's starting a push mower, and just like that, I'm breathing on my own again.

When he leaves, I press my hand against my heart. It beats like it always has, but now I know I'm broken.

When a nurse brings my breakfast tray, I turn away. I keep my eyes closed when she checks my vitals. I keep them closed when a nurse's assistant comes in to sponge me off. The girl lifts my arms and runs a damp cloth over them, chattering the entire time.

"You're a lucky one," she says. "Still young enough to get better. Most of the people in here are old. They don't have much time left."

I realize I've never thought about time before. My life used to stretch before me to a vanishing point on the horizon, the end always out of sight. Now it contracts until it's a small dot. How much time do I have left?

A week? A month?

The aid moves to my legs, running the cloth against my skin in soft circles. I count my heart beats. Nothing seems different, but I can't trust my body anymore.

When she's finished, Mom and Lily come in. Mom sways on her feet, and Lily's skin is pale.

I turn away from them.

"Get up," Mom says. She's pushing a wheelchair. "We're taking you to see your daughter."

I don't move. What kind of mother can I be if my heart might give out at any moment?

Lily sits on the side of my bed, and I roll toward her. "She's two pounds fourteen ounces," she says. "All even numbers, so it's good. She looks like you."

My heart flutters. My daughter is three days old, and I haven't seen her yet. "Really?"

Tiny strands of brown hair have escaped Lily's ponytail. Dirt fills the creases of her fingers and smudges her left cheek. She works in the garden when she's upset.

"Really." She squeezes my hand.

Mom guides the wheelchair toward the bed and helps me into it. When she bends down to ease my feet onto the footrest, I notice streaks of gray running through her hair. I smooth them down. Suddenly I don't want to see time passing.

"She's a fighter, Rose. Like you." Mom looks at me as if I've accomplished something great, instead of merely surviving.

They wheel me out of ICU and to the neonatal intensive care

unit. Mom pushes me to a double sink next to the doors. Several plastic scrub brushes are stacked in a cabinet over the sink.

Lily grabs three of the brushes and hands them out. "Make sure you get under your fingernails," she says as she shows me how to squirt soap onto the sponge and lather every inch of my hands.

She's fast, scrubbing her hands with the brush, then scraping under her nails with a tiny plastic file. She counts as she works, and I mouth the numbers with her. We stop at thirty-two.

Lily blots her hands with a paper towel, and then dries mine for me. When we finish, Mom wheels me down an aisle lined with cube pods, each of which houses a baby in a plastic bubble. It looks like something from a science-fiction movie. Quilts in bright colors—orange, pink, and purple—cover the bubbles.

"There are so many." I whisper, afraid of disturbing the babies. I had expected crying, but other than the beeping monitors, the room is silent. Nurses bend over babies. Some of them sing. Some stroke tiny feet or hands. Others adjust IVs and oxygen sensors.

Lily turns down an almost-empty row and stops next to a bubble draped in an orange quilt. A round nurse dressed in SpongeBob scrubs pushes buttons on a monitor. She looks up when we enter. "Is this Mom?" she asks.

Mom. Hearing that startles me. I need to grow into the word.

"We've been waiting for you." The nurse adjusts something on the monitor and writes the displayed numbers on her palm. Then she folds the orange quilt down, opens a curved plastic door on the bubble, and I see my daughter for the first time.

She is tiny, so small she looks more like a doll than a baby. She is asleep, lying on her stomach. Her hands are balled into fists. A purple plaid hat covers her head, but a fine mist of hair pokes out from under it. Blonde, like mine. I touch the tips of my hair and smile.

Other than the hat, a diaper, and booties on her feet she is naked. "Can I touch her?" I ask the nurse.

"Just slide your hand into the isolet. She's having a little trouble regulating her body temperature today. It's been low, so she needs to stay in there, but she'll know you're here."

I run my fingers along her back. At my touch, she sighs and moves her head to nuzzle my hand. I melt.

"We took her off oxygen this morning. She's been fine."

I nod as if the words mean something, but I'm only half listening. I'm too busy studying the eggshell pearl of my daughter's fingernails, and her toes, which look like tiny peas.

"She knows you," Lily says.

"How can you tell?"

"She hasn't reacted this way to anyone else. She normally doesn't move much, even when someone touches her. I've never seen her lean into anyone. Have you, Mom?"

"Never," Mom says softly. I hear pride in her voice.

My baby's eyelids flicker. I lean forward, hoping for a glimpse. "Has she opened her eyes yet?"

The three women glance at each other. "Once," Mom says.

I take in their glances. "What is it? What's wrong?" A list of problems flash through my mind. Blind. Missing eyes. Cataracts.

"Nothing. Her eyes are unusual. That's all."

"Can she see?" I ask the nurse.

She nods. "We think so. Some preemies have vision problems because of the oxygen, but we don't think that's the case with her."

Lily says exactly the right thing. "Her eyes are just an unusual color. They're not dark blue. They're pale blue, like cornflowers."

"Like yours, Rose, when you were a baby," Mom says.

I run my fingers over my daughter's back. Her spine is a string of pearls. "Does that mean anything?"

The nurse shakes her head. "No, it's just unusual."

Mom leans over me. "What are you going to name her?"

"Antoinette," I say. I picked the name two weeks ago after flipping through a baby name book Lily gave me. "It means praiseworthy."

At my voice, Antoinette opens her cornflower blue eyes and turns toward me. My heart stops again, but this time it's from love.

Chapter Three

Lily sat on the edge of her bed, a well-worn book in her lap. Its white cover had grayed over the years, and the rose on the front was more peach than pink.

Tomorrow she would drive to Redbud and see Rose for the first time in years. She had already called her boss to request a leave of absence. She knew she should be packing now. Her barely used black suitcase sat open on her bed, a pile of T-shirts and jeans beside it, but she was spellbound by the old book. She flipped through the pages until she found what she wanted. As she looked down at the artist's rendering of honeysuckle, her mind drifted to the last time she had been home.

Two years ago, on the first Friday in June, Lily had called in sick to work. She shoved T-shirts and jeans into a suitcase. Then she sat in her car and counted to fifty before heading south to Redbud.

It was Rose's thirtieth birthday.

When they were children, thirty had seemed mythical, like a land they'd never visit. Like China, real but out of reach. They used to sit in the rafters of the drying barn, legs dangling over the beams, eating lavender shortbread cookies while conjuring their futures.

"Paris," Rose said once. Her daydreams played out anywhere but Kentucky. "I'll paint the Eiffel Tower and the Louvre. By thirty, I'll be exactly where I want to be."

I want to be here, Lily thought, though she didn't say it out loud. Her dreams seemed small next to her sister's.

"Promise me, you'll be there when I turn thirty," Rose said as she stretched out across the wide wooden beam. "Wherever we are in the world, we'll spend our thirtieth birthdays together. First mine, then yours."

They hooked their pinkie fingers and swore to be together. Rose might have meant they'd be together on their birthdays, but Lily had meant forever.

Yet here it was. Rose's thirtieth birthday. They were apart and neither of them had the life they imagined.

Lily had arrived in Redbud early that Friday morning. She checked into her hotel room, but instead of leaving the room and driving to Eden Farms she stood at the door, twisting the knob first left, then right, counting each turn. She was stuck. It was late afternoon before she could stop.

When she finally left the hotel, she drove north, to Richmond. She ate at a diner that looked like a 1950s museum. Her legs sweated against the red vinyl booth. She drank her sweet tea and picked at her country fried steak. Then she walked around town, ducking into antiques shops and candy stores until it was too dark to do anything except drive back to the hotel.

The following day, she drove even farther north, stopping in Lexington at the Kentucky Horse Park. She bought a ticket and watched the Parade of Breeds. She looked at the statue of

Secretariat and measured her steps' length against Man o' War's impressive twenty-eight-foot stride.

Finally, on the morning she was heading home to Covington, she gathered her courage and drove to Eden Farms. She pulled off on the side of the road and stared at the blue clapboard farmhouse where she grew up. The house stood well back from the road, the drying barn several yards to its left. Oak and birch trees arched over the drive that split in front of the house. One path led to the house and the other to the drying barn.

Their land was wedge shaped, with the widest portion of their fifty acres in the back. Most of it was cleared, but a thick stand of woods made up their back border. The commercial fields were behind the house, and on the right side were two ornamental gardens—the house garden and the night garden.

The Hastings family property bordered theirs on the left, but Lily forced herself to ignore it. After Seth completed his sophomore year in college, he decided to enter seminary. When he did so, he made it clear that there wasn't room in his life for both Lily and God. Besides, the last she had heard, he didn't live there anymore. He was probably off somewhere, saving the world.

Lily turned her attention back to her home. She wanted to climb the back porch and knock on the door, but her knees locked. She stayed where she was, on the side of the road.

As a child, she had been captivated by the Victorian language of flowers. Her interest had started on a trip to the library, where she found a heavy book with a thick white cover. Each page had an artist's rendering of a flower with the meaning the Victorians assigned to it written in script below.

She flipped through the book until she found lily. There were seven entries. White lilies meant purity. Lilies of the valley meant return of happiness. Water lilies meant eloquence. Her name could mean something different every day of the week.

She spent hours memorizing the meanings for each flower. When it was time to return the book, she hid it under her bed and told her mother she lost it. Twenty years later, she still knew that white daisies meant innocence and ivy meant friendship.

Honeysuckle meant the bond of love.

She looked down at the honeysuckle growing along the fence line and broke off three long strands of the vine. She braided them together and twined the garland through the white fence.

Then she drove home without looking back.

It was hard to believe two years had passed since that day. As Lily sat among her folded jeans and T-shirts, she prayed that the courage she had lacked on Rose's thirtieth birthday would sprout up inside of her like that honeysuckle, spreading until it was impossible to ignore.

SHE SNAPPED THE book shut when Will knocked on her open bedroom door. He cocked an eyebrow and held up a bottle of wine. "Merlot. An excellent packing wine. Cherry undertones with a hint of wood smoke." He poured two glasses, then sat in the plush chair next to the window. "Your bedroom is surprisingly drab, Lils."

Lily accepted the glass he held out to her. He was wrong. Her mother had made the blue-and-white star-pattern quilt covering the bed. The oil painting hanging on the opposite wall was from Rose—a yellow lily resting on a porcelain plate. "Bright. Like you," Rose had said when she presented it to Lily. A pewter mug filled with dried rosemary—for remembrance—sat on her dresser. Sheet music, rolled into a tight scroll and tied with a black ribbon, leaned against her mirror. And a tiny purple baby cap hung from the knob of her top dresser drawer.

Her room wasn't drab, wasn't boring. It held the most important parts of her life. Will just didn't know where to look.

"Talk to me, Lils," he said. "You're troubled. I can see it on your face."

The afternoon sunlight slanted across the floor. The tiny room was stuffy. She set her book on the bed and her wineglass on the nightstand, then crossed the room and opened the window.

The ever-present sounds of traffic and birdsong drifted in with the breeze. She pressed her forehead against the screen and watched cars drive past. "I'm fine," she said. Every three seconds, a sculpture in the artist's yard squeaked.

"Yeah, and I'm a monk." When she didn't respond, he grabbed the book from her bed. "What has you so fascinated?"

"It's a book on the Victorian language of flowers," she said as she counted the cars parked on the street. Ten.

"What?" He leafed through the pages.

"The Victorians. They assigned a meaning for every flower. They'd send each other bouquets with hidden messages." Her fingers twitched, and she laced them together. Rose was the only person Lily allowed to look through the book without her. "Sometimes I think of people as a flower. Rose was—"

"Let me guess—a rose?" Laugh lines framed his mouth.

Lily shook her head. "Oak-leaf geranium. It means lasting friendship."

He flipped through the pages until he found the flower. "Pretty," he said. "What about me? What flower am I?"

Her face heated, and she bit her lip. "Give me the book."

He drew back until he was just beyond her reach. "Come on, Lils. Play along. You need to relax a little. This day has been hard enough." He stopped flipping pages. "Here I am. A red rose. Passionate love." He grinned, and her heart turned over.

"Put the book in my suitcase when you're finished," she said. She had to focus on Rose, not the way her skin tingled when Will looked at her.

"I'm teasing. Let me help. I know this isn't easy for you." He tossed the book on top of the stacked T-shirts, then walked over to her.

Her back was to him, and he put his hand on her shoulder.

"I have to pack," she said, without turning around.

He squeezed her shoulder slightly. "Sometimes it's like there's a wall around you. You need to let people in. Talk to me."

She shook her head. Her heart was still bruised from the last time she let someone in. Besides, if she started talking, she would crack right down the middle. The only way she'd be able to help Rose was to stay strong. That meant she had to focus on the business at hand. Packing. "I have to get home. Rose needs me."

Will sighed. "If you change your mind, you know where to find me." As he walked back to his chair, he stopped. "What's this?"

She looked over her shoulder. He nodded at an old shoebox sticking out from under her bed.

"Nothing." She reached for the box, but he was faster.

"Friends shouldn't keep secrets." He let the lid slide to the floor. "Pictures." He ran his fingers across their tops. "Hundreds of them."

"Four hundred twenty-two," she murmured. She reached

for the wineglass on her night stand and took a drink, focusing on the burn in the back of her throat. There were seven similar boxes under her bed.

Will flipped through photos until one caught his eye. He held it up. Three young women stood in shirt dresses, their arms looped around each other as they smiled at the camera. He pointed to the blonde in the center. "Is this Rose?"

Lily shook her head. "My mother, Portia. Rose is just like her." Rose and Portia not only looked alike, they each saw the world the same way—a patchwork of colors and shapes.

As in everything else, Rose and Lily were opposites when it came to their parents. Rose was their mother's daughter, but Lily took after their father, Wade. Rose and Portia knew purple irises rising from a semicircle of yellow pansies would look beautiful next to the gray drying barn. But Lily and Wade knew the exact amounts of nitrogen and phosphorous to feed the plants. Gardening was a synthesis of art and science.

The science came easily to Lily. She and Wade plotted the commercial fields. They worked compost into the soil, transforming it from thick clay into light loam. Before planting, they measured the ground's pH, making sure it was a perfect neutral 6.5 (unless they were planting azaleas or hydrangeas, in which case they added coffee grounds and pine needles to lower the pH to a more acidic 5). They mapped out a field rotation schedule to build up fertility and mitigate pests. They debated the merits of buckwheat or clover as cover crops.

The art of gardening was another story. Lily and Wade ruled the commercial fields, but Portia and Rose designed the display gardens. They filled the house garden with crimson William

Shakespeare roses, English lavender, and yellow coreopsis. They trained wisteria over the gazebo, and then encircled it with pink hydrangeas. It shouldn't have matched, yet it did.

But Lily's favorite was the night garden planted against the stacked stone wall on the side of the property. Everything there was white. Astilbe and sweet alyssum. Foxglove and columbine. The flowers glowed as the sun set. Standing in the garden when fireflies came out made Lily believe in magic.

That's why Eden Farms was successful. Everyone played their part.

"I see Rose in your mother," Will said, yanking her back to the present, "but I also see you. Here, in the sharp line of her jaw. She looks stubborn as hell."

He handed Lily the picture, and though she didn't say so, her heart warmed at the thought that something of her mother lived on in her.

She studied the women standing next to her mother. It had been years, but she recognized them immediately. The plump woman on her mother's left was Cora Jenkins, who owned the Italian restaurant in town. Teelia Todd, whose family owned an alpaca farm, stood to Portia's right. The three women had been inseparable when Lily was younger. After her parents' car accident, they had promised to watch over the girls and the farm. But Lily hadn't talked to either woman since her parents' funeral six years ago.

"Mom *was* stubborn," she said. "She had to have the last word in every argument." It was strange for Lily to realize she was now older than her mother had been when that picture was taken. Gently, she placed it back in the box.

Will selected another photo and held it out to her. A young man with brown hair curling around his ears leaned against the hood of an old Ford pickup. He was smiling, but his eyes were dark, and his shoulders were tense. "Who's this?" Will asked.

"Seth Hastings. Just a neighbor." She glanced at the rolled sheet music on her dresser as she took the picture from Will.

Another photo had been stuck to its back. It fluttered to the floor, but Lily ignored it as she slid Seth's picture inside the box.

"Should I be jealous?" Will asked as he retrieved the picture that had fallen to the floor.

Of what? A ghost? Lily thought.

Will turned the other photo right side up and cradled it in his hands. He drew a sharp breath.

At the sound, Lily glanced at the picture. It was summer, and a little girl sat on the porch. The girl's head lolled back, and she gazed up and to the right, fixated on something over the photographer's shoulder.

"My niece, Antoinette," Lily said, before Will could ask. She went back to her suitcase, hoping to put an end to the questions.

Being around Antoinette made the need to count worse. *Much* worse. She counted her T-shirts and jeans, making sure she had six of each. Fancy clothes would be wasted at Eden Farms. She tucked the Victorian flower-language book under a yellow and white shirt.

Shoes. She needed shoes. She fished around in the back of her closet until she found an old pair of garden clogs.

"You never talk about her," Will said.

Shame rose up in Lily, but she was going home. It was time to face her mistakes. She dropped the shoes on top of her suitcase and sank onto the bed. "I stopped going home after Rose realized Antoinette had problems." The words came out in a rush, and her ears burned.

Will frowned. "Why?" he asked. "I thought you loved it there."

She took the picture and clasped it in her hands. "I do. I did." If she closed her eyes, she could see the farm glittering with starlight. Her mother's face, lined, but still youthful. Rose as a child, long-legged and graceful, running through the stream that rimmed their property, the tips of her blonde hair dripping wet.

Then Antoinette's face flared in her mind, and Lily began to count. She reached thirty-two before she forced herself to stop.

She looked down at the photo of her niece. The girl's eyes were too far apart, and her head looked too heavy for her neck. "Our parents died in a car accident. The day of their funeral, Rose asked me to move home and help with Antoinette and the farm."

Lily's chest tightened. She could still see Rose's face, a mix of fear and sorrow, as she had begged Lily to stay. But being around Antoinette . . . Lily sighed. "I couldn't do it. And when I realized I was wrong, it was too late. Rose was so angry."

Will looked down at his wineglass. It was almost empty. He poured some more and cocked his eyebrow as he held out the bottle to Lily. She shook her head.

"Surely she would have forgiven you—"

"I called to apologize, but Rose wouldn't answer the phone," she said. "For the first month, I called every day. I left message after message." She shook her head. "Nothing. Rose was angry. I can't blame her. Antoinette is her daughter and I . . ." The words stuck in her throat.

The first time Lily held Antoinette, it had been in the neonatal intensive care unit, and her niece was only two hours old. At a little under three pounds, Antoinette was barely longer than Lily's hand. When Lily came home on visits, she used to carry Antoinette through the fields, naming the flowers and telling her their meanings.

Life continued that way until Lily returned home when Antoinette was two. That day, Lily and Rose sat side by side on a bench next to the library playground. The sun was a ball in the sky. Everything was gold. Antoinette turned in circles on a small patch of grass and waved her fingers in front of her eyes. It wasn't a random gesture. Not like she was moving for the fun of it. Her movements were methodical. Like she was counting each flick of her fingers.

Oh, God. She's like me, Lily thought, stunned at the realization. "Something's wrong," she said when she found her voice.

"What?" Rose followed Lily's gaze. "Nothing's wrong with her. She's just playing."

Lily shook her head. She stared at Antoinette, counting each twitch of her fingers.

"She's fine," Rose said, biting off each word.

"No," Lily said, unable to tear her gaze away from Antoinette. "She's not."

The little girl's head lolled to the left. She moved her hands back and forth. One, two. One, two. She didn't stop, even when Rose scooped her up.

"Nothing's wrong with her," Rose said as she walked back to their car.

Lily looked up at the sky and counted the clouds. She didn't know anything about being a parent, but she knew about being different.

That night, when their mother asked Lily to stay, she said she had to work the next day. Then she drove home, counting the entire time.

Now she looked at Will. His blue eyes were intense. "What if I'm not strong enough to handle Antoinette?" Her fear was that she would take one look at her niece and become paralyzed, would start counting and never stop. She would disappoint Rose all over again.

She reached for her glass and drained it.

Will took her glass and set it on the windowsill.

"Do you know why half of medical school is spent in residency?" he asked.

Lily looked out the window. It was getting late. Clouds drifted in front of the sun and the room grew dark.

"You can read every anatomy and physiology book on the planet, but until you're standing next to a patient who's having a stroke or bleeding out, you don't know how you'll react. You're thrown into it, and you figure it out as you go along."

Will leaned forward until their foreheads touched. "You'll do the same."

Chapter Four

Something wild was in the air. Antoinette felt it as soon as she clambered out of the van. The temperature had dropped and wind rushed through the trees. Her mother always said April weather could turn on a dime. An hour ago, the sky had been a crisp blue. Now it was so dark it almost looked like nighttime.

Seth had parked right in front of the Bakery Barn. Years ago, Eli and MaryBeth Cantwell had turned the run-down barn in the middle of Main Street into a bakery. A small roof jutted over the entrance, and baskets filled with yellow pansies and blue violas hung from the white beams. Several metal tables sat on the concrete patio in front of the bakery. They were all empty.

The air smelled like lightning, and the scent made the tiny hairs on Antoinette's arms stand. When the rain came, the land's song would change. Right now, Antoinette heard the low moan of a cello, an eerie sound.

Antoinette flapped her hands. *Change, change.* She wanted to stand outside in the rain, listening to the land's music. She imagined water streaming down her back, flattening her hair against her head, her whole body bright with sound.

"I still say you need to tell Lily *everything*," Seth said as he led Antoinette and her mother to a table near the bakery entrance. He had been saying the same thing since they left the farm.

Antoinette's muscles felt short and her joints stiff. In spite of that, when her mother pulled out a chair for her, she didn't sit. She leaned against the table, hands curled tight against her shoulders and her head cocked to the side, listening. The music would change soon.

"The rain should hold off," her mother said as she sat down. The walk from the van to the outdoor table had been short, but she was out of breath. "At least until we get back to the farm."

"You need to tell her," Seth said again.

This was one of the few times Antoinette had heard her mother and Seth argue. It bothered her, and she pulled her hands even tighter against her shoulders.

"You don't need to protect Lily anymore," her mother said. "Besides, she was anxious around Antoinette before. Knowing *everything* will scare her away. I can't risk her leaving."

Antoinette didn't like it when people talked about her. It made her feel bound up inside, like she was tangled in rubber bands.

She tried to focus on the music, but over the cello she heard the distant buzz of traffic. She also heard a bird calling from one of the Bradford pear trees lining the square and the rush of wind in the tree leaves. But most of all, she heard her mother's voice. It was light as a bell with Seth's lower voice her counterpoint.

Her mother spoke easily. Words fell from her mouth like water flowing downstream. Seth was deliberate in his speech. Antoinette wondered whether he spent hours in silence, storing his words, savoring their taste before doling them out one by one.

"You don't know that," he said. He sat with his elbows braced on his knees, like he was waiting for something.

"Why do you care?" Antoinette's mother asked. She leaned forward and stared at him as if studying his face. "You haven't talked to Lily in years."

Seth pushed his chair back from the table and stood. "It's not about Lily," he said. "It's about what's best for Antoinette. She deserves someone who knows the whole story. And Lily's stronger than you think. Have faith in her."

"Faith was always your purview," her mother said, "not mine."

Antoinette watched as Seth walked to the corner of the patio and pulled a pack of cigarettes from his pocket. He leaned against the wrought iron railing as he shook out a cigarette, lit it, and inhaled deeply. His closed his eyes as he blew out a stream of smoke.

Her mother stared at him through narrowed eyes. "You still have feelings for her," she said.

Seth didn't answer. He took another pull on the cigarette.

Her mother pressed on. "When you talk about her, your voice softens, and you get these little lines about your eyes, as if you're smiling." She pointed at his eyes. "You're doing it now."

Seth turned away and stared out across the street. "We were talking about Antoinette. Not Lily."

"You might want to figure out how you feel about Lily before she gets home," Antoinette's mother said.

He hunched his shoulders and stubbed out the cigarette. "Thanks for the advice."

Antoinette cocked her head. He didn't sound thankful. She rose up on her toes and rocked her head from side to side, trying to loosen the tension in her body. She felt thunder in the sky.

"She has a right to know how you feel," her mother said.

Seth laughed, but it wasn't a happy sound. "She has a right to know *everything* about Antoinette."

"Touché," her mother said as she leaned back in her chair.

"There y'all are." A tall woman with hollow cheeks approached their table. Her gray hair was clipped short, and her eyelids drooped slightly. MaryBeth Cantwell. Her left hand was behind her back. "With the weather, I was afraid you wouldn't make it. They said on the radio that a storm's rolling in." Her right hand shook slightly as she shielded her eyes and looked across the parking lot. There the sky faded from gray to black.

"We can use the rain," Seth said. "The ground's starting to crack, and it's only April." He seemed grateful for MaryBeth's presence. He tossed the spent cigarette on the ground, then walked back to the table, pausing to kiss the older woman's cheek before sitting down.

"I appreciate you coming out to test my new cupcakes before the show, but I don't want y'all to get stuck here because of me." A constant tremor shook her right hand, and her head lolled to the right. She leaned down and whispered in Antoinette's ear. "Don't tell your Mama—or Seth"—she winked at them—"but I've got something special just for you."

MaryBeth pulled her left arm from behind her back. She held a small silver platter. On it sat a white cupcake swirled with pale lemon frosting. The little cake was crowned with a candied purple pansy. "I made it special for you. I'm selling them at your mama's garden show next weekend, so you tell me if it's good." She placed the plate on the table.

Antoinette had overheard her mother talking to Seth and knew MaryBeth was sick. She looked at MaryBeth's trembling hand and thought the woman must understand what it felt like to be unable to control your body. She wondered what MaryBeth's song would sound like. Would it be slow and sweet like her mother's? Or ragged around the edges, like Seth's?

The wind picked up, lifting tendrils of Antoinette's hair. She bounced once and looked sideways at the cupcake. It was lace and sugar, like the snow that covered the farm each winter.

Eli Cantwell walked out of the bakery. He looked like skin stretched across a skeleton, and when he smiled his lips disappeared. He carried two porcelain saucers. Each one held a cupcake. One cake had pale green icing dusted with coconut shavings. The other had lavender icing topped with thinly sliced strawberries.

"We didn't forget about you two," he said as he set the saucer with the green cupcake in front of Antoinette's mother. "Tell us what you think. We want to be ready for the garden show."

"You'll be ready before we are," her mother said. "Two weeks doesn't seem like nearly enough time." She peeled the wrapper from her cupcake and took a bite. "It's delicious."

Antoinette loved their yearly garden show. Her mother invited artists from all over Redbud to set up exhibits in the garden. Then she opened the farm to the public. All day people milled through the fields, gazing at the flowers and art. The air was always filled with music that day.

Thinking about it made her happy. She flapped her hands.

MaryBeth took the other plate from Eli. She held it in her bad hand, and it shook slightly. "Would you mind helping us haul some tables out to the barn before the show?" she asked Seth. "Eli and I aren't as young as we used to be."

"We've got plenty of extra tables at the farm," Antoinette's mother said.

"We'll set them up for you," Seth said.

That was one of the things Antoinette loved about Seth; he was always willing to help.

"I don't want you to go to any trouble," MaryBeth said. She set the plate in front of Seth, and as she did, her hand twitched. The cupcake ended up in Seth's lap, and the saucer shattered on the concrete.

"I'm sorry." MaryBeth pressed her good hand against her mouth. "I . . . I'll clean it up."

"Don't worry about it," Seth said. He grabbed some napkins from the dispenser on the table and wiped the icing from his pants. "That's one good thing about working on a farm. A little mess doesn't bother you." He smiled at her, but she hurried back to the bakery without noticing.

Antoinette's hands stopped flapping, and she managed to take a bite of her cupcake. She would make MaryBeth feel better by eating every last bit. Her first bite was all icing. Smooth and lemony.

Eli watched his wife leave. "She's having a bad spell. She likes doing things herself, but I don't think she can keep it up much longer." His voice wavered, and he looked older than he was.

"She seems worse than she was last month," Antoinette's mother said gently.

Eli nodded. "Her strain of ALS is particularly aggressive. I don't know what I'll do when she's . . ." He stopped and spread his hands. "God will provide. He always has. Excuse me, I'd better go check on her."

Antoinette wasn't sure about God providing. He never answered her prayers. She stared at the purple candied pansy. It looked like it was covered in glass.

"You can eat it," her mother said.

Antoinette knew that. Cora Jenkins often stopped by their house to collect edible flowers. She tested her recipes on Antoinette and her mother before serving them in her restaurant. She made flower-themed food for the garden show. Last year, she made a spinach salad tossed with tiger lilies and dried cranberries. It had been the perfect mix of bitter and sweet.

Antoinette felt the temperature drop again. She flapped her hands in excitement, then calmed enough to take a big bite of her cupcake.

Seth took another napkin from the dispenser. Most of the icing was gone now, but he kept working. He kept his head down, avoiding her mother's gaze. "Do you really think Lily will come home?"

Antoinette tapped her fingers on the table. *Why is Lily coming?* She wanted to ask, but no one paid attention to her.

"She'll come." Her mother's voice was low, but she sounded confident. "She would have come home years ago if I hadn't been so stubborn."

Seth tossed the napkin on the table, then put his elbows on his knees and laced his fingers together. "She's going to find out about Antoinette sooner or later."

"Let's hope it's later," her mother said. Then she did what

she always did when she didn't want to talk about something, she changed the subject: "Why didn't you let Lily know when you came home?"

Seth sighed and shoved a hand through his hair. "I tried. When Mom told me that Lily had moved to Covington, I found her address online and drove to her house. I parked on the street and sat in my truck, trying to get up the nerve to knock on her door." He lifted one shoulder in a small shrug. "I didn't exactly end things on a good note, and I wasn't sure she'd be happy to see me."

He shook his head. "God, I was stupid. I should have known seminary wasn't right for me. I was always more Peter than Paul."

Antoinette's mother gave a small laugh. "I always thought Peter was easier to take. At least he seemed human."

"Yeah, well that was my problem. Too human." Seth frowned. "School was about following a set of rules. I learned which people were too damaged to love and that being a good Christian meant staying away from them.

"No one was *real*. No one ever sat down and said, 'You know what, there's this place in me that's broken. I'm not sure whether God exists and, if he does, whether he gives a shit about me. I felt like I was wearing a mask the entire time I was there."

"Did you tell Lily any of this?" Antoinette's mother asked. A chilly wind was blowing and the sky darkened. Her mother shivered. "The storm will be here soon."

"Wait here," Seth said. He jogged back to the truck and returned with a sweatshirt that he wrapped around her shoulders.

"I wanted to tell her," he said as he sat down. "That's why I drove to her house that day. But just as I found my nerve to get out of the truck, Lily came outside. A man was with her. A good-looking guy, I guess. Dark hair. Neatly dressed even though it was a Saturday."

Seth reached into his pocket for his cigarettes. He pulled one out but didn't light it. Instead, he tapped one end against the table, then turned it over and tapped the other end. He repeated the action several times. "The man had his arm across Lily's shoulder, and she was laughing at something he said. They seemed . . . close."

"Did you talk to her?" Bundled in Seth's sweatshirt, Antoinette's mother looked small, but the blue tinge had left her lips.

Seth shook his head. "She had obviously moved on. I didn't want to interfere. I had hurt her enough already, so I left before she noticed me."

Antoinette's mother reached across the table and placed her hand over his, stopping his nervous fidgeting with the cigarette. "Will you be okay with her here?"

Seth pressed his lips into a thin smile. "I'll be fine," he said. "I always am."

The first drops of rain fell as MaryBeth and Eli returned. MaryBeth carried a white bakery box tied with a red ribbon, and Eli carried a broom.

"I'm so sorry," MaryBeth said to Seth. "I can't always control my arm anymore."

Antoinette knew how that felt. She took another bite of her cupcake, hoping it would cheer MaryBeth. *It's good*, she tried to say, but no one noticed. She tapped MaryBeth's leg and smiled. Her teeth were coated with icing.

No one paid attention to her. She stomped her feet. Still, no one listened.

Eli swept the shards of glass into a dust pan. "What's life without a little adventure?" he said with a smile, although his eyes looked sad.

Antoinette took another bite of her cupcake. Lemon and vanilla combined together. Two of her favorite flavors. She wanted to tell MaryBeth that she understood being different.

Antoinette tapped MaryBeth's hand. She wanted to hear the older woman's song.

"Don't," her mother said, concern in her voice.

"She's okay," MaryBeth said. "I see you finished your cupcake. Did you like it?"

Antoinette flapped her hands. *Good*, she thought. *It was good.*

"I'll take that as a yes," Eli said with a laugh, but MaryBeth's shoulders sagged. She seemed sad.

The sky started spitting rain. "We'd better go," her mother said, but Antoinette wanted MaryBeth to smile.

Seth stood and held his hand out to Antoinette's mother. "You look tired," he said. "Lean on me. I'll help you to the car."

"MaryBeth, the cupcakes are wonderful," Antoinette's mother said. "You'll sell out of them at the show." She hugged the older woman.

With her mother distracted, Antoinette caught MaryBeth's hand. Bells filled her mind. Antoinette closed her eyes and followed the threads of the song. In most places, it was light as a hummingbird's wings, but in one spot the notes were round and flat.

Antoinette hummed along with MaryBeth's song. She had just reached the part where the notes felt off, when her mother noticed. "Antoinette, stop." She grabbed Antoinette's shoulder and pulled. Through her thin cotton shirt, Antoinette felt her mother's cold fingers, but she didn't let go of MaryBeth's hand. She pictured the way the woman's song should go and hummed, correcting the notes that were off.

"Seth?" her mother said. There was an edge of panic in her voice. "She's going to seize."

Antoinette's hands tingled, and her neck twitched. She squeezed MaryBeth's hand hard.

The woman groaned. "You're hurting me, Antoinette."

"What's going on?" Eli asked.

"Antoinette, let go!" Her mother was loud, but Antoinette didn't stop.

"It hurts," MaryBeth said.

At the same time, Seth grabbed Antoinette under her arms and pulled her away. The connection broke, and the song faded.

The rain fell harder, but no one moved. Antoinette slumped against Seth, fighting to keep her eyes open. MaryBeth twisted her neck from side to side.

Are you happy? Antoinette thought. She tried to focus on MaryBeth's face, but it looked fractured, as if her eyes had traded places with her mouth. Antoinette had to look away.

"What happened?" Eli asked.

"I don't know," MaryBeth whispered. Her voice was different, stronger.

Fireworks exploded behind Antoinette's eyes, and her arms started to shake. *Not yet*, she thought, but she couldn't stop. Her eyes rolled up, and color filled her brain.

"She's having a seizure," her mother said. "We need to get her to the van."

Seth turned, but Eli grabbed his arm, stopping him.

"What just happened?" Eli said. "Look at MaryBeth. She's not shaking. Antoinette *did* something!"

The colors came faster now, brilliant blues and reds like lightning that colored the sky at night.

Just before darkness overtook Antoinette, she heard her mother's voice, soft with compassion: "Eli, you're looking in the wrong place if you're looking for a miracle. She's just a little girl."

ROSE'S JOURNAL
May 2003

—✛—

I AM A mother.

A mom.

Mommy.

I chant the word as I ease Antoinette from her car seat. If I say it enough, maybe I'll believe it. Maybe I won't shake when I hold her.

It's early. The sun is just now climbing over the hills, and the chill of the night still hangs in the air. Antoinette is six weeks old and barely weighs five pounds, yet I've never held anything heavier in my life.

Until now, she has spent every minute of her life in the NICU. Mom and Dad offered to accompany me to the hospital to bring her home, but in the past month and a half I've grown small with fear. How can I be a mother if I'm afraid to be alone with my daughter? I went to the hospital alone to prove to myself that I could.

A shock of blonde hair pokes from beneath Antoinette's purple plaid cap. Her eyes are closed, and she snuggles into my arms as if there's no place she'd rather be.

But my heart could stop beating any minute. How can she trust me when I don't trust myself?

My knees are jelly as I carry her up the back porch steps. I move carefully, monitoring my heartbeat. I go to brush my hair away from my shoulders, forgetting I cut it off four weeks ago. I am not the same person I was before I went into the hospital. I needed my appearance to reflect that. Several heartbeats pass before I can open the door.

A bundle of cinquefoil sits in the center of the kitchen table. The shrubby plant spills out of the old glass someone used as a vase. The flowers are paler than they should be, more butter yellow than lemon. I'm not sure whether something's wrong with the plant or with me.

Before I became ill, colors were vibrant. I saw pink and blue and yellow housed in a white rose petal. After all, white is a compilation of every color.

Things are faded now. I only see white. Or butter yellow in this case.

"They mean 'beloved daughter,'" Lily says.

I startle. I was so intent on carrying Antoinette without dropping her that I didn't see Lily beside the table.

My heart shudders. I take several deep breaths, calming only when Antoinette wraps her hand around my little finger. "What are you doing here?" I ask Lily.

"Can I hold her?" When Lily takes Antoinette, it feels like a huge weight has been lifted from me instead of a tiny baby.

She removes Antoinette's cap and tosses it on top of her bag, then presses her nose against Antoinette's scalp.

"Why aren't you at school?" I ask. There is a week left in the semester. Lily missed several classes while I was in the hospital, so I know she has to be behind.

"Couldn't miss my niece's homecoming. Besides, I took my exams early."

Of course she did. Jealousy swallows me. I should be graduating next Saturday. Instead, I dropped out in the middle of my last semester.

"Do you think she remembers me?" Lily rocks gently as she talks. Antoinette looks comfortable with her.

"I'm sure she does," I say, though I don't know. The nurses at the NICU know my daughter better than I do.

Lily starts singing. Not a real song. She strings numbers together to the tune of the alphabet song.

"You're home for the summer?" I ask. In spite of the envy I feel as I watch how easily she interacts with my daughter, Lily is my touchstone. I am strong when she is here.

She curls around Antoinette. Her long dark hair swings forward, screening her face. "I'm taking summer courses this year. I'll be home for the garden show, but then I'm going back to school." There's a slight tremor to her voice, and when she looks up, her eyes are red.

I am about to ask her what's wrong, when Mom and Dad rush into the kitchen. Lily hands me Antoinette and slips away.

"I thought I heard you," Mom says. "Did you have any problems? Are you okay?" She holds me by the shoulders, examining me as if I might have a heart attack right here in the kitchen. She's aged in the past two months. Frown lines stretch across her brow.

I want to reach for Lily, but the worry in Mom's eyes holds me here. "I'm fine," I say, though my heart tumbles through my chest, and I see black spots before my eyes.

"You're sure?" Dad hides his concern better than Mom, but I see anxiety in the way he holds his hands perfectly still.

I look around them, trying to see Lily, but she has disappeared.

I force a smile and turn back to my parents. "Positive." I am lying.

LATER THAT NIGHT, I sit on the edge of my bed, peering into Antoinette's crib. Is she breathing? I place my hand under her nose. I don't feel anything. Panic stings my throat. Then I feel a warm puff against my hand, and I relax.

Lily sleeps in the twin bed closest to the door. I have always slept under the window. Her soft snores fill the room. The familiar sound helps me breathe easier.

Our room is still a large square box. The walls are still painted faded rose; the floor is still scarred where Lily and I carved our initials into the soft wood beneath our beds. But Antoinette's crib changes everything.

I tiptoe across the room and sit on the side of Lily's bed. I never got to ask her what was bothering her earlier in the day. After Mom and Dad came in, she slipped out to the garden and stayed there until after dinner.

"Lily?" I nudge her shoulder.

She groans. "What's wrong?" she asks, without opening her eyes.

"Can I get in?" I crawl beneath her covers before she answers. As a child, Lily would slip into my bed at night when she didn't want to go to school the next day.

Funny how our roles have reversed.

She makes room for me, and I roll onto my side so that I can see her face. Lily is tall and dark. The exact opposite of me.

"Why were you upset earlier?" I ask. Her eyes are still puffy, and I know it's not from sleep.

She is fully awake now. "It's nothing," she says. "Is Antoinette sleeping?"

I don't want to talk about Antoinette. I want to pretend we're teenagers again, sharing secrets. "I know you. You don't cry easily."

"I cried a lot when you were in the hospital," she says. She rolls over on her back. Her lips move, and I know she's counting.

I cried then too, but I don't say so. I used to be the one who comforted her. Now that I need her comfort, I don't know how to act.

"Seth broke up with me," she finally says. "That's why I'm taking summer courses. I can't be on the farm, knowing he's next door."

Whatever I was expecting, it wasn't that. Seth and Lily have been together for so long that I think of them as one person. *SethandLily*. "Why?" She must have misunderstood him.

"He's decided to go to seminary. Apparently, I'm a distraction." She puts a hand over her eyes.

That doesn't sound like Seth. I'm about to say so, when a soft bleat comes from Antoinette's crib. I don't want to leave Lily, but she shoos me away. "Go check on her."

I hesitate. "I'm fine," Lily says. "Go get her."

This time I listen. I lean over Antoinette's crib. Her eyes are open. I freeze, hoping she'll go back to sleep. When she doesn't I say the first thing that pops into my mind. "I'm your mom," I whisper. "Do you remember me?"

"Of course she remembers you," Lily says. She flings back her sheet and sits on the side of her bed. She sleeps in one of Seth's old white T-shirts. It's only May, but her legs are already brown.

Antoinette kicks her feet and waves her hands in front of her face.

"Have you called him?" I ask as I pick up Antoinette. Her hand wraps around my finger. She has a tight grip for a little girl. As usual, her touch calms me.

"He won't answer my calls." Lily traces the lines between the wood planks with her toe.

I carry Antoinette to the rocker in the corner of the room and sit down. "I could talk to him."

Lily shakes her head. "You have enough on your plate."

Antoinette closes her pale blue eyes and nuzzles against me, causing a few drops of milk to leak from my breast.

Quickly, I lift my shirt. I haven't been able to breast-feed her yet. My first job as a mother was to carry her for nine months. My second is to feed her. Antoinette is only six weeks old, and already I've failed at everything a good mother should do.

"Your body experienced too much trauma," the nurse said at my last checkup. "If your milk hasn't come in yet, it's not going to."

I whisper a prayer. *Please, let me get this one thing right.*

Antoinette latches on and begins to suck, but within seconds she curls her fists into tight balls and screams. I want to cry. I squeeze my eyes shut and push my toes against the cold wood floor to get the rocker going. The motion soothes Antoinette, and she settles into a hiccupy sob. "Is there a flower for disappointment?"

I hadn't meant to ask the question, so I'm surprised when Lily answers: "Yellow carnations."

"But they look so happy."

Lily stands and stretches. "Appearances can be deceiving."

Antoinette opens her mouth wide, but no sound comes out. She's hungry. I need to go downstairs and warm up a bottle. I push myself up, but when I stand the room swirls.

I fall back into the rocker. Antoinette wails. "Lily," I say over Antoinette's cries. "Can you go downstairs and warm up a bottle?"

She is out the door and down the hall before I stop speaking. How am I going to get through the summer without her?

Antoinette still screams. I start rocking again, but this time, the motion doesn't soothe her.

"Hush. Hush." I place my lips next to her ear and whisper, but she doesn't stop.

"Let me take her." Mom leans against the doorway, eyes red from lack of sleep.

I shake my head. *I can do this. I can take care of my daughter.*

"Rose," Mom says in a voice so soft I almost miss it, "let me take her."

"But I'm her mother." I don't want to let go. I want to get one thing right.

"Part of being a good mother is learning when to ask for help." Mom smiles to soften her words. "Not your best quality."

She leads me to my bed and eases me onto it. She cradles Antoinette in one arm and me in the other. As Antoinette settles into her grandmother's arms, blessedly silent, I realize I will never be the kind of mother I want to be.

Chapter Five

Lily left Covington before sunrise. After 111 minutes on the road, she reached the outskirts of Redbud, Kentucky. The town was named for the trees that grow wild over the hills, making the air in early spring smell sharp and sweet.

It had rained last night, and the grass was still wet. The road was narrower than Lily remembered, and as she rounded a bend her tires slipped onto the gravel shoulder. An unwanted thought pushed through her mind: traffic fatalities were the leading cause of death for people ages eight to thirty-four.

She eased off of the gas pedal and positioned her hands at nine and three o'clock on the steering wheel. Her knuckles were white, but she didn't loosen her grip. She hunched her shoulders to loosen the knots between them.

Around her, white-plank fences stood in front of houses tucked into the hills. Puffy white-flowered Bradford pear trees dotted the landscape. The trees were invasive, able to grow anywhere, including the thick Kentucky soil. They spread like the honeysuckle in the woods behind Eden Farms, but Lily liked them. There was something to admire about a species that planted itself anywhere, even if it wasn't wanted.

The road widened slightly as it turned into Main Street and ran past Cora's Italian Restaurant, past the Bakery Barn, and Teelia Todd's shop, Knitwits. Lily passed the library with its Georgian columns making it look as if it belonged in a grander town. The farmers' market sat across from the library, taking up an entire block.

Redbud was known for Eden Farms' flowers, and in two hours the market would be full of daffodils and hyacinths, the air thick with their scent. Moms in baseball caps would meander through the aisles, towing toddlers behind them.

On impulse, Lily turned into the lot and parked in front of the Eden Farms' booth. It still anchored the market the way it had when she was young.

Teelia Todd's booth stood across from theirs. She sold hand-spun alpaca yarn. Her husband had died when Lily was in kindergarten, leaving Teelia to raise their son, Deacon, alone. On cool days, Teelia would bring one of her alpacas, Frank, to the market with her. She'd loop his lead line around a beam where he'd nuzzle everyone who passed.

Lily smiled at the memory as she walked to the Eden Farms' booth. She ran her fingers over the rough wood planks. The years fell away, and she was sixteen again, sitting on a metal stool, surrounded by cut sunflowers and hydrangeas, fanning herself with a folded price list.

Rose was supposed to help, but she usually snuck off before the day got too hot. "I'm out of here as soon as I finish school," she'd say. "Who wants to spend their life pulling weeds and spreading manure?"

Lily tried to explain the peace she felt sitting in the booth, answering questions about which flowers tolerated the heavy

Kentucky soil, or why a blast with the garden hose was the safest way to get rid of Japanese beetles, but Rose never understood.

Flowers were predictable, like numbers. Black spots on rose leaves indicated a fungus. Prune the damaged leaves, apply a fungicide, and the plant should survive. Brown hosta leaves meant the plant needed more shade or water. Move it to a shady spot or increase the waterings and it would be fine. Plants spoke a language she understood. To those who paid attention, they revealed whether they needed more phosphorous or nitrogen, less water, or a good soaking with the hose.

A large pickup truck rumbled past. In only minutes, the lot had started to fill with the farmers and artists who had booths at the market. Looking out across the market, she pictured it full. Handmade soaps. Chocolate-dipped strawberries. Hand-harvested honeycomb. Teelia's booth stuffed with yarn.

Lily wanted to settle onto the metal stool behind the Eden Farms cash register, but Rose was waiting at home, and although Lily's heart hammered nervously against her ribs she longed to see her sister.

A white truck, its bed filled with yellow snapdragons and pansies in rainbow colors, slid into the parking space next to hers. Lily dipped her head, letting her dark hair fall like a screen across her face.

"You're early. The market doesn't open for another two hours," a man said.

Even with her back turned, she knew that voice. Her heart raced and her cheeks flushed. She looked up as Seth Hastings stepped out of the truck, his unruly brown hair already streaked with summer gold.

Seth wasn't handsome. His cheekbones were too sharp, and

his forehead too broad. His dark eyes were framed by thick brows, and he was almost too tall. As a child it had made him look awkward. But now, as Lily studied him, she saw that he had grown into his body.

She flashed to an image of him at seventeen, lanky in a teenage boy way, supporting his weight on his arms as he rose above her. Despite the crisp breeze, her whole body flushed. She had no idea he was in town.

"Lily?" He frowned, looking surprised to see her.

Years ago, talking to Seth had been as natural as breathing. Now, seeing him made her mute, and she started counting. She was on six when he leaned in and hugged her. His arms were stiff, and the hug seemed more out of obligation than anything else, but without thinking she gripped him tightly. His hair still smelled like strawberries and summer.

"Sorry," he said. He pulled away and ran his hands through his hair. "I didn't mean to—"

She wanted to look away but couldn't. His hair was longer now. It brushed his shoulders, curling up around the edges. The look softened him, lessening the air of seriousness he had as a boy.

"It's like time stopped," he whispered, "and you're still seventeen."

His comment caught her off guard, and she laughed. "You know how to flatter someone, don't you?" She was thirty years old. Her hair might still be long and brown, her eyes might still be moss green, but when she looked in the mirror, there were tiny lines around her mouth and a melancholy look in her eyes that hadn't been there when she was younger.

Seth tilted his head. "No," he said. "You're the same. But

why are you at the market instead of the house?" He seemed to have recovered from the initial surprise of seeing her, and he took a step back, putting some distance between them.

That's when Lily noticed the Eden Farms' logo—a nodding lily—on his truck door. The same thing was on his green T-shirt. "You're wearing an Eden Farms' shirt," she said, shock coloring her voice.

"Rose didn't tell you?"

She shook her head. "I didn't even know you were in town." She had been so startled at seeing him again that until now she hadn't wondered why he was here. "Shouldn't you be heading up a church or off saving the world?"

"Yeah. That didn't work out so well." He shrugged and pulled his hand through his hair again. She recognized the gesture. He was nervous. "Round peg in a square hole and all. They didn't take my questioning the tenets of the faith as well as you did. I should have been sure of God's existence before entering seminary instead of hoping seminary would prove his existence to me." One corner of his mouth quirked up.

"Did it?" Lily asked.

He shook his head. "I didn't figure that out until after I came home and bought into Eden Farms. Spending time with Antoinette helped me realize that he exists, even when I can't feel his presence.

"It's funny, I used to think my messed-up life was proof that God didn't exist. But when I finally found him, it was because of a little girl whose life was more broken than mine had ever been." He shrugged and smiled.

A familiar anxiety prickled along Lily's spine as he spoke of

Antoinette. "She sounds special," she said, resisting the urge to count.

"She is," he said. "Between Antoinette and working on the farm, I feel . . . settled. Like I'm where I'm supposed to be."

Lily had signed over her share of Eden Farms to Rose years ago and no longer had a say in what happened there. So why did it feel like a betrayal to know someone outside of the family owned part of it?

An even worse feeling arose. Why hadn't Seth called her when he left seminary? Going to school had been his reason for ending their relationship. Why didn't he try to resume it once he was no longer in school?

She drew the inevitable conclusion: his feelings for her were not as strong as her feelings for him. At the thought, her knees wobbled.

Stop it, she told herself. *Focus on Rose. Coming home is complicated enough without dwelling on the past.*

The pansies in the truck bed caught her eye. Getting her hands dirty always helped her calm down. "Need some help?" She pointed at the flowers.

Seth raised his eyebrows as if he had expected her to say something else. "Sure," he said. "We can set these out, and then I'll ride back to the farm with you." He paused as if he had misspoke. "That is, if you want me to."

Lily took a deep breath and counted to eight. *You can handle running into an old boyfriend,* she told herself. Seth was just someone she used to know. Nothing more. Besides, seeing Rose again would be easier if she wasn't alone.

At her nod, he dropped the tailgate and took a pair of gloves from his back pocket. She shook her head when he offered them to her. "You know what to do?" he asked.

"I haven't been gone that long." She grabbed a flat of yellow pansies. Dirt spilled over the edge, coating her hands. She slid the flat onto a metal rack behind the counter and wiped her hands on her jeans, leaving behind a smear of mud.

Seth worked fast. There was a rhythm to the way he walked over the curb and grabbed flats from the truck, as if he moved to music Lily didn't hear. They didn't speak as they worked, but then, they never had. Between the three of them, Rose was the one who always had something to say. Without her, a soft silence stood between them.

When they shoved the last of the pansies into place, Seth tugged his gloves off and stuffed them in his back pocket. "I'll drive you back to the farm if you'd like," he said.

His tone was formal, and despite her resolve to ignore their past, she felt something small and bruiselike form in the center of her chest. She looked down at her hands so he wouldn't see the hurt in her eyes. Dirt from unloading the pansies was trapped under her nails. She focused on it as she climbed into his truck. They could return for her car later.

Seth took a deep breath, then blew it out. "I should have handled things between us differently," he said as if reading her mind. He started the truck and drove out of the market. "I didn't want to hurt—"

Lily held up her hand, cutting him off. "Tell me about Antoinette," she said as she rubbed her hands together. Dirt was everywhere. Under her nails. In the creases of her palms. "Is it bad?"

For a long moment he didn't respond. They drove a mile before he said, "It's not bad. She's different. She can't speak. She communicates by touching or pointing to what she wants. But she's smart. Rose taught her about art. I play for her. Mozart and Handel mostly."

"You still play?" Seth's father had taught him how to play the violin. It was one of the few things they shared. Lily remembered summers in the flower fields, sitting at Seth's feet as he played. Even scales were beautiful in his hands.

Seth nodded. "Antoinette connects with music and art. She spends hours staring at Rose's art books. If you ask her to find a certain painting, she'll page through the books and locate it in seconds."

The image he described didn't match the child Lily remembered. Antoinette had been almost four years old when Lily last saw her. It was during the funeral for their parents. Antoinette flapped her hands in front of her face the entire time. Then she bounced up to the rosewood coffins and banged her hands against them until Rose pulled her away.

"Did the doctors ever diagnose her?" Lily asked.

"No. At first, they thought it was autism, but that never fit. She's affectionate. Sometimes when Rose holds her, Antoinette sinks into her as if Rose is her whole world." He glanced at Lily. "It's like she's locked in her body and can't get out."

"And Rose?" Lily knew the statistics. Rose should have died already.

He tightened his grip on the steering wheel. "It's bad."

Lily's stomach twisted. She stared at the land rushing by.

Too soon, they left town and passed Seth's place. His family owned the twenty acres bordering Eden Farms. A white-plank fence marked the property line.

Before she could blink, they were at the white sign with black scroll lettering: EDEN FARMS, FLOWERS. The shoulder dipped slightly. Honeysuckle and scrub brush grew along the side of the road, but several feet of land was cleared on either side of the farm entrance.

Seth turned in, and Lily noticed a locked black iron gate in front of the driveway. "What's that about?" she asked as Seth pressed a button on the remote clipped to his visor, and the gate swung open.

"Antoinette wanders off. When she was six, I found her walking down the main road. After that, Rose installed the gate." Seth punched a button and it closed behind them. The oak and birch trees arching over the drive had budded. Soon they would leaf out, shading the way to the house.

Lily watched Seth. Small lines creased his forehead. The angles of his face had sharpened over the years. But at that moment, she saw the ten-year-old boy who had saved her from bullies all those years ago at school. Despite the way things ended between them, Seth had always looked out for her. Now it sounded like he was doing the same for Rose.

"I'm glad you were here for Rose," she said. "And Antoinette."

He bobbed his head once, an almost imperceptible nod.

The forsythias lining the drive were still in bloom, making Lily feel like Dorothy following the yellow brick road. In minutes, she would see Rose. Every muscle in her body tightened, and she started to shake. *What am I getting myself into? Will Rose still be angry? Can we ever be close again?*

Asphalt changed to gravel as the drive split, one half leading to the farmhouse and the other to the drying barn. At the intersection, a profusion of yellow daffodils bloomed. In a week or so, pink tulips would also sway in the wind.

Seth parked and shut off the engine. "I'm sorry I hurt you," he said, without looking at her. Then he climbed out of the truck and shut the door before she could respond.

Lily sat in the truck, hand pressed over her heart as if holding it in. Driving up, she felt the way she did each time she came home. Her body recalled every dip, every bump.

Seth rapped on the window. "Coming in?" he asked.

Unable to stall any longer, she stepped out of the cab. Like it or not, she was home.

Chapter Six

Early morning sunlight fell in pale streaks across the wood floor. Antoinette lay sprawled in the middle of a sunbeam, her arms stretched over her head, her legs bent at the knees. If she were a cat, she'd arch her back, then curl into a ball and let the heat sink through her skin.

The kitchen smelled like vanilla and cinnamon, which was a Saturday smell. But today was Tuesday, and the kitchen should smell like coffee and toast. Also, Antoinette should be sitting at the table with flash cards spread out in front of her.

She was homeschooled, but she didn't study math and English. Each day, Jenna, her therapist, arrived at their house carrying a black bag filled with bits of chocolate, animal crackers, and pretzels.

Weekdays, Antoinette and Jenna would sit at the table. Jenna would take two laminated flash cards and hold them up. On the cards were words like *home* and *chair* and *Mommy*. Antoinette understood the words when they were spoken, but the letters swam when she looked at the cards.

"Show me 'Mommy'!" Jenna would say in her bright voice. Staring at the cards hurt Antoinette's head, so she never looked at them. Some days when Jenna said, "Show me 'Mommy'!" Antoinette would point to her mother who often sat at the table with them, going over the farm's financial records.

"No, silly," Jenna would say as if Antoinette were two years old. "On the card. Show me which card says 'Mommy.' I'll give you an animal cracker if you get it right."

Antoinette was not a baby, and she was not a dog. She didn't want an animal cracker.

They'd continue this way until Antoinette either randomly tapped a card and by chance landed on the correct choice or, more often, started screaming.

That was usually when her mother would intervene and suggest that they were finished for the day.

But not today. Today they were up early, and her mother had already told her that Jenna wasn't coming.

Plus, they had company. Cora Jenkins sat at the large oak table, across from Antoinette's mother, their heads bowed toward each other, their voices rising and falling.

Antoinette didn't like the morning therapy sessions with Jenna, but disruptions in her schedule made her feel like there were ants crawling over her. She twisted on the ground, trying to calm the itchy feeling. Everything had felt off since last night's storm. Even her seizure had been worse than normal, and her body still didn't work right.

"Lily's the only family Antoinette will have when I'm gone," her mother was saying.

I don't need any family except you. Antoinette shoved her feet against the floor and tried to push herself out of the room, but her knees were locked. She couldn't move.

"Lily hasn't acted like family," Cora said. She stood up and walked to the counter. "I can't just sit here waiting. I need to do something. Your mother always brewed a pitcher of hibiscus tea for company."

"Lily's not company," Antoinette's mother said.

Antoinette squirmed. Her skin still itched. She wanted to leave the room. If she tapped on her mother's leg, she would understand. She would pick Antoinette up and carry her away.

Cora shrugged as she opened the blue canisters on the counter. "She hasn't been home in years. That makes her company." She measured out a cup of dried hibiscus petals and one-half cup of fresh lavender. She emptied the petals into a large saucepan, filled it with water, and then added one-third cup of sugar. She found a glass pitcher in the cabinet beside the sink and set it next to the stove. "I'll make enough to last several days," she said.

"Family isn't company," Antoinette's mother said, but she didn't tell Cora to stop brewing the tea.

Antoinette closed her eyes and focused. Everything would be better once she left the room. Her feet were bare and the floor was slick. *Move.* She willed the muscles in her legs to contract.

Nothing.

She groaned in frustration.

At the sound, her mother said, "I know. This isn't a normal Tuesday. Cora, turn on my iPod. It's docked in the speakers next to the stove."

Cora hit a button and Vivaldi's "Spring" rolled out of the speakers. Still, the familiar music didn't help Antoinette.

If Seth were here, he would play for her. His music was alive. He would slide the bow across his violin, and she would move.

"Better?" her mother asked.

Antoinette groaned. The violins soared, but they didn't mask the whir of the refrigerator or the sound of water dripping from the faucet. They didn't mask the sadness in her mother's voice.

"What should I do?" Her mother had turned back to Cora. "Pretend I don't have a sister?"

Cora took two white mugs from the cabinets by the stove. While she waited for the water to heat, she put a spoon of raw brown sugar in each mug. "You could ask Seth," Cora said. "Or me, for God's sake. Either of us would help with Antoinette. She probably doesn't even remember Lily."

That wasn't true. Antoinette remembered a woman with dark hair and moss-green eyes. A woman who looked like something that bloomed at night.

Cora put the lid back on the canister. "Have you ever thought about expanding into flower-based products? You could sell teas, handmade soaps, lotions."

The whole room smelled sweet. Antoinette squeezed her eyes shut and clenched her jaw until a hard ache formed behind her teeth. It helped her focus. She bit down harder, catching a piece of cheek between her teeth. This time her hands flopped against the floor, but her arms didn't budge.

"Seth and I have thought about it," Antoinette's mother said, "but we decided not to make any major shifts right now. Maybe once Lily's here—"

Cora sighed. "Who says she'll stay, even if she does show up? And Antoinette doesn't know her." The water finished boiling. Cora turned off the burner and fit a metal strainer over the pitcher.

"Seth called from the market," her mother said as Cora poured the tea through the strainer. "He ran into Lily there and is driving her home. Besides, it's my fault Antoinette doesn't know her aunt. I should have called Lily before things got this bad. Antoinette needs her family."

I don't need anyone except you. Antoinette tried to scoot closer to her mother, but her feet wouldn't budge.

"Seems like she's done just fine without Lily for all these years," Cora said. She dumped the spent hibiscus and lavender into a bowl by the sink. "I'm experimenting. How do you feel about candied hibiscus flowers?"

That's right. I'm fine. Sometimes when Cora spoke, Antoinette leaned against the older woman's leg. When she did, Cora's voice vibrated through her body, and Antoinette pretended the woman's words were her own.

She loved the way Cora's hair, black laced with silver, hung straight to the middle of her back. Once, Antoinette had tangled her fingers in a hunk of that hair. It was thick and coarse, and Antoinette had not wanted to let go. Thinking about it now made her hands flick open and snap shut.

Flick. Snap. She giggled at the movement.

"Antoinette might have been fine without Lily," her mother said, "but I haven't been. I was just too stubborn to admit it."

In the stillness, the house creaked. Water dripped from the faucet. The refrigerator whirred. Vivaldi's violins hummed.

"And candied hibiscus flowers sound too pretty to eat," her mother added.

Again, Antoinette thought about Cora's rough black hair tangled around her fingers. This time, she was able to lift her head and let it thunk to the floor. For a moment, everything was beautifully quiet. She could move. Quickly, before the noise returned, she pushed her feet against the floor, scooting along on her back until she was under the table.

Cora handed Antoinette's mother a mug of tea and sat down. Antoinette's mother shifted in her seat and tucked her feet under her chair. When she did, her pajama leg moved, exposing a band of skin above her slippers.

Antoinette wanted to hear her mother's song. The last time she had touched her mother, the tempo had been too slow, and every once in a while a sharp note grated against her ears.

Recently, her mother stepped away each time Antoinette reached for her. Antoinette missed the feel of her mother's hand against her cheek. She missed curling into her mother as they sat side by side on the couch, the heat from her mother's body pulsing through Antoinette like a bright orange sun. If she could wrap her fingers around her mother's ankle, everything would be better. But anxiety forced her knees to her stomach and her arms to her chest. If she were normal, she would sit up and take her mother's hand. Instead, she lifted her head and dropped it to the floor.

Thump.

Again. Thump.

The tension in her body broke when the back of her skull hit the hardwood, and she let out a happy shriek. Her mother sighed, but she didn't press her hand against Antoinette's forehead and say, "Stop." So Antoinette hit her head again.

"I worry about you," Cora said between Antoinette's head thumps.

The words made Antoinette's hands twist into tight balls. She worried about her mother too.

Her mother sipped her tea. "This is good. It tastes just like Mom's."

"Who do you think gave me the recipe?" Cora said. "And don't think I'll give up just because you ignored my remark."

"I know you worry." Her mother sighed. "But you don't need to. On my thirtieth birthday, I found honeysuckle twined through the fence. Lily had been here. As girls, we had promised each other to be there when we turned thirty. I forgot, but Lily remembered. She might have caused our rift, but I kept it alive. I don't have time to be angry any more. And I suspect Lily knows that."

"I don't know, Rose, you might be asking too much. Lily might come home, but will she stay? You asked her once before and she ran off."

"I know. But I have to try. I want Antoinette to know her family, and Lily's the only family I have left."

Antoinette drew her legs up and pushed against the floor. She was all the way under the table now. Outside, a car door slammed.

Both women started. "She's here." Her mother stood.

Antoinette shoved her body until she was at her mother's feet. She concentrated and flung out her arm.

Chapter Seven

A deep porch encircled the blue farmhouse. White rockers flanked the door, and baskets overflowing with yellow pansies hung from the eaves. It was inviting, but Lily and Seth walked around back—only strangers used the front door.

The back porch had a crisp new coat of white paint, and purple clematis scrambled up the posts. The swing where Lily and Rose used to sit and watch as storms rolled in was still there. Lily gave it a small push as she passed.

"Is it how you remembered?" Seth asked. The steps creaked under his feet.

Lily went to the clematis. The flowers were so full and heavy she was surprised the plant didn't topple over under its own weight. Last night's rain drops were scattered across the vine, each one a miniature crystal. "Yes and no," she said. Coming home was like rereading a beloved childhood book as an adult. The same, yet different.

She cupped a blossom that was as big as her hand. It was a double bloom, the petals like layers of tissue paper. "It's too early for this to flower. Did you have a warm spell?"

Seth wasn't listening. He was looking over her shoulder, through the screen door. Lily dropped the flower and followed his gaze. Inside, she saw Rose and Cora Jenkins. The skin under Rose's eyes was the color of old pewter, and she stood hunched over, as if her body were caving in on itself.

"Oh no you don't," Seth murmured as he ran into the kitchen.

Lily followed him but once inside folded herself into a corner of the room. An iPod on the counter played Vivaldi's "Spring."

Rose's gaze skimmed past Seth and lingered on Lily. They locked eyes, and Rose smiled.

Lily took a step toward her sister and only then noticed the little girl lying at Rose's feet. Her white-blonde hair fanned out behind her, and her legs were akimbo. She stretched one hand toward Rose as if trying to grab her mother's ankle.

"There she is," Seth said as he reached for the girl.

"Antoinette?" Lily whispered. The young girl was fragile-looking, like a glass figurine. Her skin was so pale it was almost translucent, and her eyes seemed too big for her face.

Startled, Rose looked down, then quickly stepped away as Seth scooped up Antoinette and tossed her into the air. Lily drew in a sharp breath, worried the girl would shatter. Without thinking, she reached for her niece, ready to catch her should she fall.

"You came," Rose said, her voice wavering for an instant as she wrapped her arms around Lily.

Lily was a head taller than her sister, and Rose's arms were thin as willow branches. Lily felt like she was hugging a child instead of her older sister. "Of course I came," she said. Her throat burned, and she clutched Rose as if afraid she might disappear.

"It's good to have you home," Cora said when Rose pulled

back. She pressed her lips into a tight line and nodded. "Rose has been on her own for too long."

"She hasn't been on her own," Seth said, his voice sharp. Antoinette struggled in his arms, still trying to reach Rose. "I've been here."

Antoinette groaned. She smacked Seth's back with one hand and reached for Rose with the other.

"Calm down," Rose said, stepping out of Antoinette's reach.

"It's not the same as family." Cora tucked her long dark hair behind her ears and directed a pointed look at Lily.

"Cora—" Rose started.

"No," Lily said. She stared at the hardwood floor, more scuffed now than it had been the last time she had been home. "She's right, I should have—"

"Not your business, Cora," Seth said. Antoinette squirmed and he tightened his arms around her.

Cora arched her brow, but she stopped talking.

Antoinette threw her head back and screamed. She put both hands on Seth's chest and pushed.

"What's wrong?" Lily asked.

"Is it a seizure?" Cora asked. "Should I call the paramedics?"

Yes, Lily thought, *paramedics are a good idea.* Epilepsy was associated with an increased mortality rate.

Seth paced, trying to calm the girl, but she continued to scream. He just held her tighter and kept walking.

"No," Rose said with the voice of someone who had been through this scene a million times before. "She's not having a seizure. She's mad. Calm down, Antoinette. You can't get down until you stop screaming."

But Antoinette didn't stop. Lily was amazed that such a loud noise could come from such a little child. The urge to count crept over Lily, and she pressed her fingernails into her palms to keep it at bay.

"Take her to the family room, Seth," Rose said. "Maybe she'll stop if she can't see me."

Antoinette's face was pinched and red, and the tears rolling down her cheeks made her hair stick to her face. Seth seemed unfazed by her behavior. He carried her to the adjacent family room and walked in circles, holding her close.

Lily counted the kitchen's wood floor planks, pressing her lips together so she wouldn't say the numbers out loud. She was on ten when Rose said, "Antoinette gets frustrated."

On the iPod, a new symphony had begun. *Vivaldi's "Summer,"* Lily thought.

"It's hard for her," Rose said, "not being able to speak."

Lily mouthed, *Sixteen,* then closed her eyes and breathed deeply.

"Still counting?" Rose asked.

Lily blushed, but she nodded.

Antoinette whimpered, and Rose peeked into the family room. The little girl slumped against Seth's shoulder. A thin line of drool ran from her mouth down his back.

Rose went to him and touched his shoulder. "Thank you," she whispered. "You can set her down now."

Gently, Seth lowered Antoinette to the floor. Her knees folded under her like an accordion, and she plopped down, spent from her temper tantrum.

Rose sank down next to her daughter.

Seth stepped back to give them room. He crossed to stand next to Lily. "You okay?" he asked in a low voice.

"I don't know." Lily watched her sister. Rose's skin had a blue tint, but her eyes were bright. "Does she do that a lot? Antoinette, I mean."

"Does it matter?" Cora asked. "You're family."

Lily repressed a sigh. "No, it doesn't matter."

"Only when she's upset," Seth said. "And with Rose's health, she has a lot to be upset about."

Rose ran her hands through Antoinette's thin hair. The little girl let out a sob. "Shh, it's okay," Rose said. As she spoke, Antoinette's eyes closed and her breathing slowed.

Lily felt like she was intruding. She stepped back and bumped into the wall. Seth touched her back, steadying her.

"You're good with her," Lily said to him.

"She's just a little girl," Seth said. "No different from anyone else."

Lily frowned but didn't say anything.

Cora turned off the music. The sudden silence filled the room. "Is she okay?" She walked over to Rose and peered at Antoinette.

Rose dropped her chin to her chest, and her shoulders slumped. "She's fine. She'll sleep for a while."

"Want me to carry her to her room?" Seth asked.

"No," Rose said. "Let's pile some pillows on the floor. She can sleep here."

Seth went upstairs to get some pillows and Cora followed.

When they left, Lily felt like a spotlight had been turned on her. "I'll just—" She gestured to the kitchen and walked to the back door. She turned the doorknob; it squeaked the way it had when she was a child.

"Don't go," Rose said. She rocked back on her heels and

closed her eyes. "I need you. I've needed you for a long time. I was just too stubborn to admit it."

Lily glanced at Antoinette and took a deep breath. Her hands shook as she walked toward her sister. This was why she came home. "Don't worry. I'm not going anywhere."

ASIDE FROM ANTOINETTE curled on a nest of pillows at one end of the family room, Lily and Rose were alone. Cora left once Antoinette was settled, and Seth was upstairs getting a quilt. Lily stood with her arms wrapped around her middle, hoping she didn't look as awkward as she felt.

The room had changed. If she had thought about it logically, she would have realized that with their parents gone, Rose would change the house to suit her needs, but home was the one place Lily's heart ruled, not her head. Over the years, whenever she thought of home, the house was frozen in time, remaining the way it had been in her youth.

The family room used to have beige walls and a desk overflowing with receipts and flower catalogs. Now the walls were moss green, and the desk was gone. Coffee-table art books were stacked on the floor. The biggest difference, though, were the black-and-white photos of Antoinette hanging above the plush couch.

The pictures were fascinating. In one, Antoinette knelt, her nose brushing the petals of a coneflower. In another she stood with her head thrown back, a wide smile splitting her face. In most of them she looked like a normal little girl.

"Did you take these?" Lily asked.

Rose sat on the couch, her elbows on her knees. She nodded.

"It's not easy getting a good picture of her. She's almost never still."

"I can tell it's your work," Lily said. "The contrast between light and dark reminds me of the plant studies you did for your college portfolio."

For the first time that morning, Rose brightened. "I haven't thought about that in years." She craned her neck and looked up at the photos. "College seems like a lifetime ago."

"Like we were different people then," Lily said, shifting nervously, afraid of saying the wrong thing.

When they were children, Rose had seemed to her like a giant. Though just over five feet tall, she filled a room when she entered it.

"We *were* different then," Rose said. "Younger, at least. Naive—"

"Scared," Lily said at the same time, their voices overlapping.

Seth returned and covered Antoinette with a blue quilt. "She calmed quickly this time," he said, placing a hand on the girl's shoulder.

Lily looked again at the photos hanging over the couch. There were seven. The odd number and their asymmetrical arrangement made her uncomfortable. She pushed her hair back from her face and plucked at her shirt. "Cora said Antoinette has seizures?" she asked to distract herself.

"Yes. And they're getting worse."

"Seizures can shorten life expectancy." Lily had not meant to say that. She pressed her lips together wishing she could recall the words. "I'm sorry," she whispered. "Of course you would know that."

"I know exactly how dangerous seizures are for Antoinette," Rose said as she sank deeper into the couch.

"Hello?" A man's voice called out as the back door opened. "Is anybody home? It's Eli."

Seth gave Antoinette's shoulder one last pat and stood. "I'll see what he wants."

Lily turned her attention to Antoinette. She was amazed that this was the same little girl who had fit in her hand when she was born. "Why did she get so upset?" Lily asked.

Rose let her head fall back against the couch. "It's complicated."

Muffled voices drifted in from the kitchen. Lily spread her hands. "What about this has been simple?"

At that, Rose smiled. "I'm glad you're home," she said.

As if Lily could have stayed in Covington, waiting for the call that told her Rose had died. "We're sisters," she said, and that explained everything.

Seth returned with Eli Cantwell. Lily remembered visiting Eli as a child. Each time their mom took Rose and Lily into town, they'd run to the Bakery Barn while their mom chatted with Teelia Todd in Knitwits. MaryBeth was always waiting for them with yellow smiley-face cookies.

Now Eli held out a bakery box tied with a yellow ribbon. "I heard you were home," he said to Lily. "Welcome back."

Lily smiled her thanks and took the box. She glanced at Eli's thin body thinking he looked like a stork, with spindly arms and legs, and a beak nose.

"Go on, open it." Eli waved his hand. "MaryBeth thought you'd like them."

Lily opened the box and peered inside at the stack of iced

cookies. They weren't yellow this time. They were pastel shades of blue and purple and pink, but each one had a smiley face. Lily grinned. "I can't believe she remembered. Tell her thanks."

Eli nodded toward Antoinette. "She still tired from last night?" he asked. "I've never seen anything like that before in my life."

"No. She's just napping," Rose said quickly. "She got upset this morning with all the commotion—Lily coming home and all. Wore herself out. She'll be fine with a little sleep."

Eli didn't seem to hear her. "Never seen anything like it," he said again.

Seth moved to stand between Eli and Antoinette. "You can get used to anything if you're around it enough. Spend some time here and a seizure won't seem like anything."

Eli nodded and his face softened. He stepped around Seth and knelt down next to Antoinette. "She sure is a blessing. MaryBeth can't stop talking about her since y'all stopped by last night. She's having a real good spell right now." He brushed a stray piece of hair from Antoinette's face.

Lily noticed that Rose looked troubled as she clenched her jaw and twisted her fingers together while watching Eli.

"You have any trouble getting home?" he asked. "I haven't seen it rain like that in ages."

"We were fine," Seth said as he put his hand on Eli's back. "I'll walk you out. I'm headed back to the market."

Eli took one last look at Antoinette and stood. "You ought to get an alarm system," he said. "Anyone could walk right in. With the way things are today . . ."

"We're okay," Rose said as she nodded toward the kitchen.

Lily followed her gaze and saw a light above the door. "Antoinette wanders off sometimes. I usually keep it on. Today's just been real busy. I didn't reset it after Seth and Lily arrived."

Lily didn't let herself watch Seth leave. She looked out the window at the hoop houses behind the commercial fields. Six. When she had last been home, there were only two. Hoop houses functioned like a greenhouse, extending the growing season, but since a hoop house was only a white plastic tarp stretched over flexible piping, they were a lot less expensive.

"Seth missed you," Rose said.

Each sister had always known what the other was thinking. Lily smiled at the realization that not everything had faded between them, but she shook her head. If Seth had missed her, he would have called. Besides, she was here to help Rose. Not to revive an old romance.

Upon hearing Rose's voice, Antoinette stirred in her sleep. She opened her mouth and a soft "Mmmmaaa" fell out.

"What do you think she dreams about?" Lily asked.

"The same things we do," Rose said. "Why would her dreams be different from anyone else's?"

"I used to dream about being you," Lily said shyly. "Everything seemed easy for you. You were the one everyone liked. You had all the friends. You were the pretty one."

"Everyone wants to be someone else sometimes," Rose said, her voice sounding young and wistful. Then her tone transformed into that of a woman who knew the weight of sorrow: "I dream about staying right here. Having more time with my daughter."

The anguish in Rose's voice finally pulled Lily across the room. She sat next to her sister, so close that their knees touched.

"Are you scared?" Lily asked as she reached for her sister's hand. It was so warm and real it seemed impossible that one day soon Rose's heart would stop.

Rose twined her fingers through Lily's and squeezed as if their linked fingers were enough to keep her in this world. "Terrified," she said as the distance that had existed between them collapsed and they became sisters again.

ROSE'S JOURNAL
September 2005

———+———

THE OAK-LEAF HYDRANGEAS surrounding the library playground are still blooming even though it's late September. Lily has taken a few days off work and is visiting. She and I sit on a park bench across from the swings, while Antoinette twirls on a small patch of grass. The blades under her feet are green, but everywhere else, they're brown. The summer has been hot and dry.

Antoinette stands on her toes and stretches her arms toward the sky. Other than the crook in her elbows and the way her head lolls back, she looks like any other child.

Except she looks younger. Antoinette is two and a half but looks half that age.

My heart clenches as I compare her to the other children on the playground. They hang on the swings and climb up the slide. All of them—even the babies—seem bigger than Antoinette.

Most of them speak.

A switch flipped when I became a mother. One day I didn't worry about anything; the next, everything became a concern, a possible source of danger.

Most of all, I worry about leaving her. Who will take care of her when I'm gone?

"Does she always do that?" Lily asks, staring at Antoinette as she turns in circles.

I look at Antoinette and notice a clump of out-of-season daisies blooming at her feet. How did I miss them before? It's a strange but beautiful picture.

"She likes to spin," I say. I keep my voice casual, as if Antoinette's constant movement doesn't bother me. But it does. As a mother, I find that everything bothers me.

I sleepwalked through Antoinette's first year. Suddenly, I was a single mother and a college dropout diagnosed with severe heart disease. The changes were overwhelming and I emotionally checked out. I wasn't a *bad* mother, but I wasn't the mother I wanted to be.

I hope I'm making up for that now.

Across the playground, a little boy laughs as he climbs the steps to the slide. He moves so easily I have to look away. Antoinette wears her body awkwardly, always on the verge of falling.

"How long will you be home?" I ask before anxiety claims me. Mom told me not to compare Antoinette to other children. Someday I'll listen.

Lily's visits have grown less frequent. After graduating early, she accepted a job as an actuary for a life insurance company in Cincinnati and bought a home on the Kentucky side of the Ohio River. When I asked why she moved, she said she needed a change of scenery. She didn't mention the breakup with Seth at all.

"Just the weekend," she says.

"Have you talked to S—"

She cuts me off. "I don't want to talk about it."

We both like to ignore our problems.

The sound of laughter sweeps over us. I look across the playground to see a group of preschoolers scrambling up the slide.

"Do you want to play with the other kids?" I ask Antoinette. She doesn't stop spinning, and I wonder if I should make her quit. No one else is turning in circles. I want to ask Lily what she thinks, but she's watching Antoinette and counting.

"Rose," Lily says, without looking at me. Her voice is so soft I almost miss it. "I think something's wrong." She nods toward Antoinette.

I follow her gaze. Antoinette has stopped spinning. Her head hangs to one side, and she flicks her fingers in front of her eyes. Her arms are bent at the elbows. She looks like a marionette.

Lily is giving voice to my own concerns, but I can't listen. If I do, my fears will become so big that they'll swallow me. My chest burns as I stand. "I need to get Antoinette home. Nothing's wrong with her." If I say it enough, maybe I'll believe it.

Eli and MaryBeth Cantwell come out of the library when we're almost at the car. MaryBeth sees us and waves. She is solid, like Mom.

"How's my favorite girl?" MaryBeth asks as she kneels in front of Antoinette. A strand of Antoinette's hair hangs in her face, and MaryBeth gently tucks it behind her ear. I try to focus on the joy in Antoinette's face instead of the pressure building in my chest.

"She's getting big." When MaryBeth looks up, I see longing in her face. I hurt for her. If anyone should have had children, it's MaryBeth.

"You think so?" I ask. "She seems small to me."

"You see her every day," Eli says. "Trust me, she's growing like a weed." He stands behind his wife and puts a hand on her shoulder. I don't think I've ever seen them apart.

Eli pulls a bunch of wrapped hand-pulled taffy from his

pocket. "We're trying something new at the bakery. Let us know what you think. You too, Lily. Are you home to stay this time?"

"Not yet," Lily says as she accepts the taffy. She is easy around the Cantwells. We've known them since we were little and they were newly married. "But if I can't find a decent bakery in Cincinnati, I might have to move back."

"Sooner rather than later," MaryBeth says. She sits on the sidewalk and pats her lap. Antoinette plops down and flaps her hands.

My heart squeezes the air from my lungs. The flapping is another strange thing Antoinette does.

MaryBeth laughs and waves her hands. "Are we birds?" she asks.

And just like that, my heart is lighter. Make-believe. How had I missed it? The pressure in my chest eases, and I fill my lungs with air. I forget Lily's concerns. I forget my own. I watch my daughter without fear, and for the first time I think we might be okay.

LATER THAT NIGHT, when the sky seems low enough to touch, I sit on the porch swing with Mom. Antoinette sits at my feet, waving her hands in front of her eyes.

The peace I felt earlier vanishes, and an image flashes through my mind: Lily in second grade, sitting on the edge of the school playground, counting blades of grass while everyone else whirled around her.

"Are Dad and Lily still out there?" I ask Mom. I know the answer. The hills around the farm are draped in red and gold; they'll be digging up dahlias until the sky is black.

After we got home, Lily disappeared into the fields. I haven't seen her since. She's different. Distant. Losing Seth changed her. She never trusted easily, but now it's like she's built a wall around herself.

Antoinette stops waving her hands in front of her face. She stares out over the fields as if counting the blades of grass. "Pretty, isn't it?" I say.

As usual, she doesn't answer.

"Antoinette." I tap her shoulder, but she ignores me and starts rocking. The uneasy feeling I had at the playground comes back.

"Mom," I say, trying to sound casual. "When did I start talking?" The books I've read say Antoinette should be talking by now.

My mother looks up at the porch roof. The white paint is flaking. She sighs. "One more thing to do." She closes her eyes, then says, "You were an early talker. You said your first word at nine months and never stopped."

I can't breathe. Antoinette is thirty months old.

"Lily was a different story," Mom says. "When she was four, her pediatrician thought something was wrong because she wasn't talking yet. *Mental retardation*, he said. He sounded like he was talking about a dog, not my daughter."

Lily is the smartest person I know. Different, but brilliant. Hearing the doctor's words makes me angry. Lily might have a few quirks, but nothing is wrong with her. That's the thing about being sisters. We fight, but love always wins in the end.

"I never went back there," Mom says. "Lily started talking in complete sentences a few months later." She pats my knee and smiles. "Antoinette will talk when she wants to. And if she doesn't . . . well, we'll love her anyway."

I try to nod, but I'm drowning. The air is too thick. I gasp, trying to force my lungs open. Then I feel a small hand around my ankle. My daughter, who doesn't even babble, starts humming. I'm so shocked, I forget my panic.

Her voice is clear as a glass bell. I am lost in her sound, and the pressure in my chest eases. I stare at her until her voice trails off.

Then her hand loosens. Her eyes gently close.

And I realize how much love feels like falling.

Chapter Eight

The sisters sat folded together on the couch for so long that Rose fell asleep with her head against Lily's shoulder. Lily leaned down, pressed her nose to Rose's thin blonde hair, and breathed in her scent. It was the same after all these years: peaches and warm soil.

Once, when they were girls, Lily had told Rose this was how she smelled. Rose put her nose to her arm and sniffed. "I don't smell like dirt," she said. Then she stomped out of the room before Lily could explain that the scent of freshly tilled soil made her feel safe.

Family legend had it that Rose was born perfect. She didn't look wrinkly like other babies. Her skin was smooth, and her eyes morning-glory blue, as if she knew from the beginning she was special and wanted the world to know it too.

Lily never saw Rose in that perfect baby stage, but their mother told the story of Rose's birth so often that Lily could recite it by the time she was four.

"What about my story?" Lily had asked once, sitting at the kitchen table while her mother pounded out biscuit dough.

"What story?" her mother said.

"You know," Lily said, impatiently kicking her feet against the rungs of the chair. "The story of when I was born." This was where she would find out why she was different. Why she felt like the world spun wild around her, and she needed to hold on tight.

Her mother shrugged. "Not much to tell. You were an easy baby. Three little pushes and you slid right out. No fuss at all."

That wasn't what Lily wanted to know. "But what did I *look* like?" She pictured herself as a baby. Maybe her fists were clenched so tight her mother had to pry them open.

"Look like?" her mother said, only half listening as she pounded the dough, sending puffs of flour into the air.

"You know," Lily said. "Rose had pale blue eyes like she just came from heaven. What about me?" She held her breath.

Her mother went to the sink and rinsed her hands. "I'm busy, Lily. You've seen your baby pictures. You know what you looked like. Go on outside and play." She dried her hands against her frayed apron and went back to work.

Lily had seen her baby pictures, and unlike Rose, she *did* have wrinkly skin and black baby eyes. There was nothing in those pictures that explained her fear that gravity was not enough to keep her from floating away.

Rose shifted in her sleep, drawing Lily back to the present. Her sister had welcomed her home, but Lily felt like the bond between them was tenuous, as if they were held together by spider's silk.

She slid out from under Rose and went into the kitchen. Here everything was the same—yet different. The white cabinets. The blue tile backsplash. The bleached oak floor. That was the kitchen Lily remembered from childhood, but small things were off. The canisters where her mother stored lavender and flour weren't to the right of the sink anymore. Now they were on the opposite end of the counter—all the way down by the refrigerator. The speckled ceramic container that sat beside the stove holding spatulas and wooden spoons was gone. The braided rag rug that lay in front of the sink was also missing. These small changes made Lily feel off balance, and she was overwhelmed by homesickness. She was a guest in her own home.

When they were younger, their mother made lavender bread each spring. The delicate bread was Rose's favorite. Before it finished cooling on the wire rack next to the oven, Rose would cut two large slices, one for her and one for Lily.

Each year, Rose said the same thing as she bit into the bread. "It tastes like love."

That's what they needed now, Lily thought. Something to remind them what they meant to each other. Something that hadn't changed over the years. She went to the jars in which her mother had stored dried lavender. She opened the lid, praying Rose had continued the tradition.

She had. The sweet scent of lavender wafted out. The flowers were fresh, which was strange because it was early in the season, but Lily didn't question her luck. She grabbed two white bowls and shook petals into one. Then she searched the refrigerator for a lemon and some milk.

Next she combined flour and sugar in the second bowl, then set it aside as she poured milk into a small saucepan and sprinkled the lavender petals over it. When the milk warmed, the lavender seeped through it, turning the mixture a soft purple. As Lily worked, she thought back to the last time she sat in this kitchen. It had been the morning she and Rose buried their parents.

THE DAY OF the funeral, snow covered the ground. Lily stood at the graveside, trying not to stare at the two gaping holes, but looking elsewhere was worse. Rose bent forward like a tree snapped by the weight of ice. Antoinette shrieked at the falling snowflakes. Behind them stood a row of mourners.

Snow caught everywhere, on Lily's hair, her eyelashes, her cheeks. It was obscenely beautiful, like standing inside of a snow globe. A minister she didn't know stood at the head of the graves reading from the Bible.

Their parents had died in a car accident on their way to a flower growers' convention in Missouri. Each time Lily closed her eyes, she pictured the accident. Her parents rounding a bend as they merged onto the expressway. Snow everywhere. Their wipers steady against the windshield but not fast enough to keep the snow from piling up.

A black Chevy Suburban sped up behind them. Horn blaring. Lights flashing. Crossing the yellow line to pass them.

Lily pictured her father hunched behind the wheel, murmuring, "Idiot." The other driver was going too fast and started to spin.

Her father cut the steering wheel hard. Maybe he thought they would make it. But they turned sideways and slid into the SUV.

Her mother screamed. The windshield shattered, showering the interior of the car with tiny glass pebbles. A sharp crack as her father's head snapped forward, hitting the steering wheel. The car rolled twice, and when it came to rest it was upside down, and her parents were dangling from their seatbelts like rag dolls. This was how Lily saw it in her mind, and she replayed it over and over.

Movement to Lily's left caught her eye, and she shook her head to clear the image of her parents' accident. She saw Antoinette flapping her hands and bouncing on her toes. Lily rearranged her face into a calm expression, hoping it masked the dread tiptoeing through her body.

Her last visit home had been in October. She and Rose had sat at the kitchen table while Antoinette stood in the corner, banging her head against the wall.

Rose bowed her head. "You were right. Something's wrong."

Lily stared at the little girl, and the urge to count grew until it burst out of her mouth. She counted each thump of Antoinette's head. Out loud.

It continued until Rose carried Antoinette from the room, and Lily was finally able to stop.

After that, Lily stopped coming home. She had spent her adult life locking her idiosyncrasies inside and was afraid that if she spent more time with Antoinette she would start living her quirks out loud. Someday she might start counting and not be able to stop.

Everything threatened to unravel when Lily was around her niece, not because Antoinette was different—though she was— but because Lily felt she and Antoinette were so much alike it frightened her.

She remembered the conversation she and Rose had the morning of their parents' funeral.

Rose had been shaking so hard her coffee cup rattled. She was thin, as if her skin were pulled too tight. "Please," she begged. "Come home. I can't run the farm and care for Antoinette by myself. I need your help."

Lily opened her mouth to say yes. Sisters helped each other.

She knew that. But when she looked at Antoinette, who sat under the table flapping her hands in front of her eyes, "I can't" came out instead.

LILY WAS TAKING the lavender bread from the oven and placing it on a cooling rack next to the sink when Rose padded into the kitchen. The room was stuffy from the afternoon sunlight streaming in through the windows, but Rose rubbed her arms as if she was cold. "How long did I sleep?" she asked. Against her pale skin, her blue eyes stood out even more.

"Just long enough." Lily gestured toward the loaf. The sloped brown crust split open along the top to reveal a light purple middle. Perfect. She ran a knife along the edges to loosen the bread from the pan.

"You should've woken me. I would have helped." Rose leaned over the bread, inhaling its aroma. "Reminds me of Mom. It's almost as if she's right here."

"I thought we could have a picnic. Like we used to." Lily flipped the pan upside down and twisted it to free the bread. For a moment they weren't women who hadn't spoken for years but girls holding a shared past.

"Except this time," Rose said, "I won't have to steal the bread from Mom." When she smiled, the fatigue faded from her face.

Lily sliced the bread and packed it in a basket as Rose woke Antoinette. In minutes the three of them walked outside and into the house garden.

Their property was separated into six areas. Thirty acres were reserved for the commercial flower fields that produced most of their income. A small greenhouse and a drying barn sat a short walk from the farmhouse. The house itself was surrounded by an acre of private gardens. There was a kitchen garden that abutted the back porch, the night garden that occupied the west side of their property, and a walled house garden. The back of their land was wooded and a small creek ran through it. Seth's property bordered theirs on the east, sharing a traditional white Kentucky board fence.

The house garden comprised several square flower beds, edged by clipped boxwoods. The beds were empty now, but in a few weeks lilacs and lilies, roses and lavender, would spring to life. A wisteria-draped gazebo stood in the middle of the garden. Large purple blossoms dripped from the latticework. Lily knew the vine shouldn't be blooming yet, but somehow it was.

She stopped just inside the stone pillars that marked the entrance.

"What's wrong?" Rose asked. Antoinette stuttered to a stop beside her.

"I forgot how beautiful everything is," Lily said.

Rose looked at her daughter. "Yes, I suppose it is."

"I missed being here." Lily looked down at Antoinette, and her stomach tightened. "She's grown a lot."

Antoinette bared her teeth and growled, and Lily stepped back. Then the girl stretched up on her toes, flapped her hands, and walked away. Her steps were slow and careful as she made her way around the garden.

"You'll love her once you get to know her," Rose said.

"I already do," Lily said. It wasn't a lie. She remembered holding Antoinette when she was only hours old. The little girl had curled into Lily as if she was someone safe.

Love had never been the problem.

Lily spread one of their mother's quilts over a patch of fresh grass in the middle of the garden and they sat down. Kentucky springs were volatile. Evenings could be cold enough for winter coats. Afternoons could be so hot the flowers wilted. Some years, snow piled up on the ground until May.

This April was hot. The heat made Lily's shirt stick to her back. She plucked at it and fanned her face with her hand. "Is everything this difficult for her?" she asked.

"A year ago things weren't so bad. Lately, though . . ." Rose called to Antoinette, but the little girl ignored her. "She's stubborn."

"Like every other Martin," Lily said. Now that they were together, she didn't know what to say. She tried to sit still, but anxiety made her fidget. A purple thread was loose on the quilt. She wound it around her finger.

Rose gave a small laugh. "I guess so." Then her voice softened. "Her seizures are getting worse. And she's so frustrated . . ."

Lily watched Antoinette. Sometimes the girl squatted and pushed her hands into the dirt. Then, just as quickly, she'd remove her hands and continue on her course.

"How much does she understand?" Lily asked. She counted as she watched Antoinette walk. Each time the girl put her foot down, Lily mouthed a number.

"All of it. She might not look or act like other kids, but she understands everything."

"She knows what's happening to you?" Lily kept picking at the loose thread. Her mother had made the quilt for her before she left for college. Purple lilies and pink roses twined around the edges. "So you'll feel at home wherever you are," her mother had said. Yet here she was, home but not *home*. For the first time in her life, she felt awkward around Rose.

"She does," Rose said. "I wish she didn't."

Lily gathered her courage and asked the question she had wanted to ask since she first arrived. "How much time do you have?" The words sounded cruel, and immediately she wished she could take them back, but she needed to know.

Rose stared at Antoinette. The little girl was at the gazebo. She placed her foot on the bottom step then removed it. She repeated the motion four times. It looked like she wanted to climb the stairs but didn't know how. "Not nearly long enough," Rose said. "Six months. Probably less."

Lily felt like she was falling. She ran the numbers. Six months. One hundred eighty-two days. *Probably less.*

Why hadn't she come home sooner? She and Rose had lost so much time.

"My heart is weakening. It can't pump enough blood through my body. My lungs are filling up with fluid." Rose's tone was so matter of fact that it sounded like she was rattling off a grocery list, not describing the way her heart was shutting down. "The worst part is needing someone to care for Antoinette. She comes with extra . . . complications."

Lily pulled the thread tighter around her finger. "Has it been hard?" How silly. Of course it had been hard. One look at Antoinette and anyone could see that.

Antoinette heaved herself onto the gazebo's bottom step. She clamped her fist around the wood railing and hopped up and down.

"When she was younger," Rose said, "Antoinette climbed

those stairs twenty times a day. She'd get to the top, then turn around and start down again. Over and over. It was exhausting. I tried to make her quit, but she screamed each time I picked her up.

"Then one day, she just stopped. We came out here, but instead of climbing the stairs she locked her knees and refused to move.

"I felt overwhelmed. I wanted to talk to you about everything. About nothing. Some days I just wanted to hear your voice." Rose spread her fingers wide and put her hand down in the grass, moving it back and forth.

"I tried to call you so many times," Rose said. "I'd have the phone in my hand, ready to punch in your number, but I was afraid. I hung up every time."

"Why?" Lily asked. "You didn't do anything wrong—"

"I did. I was a single mom with a bad heart and a special-needs kid. After Mom and Dad died . . ." She leaned back. Her short hair fell in messy spikes around her face. "Being mad at you was easier than dealing with everything else. Plus, I needed help, and I was afraid to ask you again. Now I don't have a choice.

"Seth is here, and Antoinette loves him. He's been a father to her, but he's not *you*." Rose's eyes looked tired, as if decades had passed instead of only six years. "I don't have time to worry about the choices I've made in the past. I miss you. You're the only family Antoinette has left. Will you help me this time?"

Lily didn't say anything. She was afraid she would open her mouth and the wrong words would fall out again. Instead, she reached into the basket and held up a piece of lavender bread. She handed it to Rose, hoping that one act spoke for her.

Rose took a bite and looked up. "Funny," she said. "It still tastes like love."

ROSE'S JOURNAL
December 2006

———+———

THE WAITING ROOM at Cincinnati Children's Hospital's Department of Developmental and Behavioral Pediatrics is too small. Children are everywhere. Some shove beads through a wire maze bolted to the floor in the center of the room. Others bounce on their toes, hands curled against their shoulders, as if afraid to touch anything. One boy stands in the corner, banging his head against the wall while a woman—his mother?—tries to hold him still.

I can't watch.

Antoinette sits on the chair next to me, bouncing. Her small green coat is folded over the armrest. She is three and a half. Her feet don't reach the floor. To bounce, she pushes against the armrests, lifting herself out of the seat. Then she lets go. Gravity does the rest.

It took three months to get this appointment. Now that it's here, I want to be somewhere else, anywhere else.

This morning, Dad held Antoinette as he paced the kitchen. She arched her back and groaned. In the past three years, he has grown soft around the middle and most of his hair is gone. He puffed as he tried to calm Antoinette. "What do you want, sweetie?" he asked. He is big enough to wrap his arms around her twice, but Antoinette is difficult to contain.

"She wants to get down," I said. After scheduling this appointment, I started making lists. The first time Antoinette walked. The first time she crawled. Her first bites of solid food. There had to be something that would prove she was normal. The lists were in my purse somewhere, but I needed to find them.

"We can cancel our trip," Mom said. They were attending a commercial flower growers' conference in Missouri. It was the first weekend in December and a light snow had fallen.

Antoinette rocked back and forth in Dad's arms like a metronome. I found the crumpled pages on the bottom of my purse and flattened them on the kitchen table. "We'll be fine, Mom."

Antoinette shrieked.

"Just put her down, Dad," I said as I dumped everything back into my purse.

As soon as Antoinette's feet touched the ground, she toddled over to me, her gaze locked on something over my shoulder. When she reached the table, she buried her face against my knees and wrapped her arms around my legs. Then she sighed with contentment as if I were her whole world.

Now, in the waiting room, she sighs the same way and stops bouncing. She leans into me, and despite the pressure building in my chest, I smile. She's happy. That has to count for something.

Finally, the waiting room door opens, and a nurse in pink scrubs says, "Antoinette Martin?"

I pick up Antoinette's green coat, take her hand, and follow the nurse out of the waiting room. As I walk, I remember the last thing Mom said before they left. "You're still her mother. Nothing can change that."

But that's exactly what I'm afraid of. What if I can't mother a broken child?

SOMEONE PAINTED BLUE and yellow fish on the walls of the exam room. White bubbles float from their mouths to the ceiling. All of a sudden, I'm Lily. I count the fish. Five. Then I count the bubbles. Seventeen.

Not good. My chest tightens, and I slip a nitroglycerin pill under my tongue.

"Is she always so tactile?" Dr. Ketters asks. She is at least sixty. The gold buttons on her purple dress gap about the middle, and two inches of white slip show beneath her dress.

Antoinette sits on the exam table, scratching her fingers across its surface. *Phft. Phft.* She laughs at the sound her fingers make. Her green coat is next to her. It's so tiny.

Dr. Ketters stands in front of Antoinette, studying her. She hasn't listened to Antoinette's chest or looked in her eyes or ears.

"She touches everything," I say. That must be normal. Kids grab things. "I have lists." I give the crumpled sheets to the doctor. "When she walked. What she eats. Textures she likes . . ."

Dr. Ketters glances at my papers, then puts them aside. "Does she make eye contact?" Like a magician, she pulls a pink feather from her lab coat pocket and waves it in front of Antoinette.

Antoinette ignores it. She looks up and to the left. "She stares at paintings for hours," I say. I stopped painting after Antoinette was born, but I still have my art books. Antoinette and I flip through them at night. "And music. She loves music." The nitro pill has dissolved, but my heart still hurts.

Dr. Ketters jots some notes in Antoinette's file. She has been in the room for less than five minutes. When she looks up and smiles softly, I know something is wrong.

"Antoinette displays a lot of autistic behaviors," she says.

"She's not classically autistic. She's affectionate." Right now, Antoinette is leaning into me, lacing her fingers through mine.

"You don't see that a lot in autism," she says, "even though it's a spectrum disorder, and people can be anywhere from high functioning with Asperger syndrome to severely impaired." With the words *severely impaired*, her eyes slide to Antoinette.

I nod as if we are talking about the weather, but I don't want to hear anything else. I set Antoinette on the ground, ignoring her upraised hands. I gather her green coat and hold it out to her. "Thank you for your time. Come on, Antoinette. Put your coat on."

Antoinette flaps her hands and pushes the coat away.

Dr. Ketters continues as if I haven't said anything. "I can't give an exact diagnosis. She doesn't fit neatly into any one category. But I can tell you that she will most likely require lifelong care."

Please stop talking. The pressure in my chest grows until I think it might explode. I shake the coat at Antoinette. "Antoinette. Let's go."

"Is her father in the picture?" The sympathy in the doctor's voice is painful.

Finally, I drop Antoinette's coat and shake my head. I'm dizzy with grief. "It's just me."

"Institutions are nicer now. Caring for her by yourself is going to be hard."

I lose my breath and I feel something crushing my chest. Then I feel a small hand in mine. When I look down, Antoinette's eyes are closed and she's humming.

She hasn't hummed since last September, and I realize how

much I missed the sound of her voice. The pressure in my chest eases. Her touch has always made me feel better. When I pick her up, she closes her eyes and rests her head on my shoulder.

Dr. Ketters is still talking when I walk out of the exam room, but I'm not listening. As we leave, I think of the second list I made. The one I didn't show the doctor. On it, I listed the way Antoinette's fingers clasp mine when we walk in the garden. The way my heart beats easier when she is next to me. The way she taps my back, and I know it means *I love you*.

LILY'S HOUSE HAS a view of the Ohio River. I see a slice of the river through the window above the kitchen sink. It is late afternoon, and the day has turned gray.

Antoinette slept briefly in the car on the drive from the hospital to Lily's house. Twenty minutes. When she woke, I picked her up and whispered in her ear. "Do it again." Then I hummed, trying to re-create the noise she made at the doctor's office. She didn't make a sound.

Now in Lily's house, she sits on the floor, tracing her fingers along the grout lines in the tile. Lily and I lean against the kitchen counter. I am too agitated to sit.

"The doctor said something's wrong?" Lily asks. She taps her fingers against her leg.

I nod, because I can't say the words out loud.

Something is wrong.

With my daughter.

"I'm sorry," she whispers. I see my pain reflected in her eyes.

"Will she get better?" Lily starts counting. Her lips barely move, but I know what she's doing. If I thought counting would help, I'd do it too.

"No," I say. "She won't get better." The words crush me. I drop my head to my hand. "Could I get a drink?" Though it's cold outside, Lily's house is warm.

Antoinette is sitting in front of the sink, and Lily avoids walking near her. Irritation flashes through me. Antoinette isn't contagious.

I had hoped that stopping by Lily's house on the way home from the doctor's office would help me feel better. Instead, I feel worse. Lily is more reticent than usual.

A holly wreath hangs from a brass hook on the door leading from Lily's kitchen to her deck. I picture her walking alone through a parking lot filled with cut Christmas trees, selecting the wreath.

Lily takes a glass from the cabinet next to the sink and drops some ice into it. She fills it with tap water, watching Antoinette the entire time. Then she hands me the glass.

I set it on the kitchen counter. "I miss you."

"Is there a treatment?" Lily asks. She looks at Antoinette, who has closed her eyes and is rocking side to side.

I don't want to talk about it. "Mom and Dad are at a conference in Missouri. Come home with me. Just for the weekend." I don't want to be alone. I don't want to think about Dr. Ketters's words. How can I provide a lifetime of care when I don't have a lifetime left?

Antoinette kicks her heels against the floor.

Lily appears mesmerized. "I can't," she says. "Not this weekend."

"It's getting late," I say. "I need to get back to the farm." I drink the water, and as I take my glass to the sink it slips from my hand and shatters on the tile floor.

I kneel to pick up the glass shards and slice open my index finger. Bright red blood drips from my hand, staining the floor.

"Are you okay?" Lily grabs a napkin from the table and presses it against my finger. In a minute, it's soaked through with blood. She folds it until she finds a clean section and dabs at the cut. "I think you need stitches."

"I'm fine." I don't need her help. I take the napkin and press it against the cut.

"I'll wrap it for you." She runs to the bathroom and returns with a Band-Aid. "It's deep," she says as she holds my hand under water. She dries it and applies the bandage.

As she does, I feel a hand against my leg. Antoinette taps my leg and raises her hands. "It's okay," I say as I pick her up. "Mommy's fine."

Antoinette rests her head in the crook of my neck and pats my cheek. Then, for the second time today, she hums, and I forget the pain in my finger.

"How about next weekend?" Lily is saying. "I'll come home then."

I nod absentmindedly and walk toward the front door. I'm fixated on the sound coming from my daughter's lips.

"I miss you too," Lily says, but she sounds unsure of herself. She hugs me and holds on tight.

A tall man with dark hair is standing on Lily's doorstep when she opens the door. "Didn't know you had company, Lils," he says.

He is handsome in a too-perfect kind of way. Not at all the type of guy I picture Lily with. "We're just leaving," I say as I carry Antoinette to the car.

The man nods his head and waves his hand in a flourish as if tipping a cap. "Will Grayson, at your service."

I nod, but I'm not paying attention. I'm fascinated by the sound of my daughter's voice.

LATER, I PUT Antoinette to bed. She slept the entire trip home, and she was still asleep when we pulled up to the farm. I don't blame her. It's been a busy day.

It's only after settling her into bed that I remember my finger. I go into the bathroom and sit on the edge of the tub. It doesn't hurt, but I want to clean it again.

I undo the bandage, expecting to see a long gash on my finger, but my skin is intact. There isn't a single mark anywhere.

Chapter Nine

Antoinette kicked off her shoes and curled her toes into the grass. The air at the farmers' market was thick with humidity, and the canvas tent shading their booth only served to trap the heat.

She turned in slow circles, listening for the land's song. Today she thought it sounded like redemption—a French horn low and soft—but she wasn't sure. Everything was muffled.

Since her seizure at the Bakery Barn, her muscles had been tight, and the world often went silent. Yesterday she had shoved her hands wrist deep into the ground. That far down the soil was cool. She squeezed the earth between her fingers and listened, but she hadn't heard a thing.

Today she could hear the music, but she had to work to do so. If she didn't concentrate, the sound slipped away completely.

Three customers browsed their booth. Two women walked through the main aisle, and a man wearing a Go Green! T-shirt knelt among eight-inch pots of English lavender. Racks of pansies and violas lined the sides of the booth, at the center of which two white work tables formed an *L*. Antoinette's mother worked at one, and Lily at the other.

Gallon pots of azaleas and rhododendrons sat below the table where Antoinette's mother put together an arrangement of white tulips and daffodils. She used an old steel watering can as the container and selected flowers from buckets of sugar water. The green buds had just cracked open. "Never use flowers in bloom," her mother had said once. "They don't last as long."

Lily sat on a metal stool behind the cash register at the second table. Cut yellow pansies lay scattered across its surface. She twirled one between her fingers. "I can't remember the last time we worked the market together," she said.

Antoinette glared at Lily. *Shut up.*

"Not my best moments," her mother said with an awkward laugh. They seemed uncomfortable around each other—Lily fidgeting and Antoinette's mother's voice too bright.

"I can't believe you never told Mom I used to leave you here alone," her mother said.

Antoinette would have left Lily too. She'd leave right now if she could. It was Wednesday. She should be at home with her therapist. She'd rather spend the morning pointing at flash cards than at the market with Lily.

That morning, her mother had looked at Antoinette and said, "How about we spend the day together? It'll be a girl's day. Just you and me and Lily. You two will love each other." Her mother's smile was too wide, and at Lily's name the excitement that fizzed through Antoinette's body died.

Not Lily. She tried to shake her head, but her neck muscles wobbled, and her chin fell to her chest. Lily had only arrived yesterday, but Antoinette already knew she was *not* going to love her. She already had a mother. She didn't need another one.

Plus, Lily's name was wrong. The lilies in the house garden

were yellow and orange and pink, but there was nothing bright about her aunt. Her hair was brown like tilled soil, and her eyes were a deep mossy green. She was more oleander than lily. Antoinette imagined the flower blooming in Lily's footsteps. *Beware*, it would say as she walked past.

If Antoinette could bite Lily, she would. She opened her mouth and snapped it shut.

Lily flinched. "I'm making things worse," she said. "Maybe I should go home."

Antoinette flapped her hands. *Yes! Go home!*

"Give her some time," her mother said. "She doesn't know you yet."

I don't want to know her. Antoinette growled at Lily.

Lily dropped the pansy she had been holding. It fluttered to the ground, and when she walked away from the cash register she stepped on it. "Are these from the greenhouse?" She stopped in front of the lavender. "I didn't see them when I walked through yesterday." She knelt and lightly touched each plant. Her lips moved, and it looked like she was counting. She whispered, "Twelve."

The strangeness of it made Antoinette pause.

Her mother trimmed a dogwood stem and inserted it into her arrangement. The red branch was stark against the white flowers.

Lily shook her head. "They shouldn't be blooming now. Everything's out of sync." She pressed her hands into the grass as if the earth was spinning too fast.

"Lily Martin!" Teelia Todd, who sold hand-spun yarn in the booth across from theirs, walked toward them. Teelia was wiry, and her skin as brown as a walnut. Her gray hair swirled around her head in a mass of curls. She carried a milk crate filled with yarn. Frank, one of her alpacas, trailed along behind her.

Antoinette liked Frank. His white fleece was soft, and sometimes he pressed his nose against her shoulder. She shook her hands and wiggled her fingers. She wanted to touch him.

"You found your way back to us," Teelia said as she set the crate on a table in her booth. Frank was out of Antoinette's reach right now, but she stretched toward him anyway.

"I knew you weren't a city girl." Teelia tied Frank's lead line to her booth and hurried over to them

Frank hummed. Antoinette loved the sound. She pressed her lips together and sang along with him.

"Is that Frank?" Lily asked as she stood up. "I can't believe he's still around."

Teelia nodded and hugged Lily. "I'll be gone long before he is. We all missed you."

No. Not everyone. Antoinette stopped humming and again tried to shake her head.

"Now that you're home," Teelia said as she released Lily, "maybe Seth won't seem so lost."

"Oh, Seth and I aren't . . ."

"I don't think Seth is lost," Antoinette's mother said. She inserted a white daffodil into the watering can and tucked moss around its stem. "A little too serious, maybe. But not lost."

Antoinette stretched up on her toes and walked to her mother's side. She opened her fingers and placed her palm against the old steel can. The metal was so cold it made her teeth hurt. It felt like Christmas and icicles and knee-deep snow.

"Maybe 'lost' isn't the right word," Teelia said. She paused. "'Agitated.' That boy is agitated. He looks like he's searching for something."

Standing this close, Antoinette saw her mother's pulse beating below her jawline. It wasn't a steady thump-thump. It was more a thump-pause-pause-thump.

Antoinette reached for her. She wanted to hear her mother's song, but her mother walked across the booth to Lily.

Antoinette balled her hands and stamped her feet. Lily needed to *go away*.

"You know Seth," her mother said. "He's probably pondering the meaning of life. Besides, it's spring. Opening the farm is a lot of work. If he's more bothered than usual, that's why."

Her mother was wrong. The last two nights, Antoinette had looked out of her bedroom window. She expected to see deer at the edge of the woods. Instead, she'd seen Seth coming in from the drying barn, carrying his violin. He only played in the barn when he was upset.

"I've known that boy since he was six years old, running around covered in bruises from his father," Teelia said. She pointed at Lily. "The only time he had any peace was when he was with you. He hasn't been himself since y'all broke up."

Lily pressed her thumb against her index finger and then moved it to her middle finger, her ring finger, her pinky. With each touch, she whispered a number. "That wasn't my doing," she finally said.

"The garden show's in less than two weeks," Antoinette's mother said to Teelia. "Are you ready?"

"Almost," Teelia said. "I want to do a spinning demonstration this year. Do you think Seth could come over and pick up the enclosure for Frank and a few crates of yarn? I'm getting too old to haul everything around myself."

"I'm sure he won't mind," Antoinette's mother said.

"Maybe Lily could come with him and help out." Teelia

winked at Lily, and at the same time Frank resumed humming. Antoinette swayed along with him.

"I don't know if that's a good idea," Lily said. "Things aren't the same as they used to be. We're not"—she waved her hand from side to side—"together. Besides, I only got home yesterday, and he seems fine without me."

"Haven't you learned yet?" Teelia asked. "Just because a man *seems* fine doesn't mean he *is* fine. Trust me, even if he doesn't know it yet, that boy needs you."

Frank's humming had grown steadily louder. He wagged his head back and forth. It looked like fun. Antoinette dropped her chin to her chest to imitate him. When she did, she lost her balance and pitched forward.

Right into her aunt.

Lily grabbed Antoinette's shoulders. "You okay?" she asked.

Antoinette bared her teeth and growled. *Don't touch me!* Her arms twitched and flew up over her head.

Lily let go and backed away. "What did I do?"

Antoinette's mother sighed. "Nothing. She just doesn't know you yet."

That wasn't it. Antoinette could have known Lily her entire life, and she still wouldn't like her. She growled. The few customers in the booth stared.

"I'd better get back," Teelia said. She took Lily's hands. "Your parents would be proud of you for helping out." Then she headed back to her booth.

The man in the Go Green! T-shirt came up to the cash register and set three pots of lavender on the counter in front of Lily. "I've never seen lavender bloom this early," he said.

"Neither have I," Lily said. She brushed the gray foliage.

"Would you like to pick out another one? I plant mine in groups of four."

"I've only got enough room for three." He held out a bill.

Lily didn't take the money. Again, she touched the plants, counting as she did. Her behavior was strange. Antoinette cocked her head to the side and watched.

Lily said, "Three." Then she recounted, as if she would come up with a different number this time. "You could plant two in the garden and two in containers in your kitchen. I do that. Then when I make lavender bread or lavender cookies, it's easy to snip off some flowers."

"No, I don't—"

"Here." Lily selected another plant. "We're running a special. Buy three, get one free."

"I don't want four." The man sounded irritated.

"Lily," Antoinette's mother said, "he doesn't want it."

Lily put the four plants on a cardboard box lid and shoved it toward him. "Take it."

"You're one weird lady," the man said as he walked away.

Antoinette giggled. She flapped her hands and turned in a circle. *Weird Lily. Weird Lily. Weird, weird, weird.* For once, she wasn't the only strange one.

"Tell me something I don't know." Lily swept the remaining yellow pansies from the table. They fluttered down, creating spots of gold in the grass.

Antoinette's mother stepped back to look at her flower arrangement. She plucked out a flower that was too tall and trimmed its stem before reinserting it. "Do you remember the garden show before you left for college?"

Lily's cheeks turned bright red. "Of course I do."

Antoinette's mother laughed. "I thought Mom was going to have a heart attack when she found you and Seth kissing in the drying barn."

Lily shook her head. "That was a long time ago."

Her mother sat down on the stool and brushed her hair back from her forehead. Her cheeks had a pink glow, but dark circles sat under her eyes. "You should talk to him. I know he missed you. He carries a picture of you in his wallet."

Go away, Lily, Antoinette thought. She slapped the table.

Her mother glanced at her, then dunked a measuring cup in the bucket of water she kept under the table and drizzled it over her flower arrangement.

"Is he okay?" Lily finally asked.

"You know better than to listen to Teelia," Antoinette's mother said. "She exaggerates. If he's troubled, it's the stress of the show. It's in a week and a half. Plus, he's been taking on more responsibility around the farm as I've been slowing down."

When Lily spoke, her voice was soft and tentative. "Maybe you should cancel the show this year. Not just for Seth, but for everyone involved."

Antoinette's mother shook her head and went back to work on her flower arrangement. "I want to keep everything the same for as long as possible."

That was exactly what Antoinette wanted. Which meant Lily needed to go home. She snapped her teeth shut. She might not be able to say *I don't like Lily*, but there were ways to communicate without language. Her mother would know that when she chomped down on nothing but air, it meant *I don't like Lily*.

Sure enough, her mother glared at Antoinette. "Stop it, Antoinette. That's not funny."

Antoinette stopped biting the air, but her mother was wrong. It *was* funny. She shrieked. *Bite. Bite. Bite*, she thought as she circled past shelves packed with flowers.

A woman trailing a toddler placed two potted azaleas on the counter. "They like acidic soil," Lily said as she rang up the plants. "Work coffee grounds around their base when you plant them."

That was true. Antoinette remembered pressing her fingers into the ground near the azaleas flanking the drying barn. The sharp taste of lemons always filled her mouth.

Antoinette stretched up on her toes and walked to the edge of their tent. Frank saw her and hummed. No one was watching. She could slip away, pet Frank, and be back before her mother noticed she was gone.

Antoinette felt light with anticipation. For once her body moved easily. Her knees didn't pop, and her arms didn't fly skyward.

She was halfway to Teelia's when her mother looked up. "That's too far, Antoinette."

From somewhere behind her, Antoinette heard her mother's voice. "Lily," she said. "Could you go bring her back?"

Lily's voice was soft. "How do I do that? Will she listen to me?"

"Just pick her up and bring her back here."

Antoinette hurried. Lily was *not* picking her up. Antoinette would pet Frank, and then she would walk back to the booth by herself. She didn't need Lily. She didn't need anyone except her mother.

She imagined running from Lily, and she moved so fast the wind tugged her hair back from her face. Two more steps and she'd bury her face in Frank's neck. She stretched for him.

Just before her fingertips touched his soft nose, Lily snatched her away.

Antoinette arched her back and screamed. *Don't touch me! You're not my mother!*

Lily tightened her arms around Antoinette's waist and started counting. "One. Two. Three. Four." Her voice shook.

Antoinette flailed her arms and kicked her feet. She screamed until her throat burned. She flung her head back and raked her nails down Lily's arms. Blood beaded up from the cuts she made, but Lily didn't let go.

Antoinette kept screaming. *I hate you!* She imagined yelling the words so loud all of Redbud would hear.

They were back at the booth, but Lily didn't set her down. Antoinette kicked her feet, aiming for Lily's shins, but this time her body didn't cooperate. She didn't hit anything.

"Antoinette, stop! You're hurting Lily." Her mother put her hands on Antoinette's face, trying to hold her head still.

Lily kept counting. "Ten. Eleven. Twelve." Her arms trembled, but she didn't let go.

Leave us alone! Antoinette screamed until she was empty. Until her mother felt so far away that Antoinette couldn't reach her, even when she stretched out her arms as far as they would go.

Chapter Ten

Any confidence Lily had in her ability to be Antoinette's guardian evaporated as she carried the girl out of the farmers' market. Her arms bled from multiple crescent-shaped gouges. Her muscles shook from the effort it had taken to hold on to the girl while she flailed. And now her hands were numb. She wiggled her fingers to get the blood circulating, but it didn't help.

When she realized she was counting, she shook her head and forced herself to stop. Instead, she focused on the spruce pines edging the parking lot. Three trees stood in front of their van. On all three, the needles along the lower branches were brown, most likely caused by a fungus. If the branches weren't cut all the way back to the trunk, the fungus would spread and the trees would die. Even with immediate pruning, it might be too late.

"I don't know what got into her," Rose said as she walked beside Lily.

Antoinette sagged in Lily's arms, heavy as a bag of wet potting soil. Her behavior wasn't mysterious to Lily. The girl didn't like her.

"Let me take her," Rose said. Her cheeks were pale, and though she tried to hide it her breathing was labored.

Lily wanted to hand Antoinette over, climb in the van, and speed back to the farm. Instead, she hoisted the girl up to get a better grip, and said, "We're fine."

Antoinette let her arms flop back and her head nod forward. *Someone so small should not be this hard to carry*, Lily thought.

They were at the van when a white truck turned into the lot. The sound of Beethoven's Symphony no. 7 poured through the windows. Seth. Rose had called him to take over the booth after Antoinette's meltdown.

Seeing Seth made Lily's skin feel like it was on fire. She thought she had stuffed her feelings for him so far down that they had died, but the moment she saw him at the farmers' market, everything came roaring back.

If Teelia was right and he was troubled . . . Lily tried to suppress her concern but couldn't. From the day Seth's mother showed up at their back door, holding his violin, Lily and Seth had been inseparable. She could no more turn off her feelings for him than she could turn off her need to count.

Lily had been eight years old the day Seth's mother unexpectedly showed up at their house. She was sitting at the kitchen table with her mother, stringing green beans, when they heard a knock on the door.

"Who could that be?" her mother said. She dropped the beans she had been holding into the bowl and went to the door.

Lily shrugged and kept stringing beans. She loved snapping the tops then zipping the string free.

Snap. Zip. Snap. Zip. It sounded like summer.

"Margaret," her mother said. "What a surprise."

Lily looked up. The only Margaret she knew was Seth's mother, but that couldn't be right. She never went outside. Lily got up from the table and went to the door. To her surprise, Seth's mother stood on their porch.

Lily stared at her. Margaret was nothing like Lily's mother—she was darker and a head taller. Though she shared Seth's dark eyes and angular face, she seemed insubstantial, as if the wind might blow her away. Once, Lily saw her standing on the front porch of the Hastings' family farmhouse. When Margaret noticed Lily, she jumped like a startled jackrabbit and hurried back inside.

Now Margaret stood in their kitchen, holding Seth's violin case. "I can't stay," she said, glancing over her shoulder. "Would you mind if Seth stored this in your drying barn? His father taught him to play several years ago, but now . . . well, his dad wasn't feeling so good the other night. A little woozy, I guess. Anyway, he accidentally stepped on Seth's first violin."

She smiled and gave a small laugh, but her lips were so tight they were colorless. "I . . . I didn't want Seth to stop playing so I bought him this one myself." She held out the violin she carried. "Sometimes his dad gets a little . . . clumsy. I'd hate for Seth to lose this one too."

Lily's mother didn't blink. "I've read that plants respond to music," she said. She wiped her hands on the blue-and-white dishcloth hanging on the stove handle. "Maybe he could play for them? It would be better than just storing it. And he'd be helping us out. The harvest was low this year, music might boost production."

That was a lie. The harvest had been so big they had to hire high school students to help out.

A look of gratitude flashed across Margaret's face. "If it's no bother—"

"No trouble at all." Lily's mother took the violin. She paused a moment before adding, "Of course, he'd need to be over here more. He wouldn't be home as much."

Lily didn't know how it was possible to look pained and relieved at the same time, but Seth's mother did. Her shoulders relaxed and color returned to her lips, but her eyes filled with tears as she whispered, "Thank you."

After that, Seth came to the farm every day. He played warm-up scales in the drying barn, then went out into the fields and played.

Three weeks later Lily noticed Seth had a bruise. He was running scales in the drying barn while she sat on a straw bale, looking through her Victorian flower book. She stopped at a drawing of rose acacia with soft pink flowers. It meant friendship, but so did ivy. "Acacia or ivy?" she asked Seth without looking up. "Both mean friendship."

Seth didn't stop playing. He was used to her calling out plant names. "I don't know what acacia looks like," he said as he climbed the scale.

She got up and brought the book over to him. "Here's a picture."

He flicked his eyes over to the book. "Pretty," he said. "Use that one." He played down the scale now. When he raised his arm to move the bow, his sleeve fell back. A green-and-yellow bruise encircled the top of his arm.

"What'd you do? Walk into a wall?" she asked. She put the book down and pushed his sleeve up. "It looks like a handprint." She touched his skin, trying to fit her fingers into the four long bruises that wrapped around the top of his arm.

"It's nothing," he said, pulling away.

Lily was only eight, but she knew a hand-shaped bruise wasn't *nothing*. "Was it one of the boys at school?" They teased her for counting; maybe they bothered Seth too. But even as she asked, she realized the handprint was twice as big as her hand.

"Oh, your da—" she started as understanding clicked into place. Her mother's lie about the harvest. The fear in Margaret's eyes.

Seth snapped open his violin case. He put the instrument away without wiping it down. "Don't feel sorry for me," he said. His eyes were hard, and he held himself tall and rigid. He glared at her, as if daring her to let the tears stinging her eyes fall.

Lily didn't say anything. She grabbed his hand and led him to the straw bale where she had been sitting. When he sat down next to her, she opened her book to the page for ivy.

Acacia was pretty, but ivy was permanent. The dark green leaves weren't flashy, but ivy grabbed on to walls and fences and wouldn't let go. Even if you cut it back, shoots popped up in unexpected places. It took years to root out ivy. "This one," she said, pointing to the picture. "This is friendship. It lasts."

LILY WAS STILL thinking about Seth when they got back to the farm from the market. People hadn't been as willing to report abuse back then, especially in Kentucky, where folks tended to mind their own business.

Lily knew the instability in Seth's childhood had created his need to understand *why* life was hard. They spent hours sitting in the rafters of the drying barn, pondering God's existence. And if he did exist, why did he let bad things happen?

They never found the answer to that question.

Would things have been different for Seth if someone had reported his father? Maybe, but "different" might not be better. Most likely, Seth would have been carted off to a foster home and who knows what would have happened there.

And despite the pain his father caused, Seth still loved him. Lily thought that was why Seth had never stopped playing the violin. It was one good thing they shared.

"Earth to Lily," Rose said when they parked. She waved her hand in front of Lily's face. "You've been lost in thought the entire drive home."

"It's nothing," Lily said. "Just remembering the way things used to be." She glanced over her shoulder at Antoinette in the back seat. "Want me to carry her in for you?" She didn't actually want to touch Antoinette, but she wanted to talk about Seth even less. She used to tell Rose everything, but she had only been home a short while, and the bridge between them still felt tentative.

"Could you? She's so big it's hard for me to carry her." Rose smiled apologetically. "I lose my breath easily nowadays."

As Rose made her way to the back porch, Lily opened the van's back door and reached for Antoinette. The little girl shrank away from her touch, but she didn't resist when Lily picked her up. Lily carried her stiffly. "Don't scratch me this time. Okay?" she said. The porch steps creaked as she climbed them.

Lily eased Antoinette onto the swing next to Rose. Antoinette leaned into her mother much like a sunflower turning toward the sun.

"Sit with us," Rose said. She patted the seat next to her.

Lily shook her head. The urge to count had been pounding through her since they left the market. She needed to get inside before it exploded, forcing her to number the wooden slats of the porch floor or the pebbles in the gravel drive. She said the first thing that popped into her mind. "I need to make a phone call."

After the words left Lily's lips, she realized they were true. She wanted to talk to Will. She had dreamed about him last night, something vague and troubling she couldn't quite remember. When she woke, the room seemed full of his voice.

Rose looked hurt. Lily could tell she was trying hard to mend things between them, and just like always Lily was running away. She paused before slipping inside. "Tonight," she said. "I promise. We'll sit on the porch and tell stories, just like we used to when we were kids."

Rose looked up. Her face was earnest, and her blue eyes were clear. "Antoinette will love you. You're too much alike for her not to."

Lily pictured sitting on the swing with her niece. Antoinette would smack her hands against the armrests while Lily counted the stars. Both of them trapped. "That's what I'm afraid of," she said as she stepped inside.

She went upstairs and walked down the hall toward the guest room. Once there, Lily sat on the corner of the bed, took out her cell phone, and called Will.

He answered on the first ring, as if he had been waiting for her call.

"Will." She closed her eyes as she said his name.

"Bored out there already?" he asked. "How is it in Sticksville?"

She sighed into the phone. "Everything feels . . . off." She thought about the strange things that had happened since returning home. Seth's presence. Flowers blooming at odd times. Antoinette. She was in a category all by herself. Lily ran her hand over the scratches on her arm.

"Why? Did you lose a tractor-pulling contest? Maybe I should come down and cheer you up. Adding a little Will to your life makes everything better."

She laughed in spite of everything. "Yeah. That's all I need."

"If it's that bad, come home. We miss you here. Your plants are droopy. I didn't have anyone to talk to last night. And get this, our neighbor even asked where you were. I didn't know Soup Can Artist could talk."

The allure of her house was strong. After this morning with Antoinette, Lily wanted to jump in her car and drive there right away. Covington was two hours north. She could be there before dinner.

But the thought of disappointing Rose again made her stomach tighten. She traced her toe along the grooves in the hardwood floor. "Rose wants me to be Antoinette's guardian," she said. "I don't think I can do it." Shame made her whisper the words.

Will tapped his fingers against the phone. When he spoke again, his voice was steady and calm. Far from the animated Will she knew. "Lils, I've treated kids with special needs in the ER, and what you've got to remember is that they're still just *kids*. People get all tied up believing that they're different. That they don't want the same things we do. But that's not true. They want friends. A family. They want to be loved. To be accepted. Just like everyone else."

Lily pressed her fingers against the bridge of her nose. A dull throbbing rose behind her eyes. "Tell me I can do it," she said. "Tell me I'm strong enough."

"Lils, you cleaned my incisions after surgery. You sat with me during chemo. You saw me almost completely bald. If you can do that, you can handle one small girl, even if that girl is a little different. Trust me. When have I ever been wrong?"

She laughed softly. "Do you want me to list each time?"

Will didn't play along. "I mean when it counts. Have I ever been wrong when it comes to something like this? Something that matters?"

She paused, thinking back over the years. "No," she admitted. "You haven't."

ROSE'S JOURNAL
June 2007

——+——

I'M THINKING ABOUT Lily when the phone rings. Antoinette giggles at the shrill sound and kicks her heels against the wood floor. She sits at my feet as I clean up from dinner.

I don't answer the phone.

There are two dishes in the sink—mine and Antoinette's. I dunk my hands into the lukewarm water and brush the bread crumbs away. Mom would be appalled. "A growing girl needs more than a grilled cheese sandwich for dinner," she'd say.

I shy away from the thought. Thinking about Mom and Dad makes me feel bruised inside. If I had accepted Mom's offer to come with me when I took Antoinette to the specialist in Cincinnati, they'd be alive today.

I've examined my journal entries from that weekend. If I had known that was the last time I would see my parents, I would have recorded everything: the shirt Mom was wearing; her shade of lipstick; the number of hairs on Dad's head. As it is, I know that Dr. Ketters wore a purple dress with gold buttons when she told me to institutionalize my daughter, but I don't know what my mother looked like when she got in the car and drove away.

The phone rings again.

Though the window above the sink is open, the house is too quiet. I need the night to seep in. I pull the drain in the sink and watch the suds swirl away. Then I rinse the plates and dry them with a dish towel. The plates are white. The towel is white. I miss color.

The answering machine clicks on after the third ring. I hear Lily's voice. "Rose. Pick up the phone. I'm sorry. Talk to me." She is crying, and so am I, but I can't move.

I miss my sister, but Antoinette deserves to be surrounded by people who love her, not by people who are afraid of her. I failed when I was pregnant by not carrying her long enough. I won't fail now. No one will hurt her. Even Lily.

The sweet scent of honeysuckle drifts through the window. Suddenly I'm a child again, sitting with Lily under honeysuckle vines blooming at the edge of the creek. Their branches were so heavy with flowers they arched downward. As we watched, a doe crept out of the brush and lifted her nose to the wind.

I held my breath.

"Do you think I could touch her?" Lily whispered.

"Hush," I said. "You'll scare her off." I was the big sister who didn't have patience for the dark-haired little girl always tagging along behind me. I was the one who was embarrassed when her sister stared at the sky and counted the stars.

Lily was mesmerized by the deer. "I'm going to touch her," she whispered. She crawled out from under the bush.

When Lily moved, the doe lifted her head and sniffed the wind. She tilted her head to the side and stared right at us.

"Don't!" I grabbed Lily's arm, trying to keep her with me, but she was too far ahead.

The doe froze, and Lily stopped. Her lips moved as she counted. She waited for so long I thought she'd give up and come back to me.

Then the doe slowly dropped her head to the creek. My heart raced as Lily crawled closer. I wanted to follow her, but fear held me back. When Lily was an arm's length away, the deer lifted her head and bounded through the brush.

Lily didn't touch the doe that day, but between the two of us, she was the one who wasn't afraid to try.

She's still trying, I think as I listen to her voice on the answering machine. If I was anything like her, I'd pick up the phone and beg her to come home.

Instead, I wait until she's finished talking and then click Save. Later tonight, I'll replay this message along with the dozens of others she's left since December.

Just then, a knock at the door startles me. I peer through the window. "Seth!" Surprise makes me throw open the door. It's been years since I've seen him.

"Lily's not here," I say, without thinking. "She doesn't live here anymore."

"I know. I mean, that's what Teelia told me. I just got back into town. I guess you heard about my mom?"

News travels fast around Redbud. His mother died of a heart attack a few days ago. His father had died a year earlier, so Seth was alone now. I nod, and he looks down at the ground.

"I'm here taking care of things and thought I'd stop by." He is shy. As if we didn't spend every summer of our childhood together.

It crosses my mind that I shouldn't be talking to him after the way he treated Lily. I might be mad at her, but she's still my sister. Then he says, "I'm sorry about your parents," and I crumble.

He holds me while I cry into his shirt. "I loved them too," he says, and I shake harder.

When I finally stop crying, he looks over my shoulder as if Lily will appear and make a liar out of me. I almost wish she would. Antoinette leans into my leg. "My daughter, Antoinette," I say.

"God, she looks like you."

I swell with pride.

He kneels and speaks to Antoinette. "I knew your mom when she was a little thing, just like you."

Antoinette flaps her hands and shrieks.

"She likes you," I say. "She usually doesn't react this well to strangers."

He straightens and stuffs his hands into his jeans pockets. "It's been years, but I hope I'm not a stranger."

"Of course not." I stand back and open the door wider. I ignore a twinge of guilt that makes me feel I'm betraying Lily by speaking to him.

When he walks in, he stops in the middle of the kitchen and turns in a slow circle. "It's the same," he says. Which is funny, because to me, everything has changed.

AN HOUR LATER, we walk through the night garden. The air is cool, and the flowers are budding. So are dandelions and chokeweed.

Mom and I spent weeks planning the night garden. I still have our plans in my old sketch pads. White lilies line the path and moonflowers scale the wrought-iron arch at the entrance to the garden. At night, the arch fades and the moonflowers look like they're floating. Lily used to say it was magic.

I haven't been here since Mom died, and it shows. Weeds are everywhere. I can't look at the ground without that bruised feeling rising up in me, so I look up. The sky is a combination of blue-and-gray swirls, like Van Gogh's *Starry Night*.

Antoinette walks ahead of us, on her tiptoes like a ballerina. Before the doctor told me that toe-walking was a sign of developmental delays, I thought it was cute. Now it's a reminder of everything that's different about her.

Halfway across the garden, she stops and kneels under a maple tree. Snowdrops bloom in a semicircle around her. Odd. I don't remember planting the flowers. It's too late in the season for them. They bloom in early March.

A page from Lily's flower language book pops into my mind. Snowdrops represent hope. The passing of sorrow.

The maple trees have dropped their helicopter seeds, and Seth sweeps them from a stone bench in the center of the garden.

I'm about to sit when I see that something has captured Antoinette's attention. A sparrow lies on its side under the tree. Its wing is outstretched, its head twisted to the side. Its eyes are open. Antoinette reaches for it.

"Don't touch!" I say as I hurry over. "It's dirty."

It's silly, but I cry when I see the bird. Antoinette kneels and softly strokes its head. She runs her fingers across its wing, and all the while she hums. She is careful, as if aware that death is a solemn thing. I don't have the heart to pull her away.

When she stops humming, her head twitches slightly, and the left side of her mouth curves upward. She suddenly looks sleepy and closes her eyes and lists to the side.

"Come on, let's go," I say.

When I bend down to pick her up, the bird hops to its feet.

I gasp and fall back. "Seth!" I point to the bird as it spreads its wings and jumps into the sky.

"Did you see that?" I ask. "The bird. It was dead." I am giddy. Death has surrounded me for so long that this small life is absurdly precious. I start laughing and can't stop.

Antoinette flaps her hands, and I pick her up. She is heavy with sleep.

"Did you see the bird?" I ask Seth as I hurry back to the bench. I shouldn't be carrying Antoinette. Though she is small, she's heavy for me. I'm winded by the time I sit next to Seth, Antoinette on my lap.

"It was probably stunned," he says, "like when they smack into a window but then later fly off."

I look at the snowdrops. I think of the way my heart eases at Antoinette's touch. The cut on my finger at Lily's house, how it healed. Coincidence can't explain everything. I want to tell Seth, but he's right. I've seen birds hit our kitchen window, fall to the ground, and lie there for several minutes before flying off like nothing happened.

"Mom's funeral is tomorrow," Seth says, breaking into my thoughts. "I'd like it if you were there. She didn't have a lot of friends. And with my father gone—"

"Of course," I say, forgetting the bird. "I'll be there."

Antoinette sinks into me. "How long will you be in town?" I ask. I have other questions: Where have you been? Why didn't you come back before? And most of all: have you talked to Lily? But I don't ask them.

Seth picks a piece of long grass and splits it down the middle. Then he ties the thin pieces into a knot. He does the same thing with several other long pieces until he has a grass necklace. "Here, Antoinette." He slips it over her head. She shrieks and flaps her hands.

"That means she's happy," I explain.

"I have to close up the house," he says. "Get everything sorted out. Should take a month or so."

"What about work? Don't you have a church or something?"

He presses his lips together and looks down at his fingers. "Didn't exactly work out."

I don't press for details; he doesn't seem to be in the mood to share, and I'm not surprised. Seth always had a philosophical bent, but he wasn't a conformist. I never could picture him among men who spent more time making sure women stayed out of the clergy than feeding the hungry.

"If you need a hand while I'm around . . ." He gestures toward the night garden.

"Thanks," I say, "but I don't know how much longer I'll be here." The words hurt as they come out. A few years ago I would have given anything to leave the farm. Now it's the only place I want to be. "I can't run it by myself." The season's only beginning and already I'm behind. Several rows of daffodils died because I didn't harvest them in time.

"You're thinking of selling?"

"I don't have much choice. I've got a kid. I'm sick."

Seth looked at me in surprise.

"I developed a heart problem when Antoinette was born. I can't handle the farm by myself." I gesture to the weeds growing at our feet. Pride keeps me from mentioning Lily's phone calls.

"What about Lily?" he asks, as if he's reading my mind.

"We had a falling out. She sold me her share of the farm."

He doesn't ask what happened, and I don't offer details. We both have sore spots when it comes to Lily.

I hate the thought of giving up the farm. Antoinette loves

it here, but I lose my breath walking from my bedroom to the kitchen. I can't manage a fifty-acre farm alone.

"What if I stick around a little longer?" he asks. "Help you get things under control."

"I can't ask you to do that," I say, but in my heart I'm screaming for help.

"You're not asking," he says. "I'm offering. Growing up, this place was more of a home to me than my own house. Let me help."

It's late, and I'm sitting in the middle of a weed patch. But I look at the snowdrops. I think of the bird flying. And for the first time in a long time, I feel almost weightless with relief.

Chapter Eleven

The next afternoon Antoinette followed Seth to the drying barn. The flagstone path radiated heat. She stepped from the stones to the Elfin thyme ground cover. Her feet brushed the tiny leaves, releasing the strong scent into the air. The plants held her footprints for a second, and then sprang back as if she hadn't been there at all.

Her mother was at the house, sitting next to Lily on the porch swing. They sat on opposite ends of the swing, not close to each other like sisters should. Antoinette growled, but the drying barn was too far away for them to hear. A hard knot sat between her shoulders. She rolled her head from side to side, but it didn't help.

Other than the thick trees lining the creek bank, this was the only spot of deep shade on the farm. Birch and oak trees, their branches interlaced and their roots tangled, encircled the barn. Hostas, ferns, and pink bleeding hearts poked through the soil. A semicircle of dead pansies stood to one side of the barn. Antoinette stretched up on her toes and walked toward them.

"Oh no you don't," Seth said as he pulled her away from

the flowers and guided her into the drying barn. "You stick with me."

It was at least ten degrees cooler in the barn. Sawdust covered the floor and drying lavender hung from the rafters. Steel buckets hung from metal hooks along one wall and wheelbarrows were stacked up against another. Seth upended one of the wheelbarrows and placed several steel buckets into it.

Antoinette tapped the wheelbarrow and raised her hands.

"You want a ride?" Seth asked.

Antoinette flapped her hands. *Yes!*

He laughed and picked her up. "You're getting big." He gave her a tight squeeze then settled her into the wheelbarrow.

"Hold this for me." Seth pressed his iPod into her hands. It was hooked to a wireless docking station. "Are you up for a music lesson?"

Antoinette flapped her hands. She didn't need paper to communicate with Seth. She held the iPod while he scrolled through the songs on his playlist. "John Hiatt on the way to the fields? Classical while we work?"

She bobbed her head. Seth loved music almost as much as he loved the farm. He taught her the names of the instruments and how to tell if a piece was written in four-four time or three-four time.

He pressed Play on his iPod, and Hiatt's "Thirty Years of Tears" started. Then Seth grabbed the wheelbarrow's handles and pushed Antoinette out of the barn. "Hiatt has a great southern folk sound," he said. "This song is in three-four time. Like a waltz."

She rode with her back to Seth so she could look out over the land. The tree leaves were the new green that only came in spring. From the woods, a whip-poor-will called and a mock-ingbird sang. She tapped her finger against the side of the wheel-barrow, the sound blending with the birdsong and the music until Antoinette felt like she was singing along.

Seth added his voice to the mix. He harmonized easily with Hiatt, the birds, and the wind. He was part of the land.

The song ended when they reached the daffodil field. Seth lifted Antoinette from the wheelbarrow and directed her to a wooden bench at the head of the row. He set the iPod beside her, then squatted in front of her and grinned. "I'm quizzing you today. I think I can trip you up."

He started a playlist then grabbed a steel pail. "The first song's a freebie. You'll get it no problem."

This was the way she learned best. Studying things she loved with people who understood that not speaking was *not* the same as not comprehending.

Over the iPod, a piano started playing. Antoinette raised her chin and flapped her hands. "Für Elise." Beethoven.

Seth laughed. He was at the spigot that stood at the head of the row. "I told you you'd know this one. It's too easy." He hung the pail from a hook and turned on the spigot. To keep the flow-ers fresh, they had to be placed in water as soon as they were cut.

"We'll do tulips and daffodils today. Maybe the last of the hyacinths if we have time. Your mom asked me to keep back some of the flowers for her to make bouquets for the market. You're in charge of those, okay?" He turned off the water and set the bucket by her feet. The next song started while Seth filled a second bucket. A violin held a single note for several beats, then an organ joined in, giving depth to the piece.

Seth took the pail and bent down among the daffodils. The

muscles in his shoulders were tight with effort as he dug out weeds and clipped buds for market. Soon a thin sheen of sweat covered his arms.

The music still played. The violins were soaring now. Antoinette imagined them as birds looking down over the trees.

Seth straightened and swiped the back of his hand across his forehead. Sweat and dirt streaked his arms, and his brown hair curled around his shoulders. "Mozart?" he asked.

Antoinette sat still. Mozart's music was lighter.

"Beethoven?"

She almost popped out of her seat but caught herself just in time. No. Beethoven's violin concerto started with oboes. This was Bach. "Air on the G String."

He dropped his pruning shears into the bucket of daffodils at his feet. "I can't fool you, can I? You know it's Bach, don't you?"

Antoinette flapped her hands and shrieked. *Bach*. If she could say his name, it would come out like a growl.

Before Seth came to the farm, she used to study men in the grocery store, wondering whether one of them was her father. Her mother was beautiful, and she could speak. No one would want to leave her. But a child who couldn't speak? Couldn't control her body? That was a reason to leave. She imagined her birth father taking one look at her and running for the hills. She hoped someday her mother would tell her about him. But she didn't know how to ask.

Seth grabbed the smooth green stem of a budding daffodil, cut it at an angle, and dropped the flower in the bucket. He made his way down the row, leaving the tight buds that weren't quite ready. Plantings at the farm were staggered to extend the bloom time.

A new song started. This one was easy. "The Grand Theme" from Tchaikovsky's *Swan Lake*. Before Seth could throw out a name, Antoinette stood, raised her arms above her head, and spun on her toes. She moved so fast her knees almost folded.

"You're right," he said as he watched her dance. *"Swan Lake.* Tchaikovsky."

Antoinette stopped spinning and grinned. Now that Seth was here, she didn't search for her father in grocery stores anymore.

The bucket at his feet was full. He picked it up and hoisted it into the wheelbarrow. "Did I ever tell you that my dad was a musician?" he asked as he grabbed another empty pail. "He's the one who taught me."

He hadn't told her. She shook her head from side to side. Seth didn't often talk about his childhood.

"When he was in a good mood, he used to quiz me on the composers." One corner of his mouth quirked up.

Antoinette tried to imitate him, but she grimaced instead.

"Don't worry," he said. "You're better than I ever was. I couldn't tell Bach from Beethoven until I was fourteen." He tousled her hair as he walked down the row.

He walked back to the row where he had been working and knelt. "My dad was first chair violin for the Cincinnati Symphony Orchestra," he said without looking up. He cut three daffodils and put them in the pail. "My mom also played, but she wasn't as good. She was a high school music teacher. My parents met when my mom brought a group of students to the symphony."

The pail at his feet was getting full, but he added a few more daffodils. "It's funny. My dad taught me the violin, but when I play I think of my mother. When my dad wasn't home, she'd put on CDs of Bach and Beethoven. I was little then. I'd stand on her feet, and she'd waltz me around the house." He smiled at the memory.

Antoinette looked out beyond the daffodil bed, across the rows of raised soil. Several rows down, bright green tulip leaves unfurled like flags. She understood how Seth felt. Antoinette saw her mother in every inch of the farm.

"She would have loved you. My mother, I mean." Seth stopped working and looked up at her. "I know it's been hard on you . . . your mother being ill and all. It's never easy to lose a parent. No matter how old you are. But you should know, your mom's trying to look out for you. Lily's her sister. You should try to get to know her. Your mother loves her. You will too if you give her a chance."

Antoinette started rocking. Other than Seth, no one talked to her about her mother's illness. Most of the time, she loved that he talked to her about things others wouldn't, but right now she didn't want to hear what he was saying.

"I used to wonder why bad things like this happened," he said, "especially to good people like you and your mom. I spent a lot of time trying to find the answer to that question, and I still don't have it.

"But I do know that Lily's here to help your mom." He paused for a moment before adding, "And you. I think you should let her."

Some small part of Antoinette wanted to clamp her hands over her ears. She knew her mother was sick. Very sick. It made her feel small and helpless in a way that nothing else did. But she did not want—no, she did not *need*—Lily's help. Antoinette could take care of her mother alone.

Seth nodded toward the house, and Antoinette turned to see what he was looking at. The back porch was just visible from the daffodil field. Antoinette saw the porch swing where her mother and Lily sat, a wide space between them. From this far away, they looked like dolls.

Seth cut another daffodil and added it to the pail. "A long time ago—before you were born—Lily was my best friend. I felt comfortable around her. I could be myself. You know?"

He looked at Antoinette as if to see whether she understood. But she had never had a friend like that, other than her mother of course, and she didn't count. She wondered how it felt to have someone who saw through to the inside of you and loved you anyway.

"It's rare to find someone who knows all your secrets and still accepts you. My dad could be . . . difficult," Seth said. "On the nights that were especially hard, I'd sneak over here and toss pebbles at your aunt Lily's window until she woke. She'd sneak me inside, and I'd lie down on the floor between your mom's bed and Lily's.

"Your mom would fall right back to sleep, but Lily would stay up with me, talking until I could close my eyes."

He sat back on his heels and laughed. "Your grandma found me there once. I was twelve. I thought she was going to skin me alive, but she just leaned against the doorframe and said, 'For God's sake, Lily, don't make the boy sleep on the floor. Put him in the guest room.' Then she went downstairs and made me a plate of scrambled eggs."

The pail at Seth's feet was now full. He stood and picked it up, sloshing a bit of water over the edge. As he placed it in the wheelbarrow, he said, "You need to give Lily a chance."

Antoinette shook her head hard. Seth could like Lily if he wanted to, but she didn't even want to try.

Chapter Twelve

The sun was setting behind the hills as Lily followed Rose and Antoinette to the drying barn. The temperature had dropped, and the wind picked up. It felt like a storm was coming. She kept some distance between herself and Antoinette. *I can't do this*, she thought every time she looked at her niece. But how could she abandon Rose again?

She kept going back to her conversation with Will. He believed she could handle Antoinette, but Lily wasn't convinced. She started counting her steps.

A series of flagstone paths wound through the farm, but the one leading from the house to the drying barn was more worn than most. The barn was only a few yards away, directly across from the house. Bright pink azaleas flanked its entrance, with a stand of birch and oak trees to the right.

It hadn't always been a drying barn—at least not an herb-drying barn. Years ago, when Lily and Rose were still young, their father had converted it from an old tobacco barn. He ran electricity to power a commercial freezer and installed lights and a phone line.

The rafters, from which farmers before them had hung

tobacco, were perfect for drying lavender, basil, and other herbs. The plants were bound into bundles, then hung from the beams. Securing them had been one of Lily's jobs, and once that was done, she'd stretch out across one of the rough beams, surrounded by the warmth of the barn and the smell of the drying flowers. There she pictured a future in which she and Rose and Seth ran the farm together.

Back then, she never would have imagined spending her adult life away from this place.

"You're falling behind," Rose said, looking over her shoulder. "Same as always, isn't it?"

Rose held the barn door open for Antoinette, then flicked on the light.

Lily shivered as the wind picked up. She hurried into the barn, accidentally bumping into Antoinette. The little girl growled.

Lily stepped back, then walked a wide circle around the girl. She didn't know how to handle a normal child, much less a child like Antoinette. "I don't know how to be a mother," she said, her voice a whisper. Parenting wasn't math. There wasn't a child-raising formula. No $x + y$ = perfect parent.

At the word *mother*, Antoinette bared her teeth.

"And you think I did?" Rose zipped up her faded green jacket. The barn kept the wind off them, but Rose was cold all the time now. Her face was whiter than usual, and her lips were rimmed with blue. "When Antoinette was born, I cried every night until she was six months old. Mothering isn't something you're born knowing. You figure it out as you go along."

"She doesn't like me," Lily said as she watched her niece shuffle through the cedar shavings on the barn floor.

Seth had left a steel bucket full of daffodils and tulips on a table at the far end of the barn. Rose went to one of the shelves and took down a handful of water tubes. They would fill each of the tubes with water and preservative and then insert one stem into each tube.

Wind whistled through the cracks in the barn's slats. The sound was eerie, and Lily counted the seconds until it stopped.

Thirty-three. An odd number. Not good.

"Fill these for me," Rose said as she handed Lily the tubes. "And Antoinette will love you. You just need to give her time."

"How can you say that?" It wasn't a rhetorical question. Lily really wanted to know. "Weren't you at the farmers' market? She hates me." Lily went to the sink in the corner.

"It's not that bad. Give her time." Rose selected a daffodil and trimmed its stem.

"It's a little early to be doing this, isn't it?" Lily asked. "We've got, what, ten hours until the market tomorrow? The tubes will only keep the flowers fresh for six hours. Besides, the wind is really picking up out there."

Normally, Lily loved storms. She and Rose used to sit on the porch swing and watch the clouds roll in. They'd count the seconds after lightning flashes: "One Mississippi. Two Mississippi," squealing in delight as the time between seeing the lightning and hearing the thunder lessened. But tonight Lily felt off balance. She wanted to be inside the house, preferably in bed with a mug of hot chocolate.

"I know," Rose said. She trimmed another daffodil before plopping it back in the pail. "I won't insert the flowers into the tubes until right before the market tomorrow. I like getting everything ready the night before. It makes things easier in the morning. Put the tubes here." She indicated a plastic container on the table. "And we'll be finished before the worst of the storm."

Lily sensed Antoinette watching her as she placed the filled tubes in the box. She tried to ignore her niece, but even with her back turned, she felt the little girl's stare. "Mom didn't do it this way."

Rose shrugged. "Mom didn't have Antoinette to deal with. Mornings aren't always easy with her."

Lily glanced at Antoinette, who growled and started walking in circles.

"Change always came easy for you," Lily said to Rose as she turned from Antoinette.

Rose flinched. "Easy? You think this has been easy for me?"

"Easier than it is for me, I mean."

Rose frowned. Two sharp lines appeared between her eyes. "I'm dying. I'm leaving my daughter. You think that's easy?" Her voice went up a notch.

Lily shook her head. "I don't mean it like that. Things come easier for you. People like you." At school, Rose had always been surrounded by friends. Lily was lucky if she made it through lunch without someone "accidentally" spilling milk in her lap.

"People like you too, Lily. You just don't let anyone get close to you. So what if you have a few odd habits? We all do. Most people are just better at hiding them—" Rose stopped talking. "Where's Antoinette?"

"By the door," Lily said as she turned around. The door was open. "She was right there."

"Antoinette?" Rose hurried outside with Lily close behind her.

Rose stopped abruptly. Antoinette was kicking her feet through a semicircle of dead pansies. "You can't run off like that," Rose said.

Antoinette kept swishing her feet through the flowers. When she saw Lily, she growled.

The anxiety Lily had felt since coming home threatened to explode. She started to count.

Now that they had found Antoinette, Rose resumed her conversation with Lily. "You said earlier that you used to dream about being me. Well, I'd give anything to switch places with you. You're the one who will be here when Antoinette finishes school. You'll see what she looks like at twenty. At thirty. That's something I can only imagine."

Rose glanced at Lily's lips, which moved as she counted, and grabbed her shoulder. "Are you listening to me?"

At the same time, Antoinette started humming.

Lily stopped counting. "What's she doing?" she asked.

Antoinette was now kneeling in the middle of the dead flowers. She had closed her eyes and was running her fingers over the browning petals as she hummed.

"Shit!" Rose said. "Pick her up. Pull her away from the flowers."

"Why? They're dead. She can't hurt anything." The wind lifted Antoinette's hair, swirling the strands around her head.

Rose's face, already pale, went paler still. "Help me, Lily. I can't lift her."

The desperation on Rose's face spurred Lily into action. In four steps, she was at Antoinette's side. The girl kept humming as she pushed her hands deeper into the soil.

"Your mom wants you to come with me," she said. As she

reached for Antoinette, she prayed the girl wouldn't scratch her again.

Just before they touched, Antoinette stopped humming.

"Pick her up!" Rose yelled over the rising wind.

At the same time, Antoinette looked Lily right in the eye and smiled.

Lily's skin prickled.

"We're too late," Rose whispered.

Antoinette slumped forward, and the dead pansies blushed back to life.

"Oh my God!" Lily stumbled back. "It's not possible." She forgot about the mounting storm, knelt, and cautiously touched a flower petal. It was fragile and unbelievably soft.

Then Rose was there. "Don't let her seize this time," she murmured as she turned Antoinette onto her side.

A statistic flashed through Lily's mind: a major cause of death in epilepsy was asphyxiation due to the inhalation of vomit. She shook off her wonder at the flowers and helped Rose hold Antoinette on her side.

"Is she seizing?" Lily asked. She had never seen a seizure before, but she thought there should be shaking involved. Antoinette was still.

"No," Rose said. "She's sleeping."

Then Rose's earlier words flashed through Lily's mind: "Don't let her seize *this time*."

"You knew." Lily gestured to the now-brilliant yellow pansies.

"She's done this before." Everything she had seen since coming home flashed through her mind: the clematis over the porch, the wisteria draping the gazebo, the lavender at the farmers' market— all flowers blooming out of season.

Rose kissed her daughter. "Yes. I knew." The anger in her voice had evaporated. "Flowers. People. She fixes them all. Antoinette's the reason I'm still here. I would have died long ago if not for her."

Lily stared at her niece, numb with wonder. One thought went through her mind. If Antoinette could do this, she could heal Rose.

She could *heal* Rose.

"The healings are temporary," Rose said, dashing Lily's hope before it could fully form. "She seizes with more complicated healings, like my heart condition. And the seizures are getting worse each time. She'll die if she keeps doing this."

Tentatively, Lily stroked Antoinette's hair, unable to believe what she had just witnessed. Lightning flashed, and automatically she started counting. "One Mississippi. Two Mississippi. Three Mis—" A crack of thunder stopped her.

Rose touched Lily's shoulder. "The storm's getting closer. We need to get her back to the house. She'll sleep for a while now."

The wind had begun to roar and rain had started to fall, but Lily couldn't move.

"Come on, Lily," Rose said. "I need your help. I can't carry her anymore."

Slowly, Lily lifted her niece and followed Rose back to the house. As she did, she counted each step away from the spot where Antoinette had performed a miracle.

ROSE'S JOURNAL
June 2008

———+———

I MISS MY sister.

More than a year has passed since I spoke to Lily. Every time I pass the phone, I chant, *Ring!* But Lily doesn't call.

I've started talking to her in my mind. I tell her about the flowers we're growing. I tell her that Seth keeps an old picture of her in his back pocket. I tell her that Antoinette loves flowers the way she does.

Then I remember the way she shrank from Antoinette during Mom and Dad's funeral, and I feel a rush of anger. I love Lily, but I live for Antoinette.

Right now, Antoinette toddles toward the Bakery Barn. I count her steps as if, like Lily, I need numbers to make the moment last. A small garden filled with purple petunias, pink zinnias, and yellow daylilies frames the bakery entrance. The zinnias and daylilies are bright, but the petunias have wilted. The sun is directly overhead. It burns my shoulders and the top of my head.

As Seth and I walk to a metal table, I shield Antoinette's view. If she notices the flowers, she'll have a meltdown. When she sees a flower bowed under the summer heat, she stomps her feet and flaps her hands. She seems to have an emotional connection with nature. She only calms after I water the plant.

The patio is empty. Seth selects a table next to the door. His skin is tanned a deep brown, and his hair is streaked with gold. When we were kids, he walked as if he carried a heavy burden, and he rarely smiled. Now he sings while he works, and sometimes Antoinette hums along with him. It seems he has found his place in life.

"Can you watch Antoinette?" I ask him. "I need to talk to MaryBeth." I want to head off Antoinette's meltdown if she notices the plants.

"Sure. But when you come back, I want to hear what the doctor said." Since returning home, Seth has driven me to the cardiologist every three months.

I nod, then pop into the bakery. A young girl with spiky hair and a nose ring mans the counter.

"Is MaryBeth around?" I ask.

The girl rubs her nose ring, a small diamond stud. "I think she's in the back." She points to a room separated from the front of the store by a thick brown curtain.

I walk around the counter and sweep back the curtain. "Eli? MaryBeth?"

The room is well lit. MaryBeth leans over an antique desk that's covered with receipts. Half-moon glasses perch on her nose. Her short hair is messy. She looks like she's been working since the dark morning hours. Judging by the rows of cookies and cupcakes in the bakery case, she probably has.

"Rose!" Her arms are thin but strong, and her tight hug reminds me of Mom. I don't want to let go. "Is my favorite girl with you?" she asks.

"She's outside with Seth. That's why I'm here. Your petunias are a little droopy. Antoinette can't stand seeing flowers in distress. If you've got a watering can, I'll take care of them."

MaryBeth drops her glasses on the desk. "Well, we can't have her getting upset, can we? I've got a can under the sink."

I don't mean for MaryBeth to stop what she's doing, but she waves away my offer of help. "Go sit with Seth and your daughter. I'll be out in a minute." She steps back and looks at me. "And get something to eat. You look hungry."

I've lost weight, but I didn't think it showed. Between working the fields and caring for Antoinette, I'm so tired I often go to bed without eating. Seth's help makes it easier, but he's not the one who wakes when Antoinette has a nightmare. He's not the one who lies in bed staring at the ceiling, wondering who will care for her after I'm gone. I stop at the counter and order three cupcakes from the girl with the nose ring.

Antoinette is sleeping on the ground beside the garden when I come outside. Her hands are covered with dirt.

"Did she scream herself out?" I set a cupcake in front of Seth. It's his favorite, chocolate cake with vanilla icing.

"No," he says as he peels back the paper wrapper. "She saw the flowers, stuck her hands in the ground, and started humming. After she finished, she leaned over and closed her eyes. I think the heat got to her. No one's here, so I let her sleep."

I set the other cupcakes on the table and kneel beside Antoinette. Her eyelids flutter when I stroke her shoulder. "Wake up, sleepyhead. You can't just lie down on the sidewalk and take a nap."

She smiles, and I feel full of light. Antoinette isn't an easy child, but she's *my* child. My past, present, and future are in each breath she takes.

I don't notice the petunias until I help her sit. When I do, I blink twice. "Did I miss something? They were droopy and brown before, right?" The flowers beside the door are a purple so bright it almost hurts my eyes.

Before Seth answers, MaryBeth arrives with a watering can and walks to the flowers. "I thought you said they were brown. I'm no gardener, but they look okay to me."

I shake my head and guide Antoinette to the table. She grabs a cupcake and squishes her hand in the icing. "I must be seeing things. I could've sworn they had wilted."

June isn't Kentucky's hottest month—that would be August when the air burns your lungs—but sweat popped out along my arms as soon as I walked outside. I chalk up my confusion to the heat.

Antoinette shrieks—her happy sound. White icing coats her hands and her mouth. I laugh. "You like that?"

Antoinette flaps her hands. Then she takes another bite of her cupcake. Most of it makes it to her mouth. When she grins, chocolate crumbs coat her teeth.

"There's plenty more where that came from," MaryBeth says. "Eli will be sorry he missed you. He went home after the morning rush. A bakery's not the best place to be during the summer. All that heat.

"Speaking of which, I'll bring out a pitcher of sweet tea," MaryBeth says. "Y'all can't sit out here without something to drink."

As soon as she leaves, Seth says, "What did the cardiologist say?"

I hear him, but I can't get my mind off the flowers. "Did you see the petunias when we arrived? Were they wilted?"

I don't know what I want him to say. If he says no, I'm seeing things. If he says yes, well, I don't know what that means.

"The cardiologist?" he insists. "What did he say?"

I take some napkins from the dispenser on the table and wipe Antoinette's hands and mouth. She finished her cupcake, but more of it is on her face than in her stomach.

"He did an echocardiogram. My ejection fraction was thirty-five percent." Somehow I keep the fear from my voice.

An echocardiogram measures the amount of blood the heart pumps out. Anything over fifty percent is good. Thirty-five percent is low. It means I'm at significant risk for a heart attack.

Thinking about it makes my chest constrict. I take deep breaths and tell myself I should be happy. It's been a little over five years since my heart gave out during Antoinette's birth. My time should already be up.

"I'm sorry." Seth squeezes my hand, and I wonder whether I look as sad as he does. He would have made a good minister, I think. I say so, but he shrugs me off.

"Too many sacrifices," he says.

I wonder if he means Lily.

I pick at the cupcake in front of me. MaryBeth makes them fresh every day, so I know it's good, but I can't eat. I clench my teeth so hard my jaw hurts. I can't talk about my health. If I do, I'll start crying and never stop.

I look at the flowers again. In the year that Seth's been at the farm, we've rarely talked about the things that happen around Antoinette. Flowers blooming out of season. The fact that I'm still here.

Voicing my thoughts seems silly, but I plunge ahead. "You saw them too." I nod to the petunias. "They were wilted before."

Seth folds his cupcake wrapper into a small square. He turns it over and presses the sharp corner into his thumb. "We're both tired from working in the fields today. Or maybe it was a shadow."

It's the closest he's come to admitting that he's seen the peculiar things that happen around Antoinette. I think about the snowdrops in the night garden. The cut that disappeared from my finger. The bird that hopped into the sky after Antoinette's touch.

"It wasn't a shadow," I say, "and I'm not *that* tired." Then I blurt out what I've been thinking for the past several months: "What if Antoinette's causing these things to happen?" I know I'm grasping at straws, but if Antoinette made those things happen, then maybe she can fix me.

MaryBeth returns holding a tray with a pitcher of sweet tea and three glasses. She sets the glasses in front of us and pours the tea.

Seth and I fall silent. I'm embarrassed by my outburst.

"I'd stay to chat," MaryBeth says, "but without Eli, I'm the only one keeping an eye on things." She hugs Antoinette before she leaves.

When Seth speaks, his voice is filled with pity, and that hurts more than his words. "She's just a little girl, Rose. She's not causing anything."

"I'd think you of all people would believe," I say in a stubborn last-ditch attempt to persuade him.

"That's not fair," he says. "There's a difference between faith in God and believing that Antoinette can do miracles."

Why? I want to ask. But I don't say anything, and we finish our cupcakes in silence.

• • •

THE BACK OF my legs stick to the wood bench running along the gazebo, which Seth painted purple and yellow last week. The colors are happy, but they don't help my mood. A bucketful of strawberries sits at my feet. Antoinette is in the middle of the gazebo, stretched up on her toes, twirling.

Seth sits beside me. He hasn't said much since we left the Bakery Barn. I can't blame him. I don't know what to say either. My chest hurts.

I pluck a strawberry from the bucket, pop off its stem, and bite into it. Fresh strawberries are my favorite part of June. I study Antoinette as she dances, trying to see past her awkward movements. Seth's right—she's just a little girl.

"Earlier, at the Bakery Barn . . . I mean, it's obvious Antoinette isn't making these things happen," I say.

Ever since Dr. Ketters told me to institutionalize Antoinette, I've been looking for some great good to balance out all of the heartache. I used to imagine Antoinette listening to one of Mozart's symphonies and then picking out the melody on the piano at Seth's house. I'd dream of her taking my old paints and producing a perfect replica of the striped fields behind the house.

"I just want to believe something good will happen."

"It already has," he says. He nods toward Antoinette, who is waving her fingers before her eyes, giggling.

He picks up a strawberry and turns it over before dropping it back into the pail. He and Lily used to spend hours picking strawberries. I haven't seen him eat one since coming home.

"Do you miss her?" I ask. I don't want to embarrass him, so I look at my feet. My ankles are swollen, one of the perks of a damaged heart. I make a note to take a water pill when we go inside. Then I steeple my fingers and press them into my chest, trying to dispel the pressure that started building earlier at the Bakery Barn.

"Every day," Seth says softly.

It's getting hard to breathe. "You should call Lily," I say. I haven't talked to her in years, but I'm still her big sister. The need to watch out for her never left me.

"Maybe someday." Seth straightens and stretches his arms over his head.

"I don't understand."

He stares out over the hills. His hair falls over his eyes. "Sometimes the best thing you can do for someone is to stay away from them. She has a new life. I don't want to disrupt it."

It's dusk; the fireflies are out. We should be in the night garden. This past spring, Seth helped me fix it up. The weeds are gone and the trellis is heavy with moonflowers and climbing hydrangeas.

Antoinette stops dancing. I hold out a strawberry. "Want it?"

My chest squeezes again. I should go inside and lie down, but Antoinette is happy, and I love seeing her that way. I want to prolong this moment.

She bites into the berry and red juice trickles down her chin.

I laugh. "Between the cupcake and the strawberries, we'll have to hose you off before we go inside."

When I lean forward to wipe her mouth, my chest tightens. It feels as if someone is crushing my heart. I close my eyes and breathe deeply, focusing on expanding my rib cage and filling every inch of my body with air.

Seth touches my shoulder. "Are you all right?"

I force my eyes open, but I keep taking slow, deep breaths.

The pressure builds, and I shake my head. My nitro pills are at the house.

Antoinette comes closer. My focus narrows to the strawberry she holds. I stare so hard I can count the seeds running up its side. I breathe. In. Out. In. Out.

"What can I do?" Seth asks, an edge of panic in his voice. "Your lips are blue. Should I call the paramedics?"

I try to say *Call 911*, but my mouth isn't working.

Antoinette drops the strawberry. It rolls toward the stairs, leaving a trail of red juice.

I need to go to the house. I try to stand, then stumble to the ground.

Seth yells my name, but I block out everything except my daughter. I fight to keep my eyes open, wanting her face to be my last sight.

She crouches beside me, and her long blonde hair touches the back of my hand. Her face is too serious for a five-year-old. My vision starts to fade. I open my eyes wider.

Antoinette caresses my cheek. I remember how strong her grip was as a baby. How could I have ever wished her to be more than she is? I want to tell her that she's perfect, but the pain has crawled into my jaw. Suddenly we're both mute.

Then Antoinette hums, and I feel like I'm being turned inside out. The pressure in my chest builds to a single concentrated point, and then it explodes outward. I arch my back and scream.

Antoinette hums faster.

I burn with pain.

Just when I think I will burst, everything stops. I lie still for a moment, afraid to move. Then I feel Antoinette's hand against my cheek.

I open my eyes. She's smiling at me.

"What happened?" Seth is beside me. He tilts my face to his. "The color is back in your face. Your lips aren't blue."

But I don't speak. I'm focused on my daughter.

I put my hand over hers. "Did you do this?"

Antoinette gives me one more brilliant smile before her eyes roll back, and she collapses. Her arms shake, and her heels thud against the gazebo floor.

"Oh God," I say."What's happening?"

Seth doesn't hesitate. "We need to get her to the hospital." He scoops her up and runs to the truck. I hurry after him, my heart beating as easily and smoothly as it did when I used to run through the fields with Lily.

"I DID THIS to her," I say. I lean over Antoinette's bed in the emergency room. Seth and I stand on either side of her, keeping watch. She had a grand mal seizure. The medicine that stopped it made her fall asleep.

"You didn't do this," he says. "The doctor said seizures are common in children with Antoinette's disabilities."

Antoinette's seizure lasted thirty minutes. Far too long, the ER doctor said. The longer a seizure lasts, the greater the possibility for brain damage.

An IV snakes out of the back of her hand. The nurse had to bandage Antoinette's arm with surgical wrap to keep her from yanking it out.

"The flowers. The bird. And now me. Antoinette's disability didn't cause her seizure, healing me did."

Seth says, "You couldn't have known," and I know he believes now. Antoinette saved me.

When we arrived, Seth told the doctors I had been having chest pain. They did an EKG, an echocardiogram, and drew blood to check for cardiac enzymes. Everything was normal. The echocardiogram—my second today—showed my ejection fraction at sixty percent.

Better than normal.

But at what price? I brush Antoinette's hair from her forehead. I don't know how, but I'm convinced she healed me and that the effort caused her seizure. Which means that I can't ever let her do this again. A broken body I can bear, but a broken heart, well, even Antoinette can't fix that.

Chapter Thirteen

L ily couldn't sleep. She lay in bed, staring at the ceiling. Every time she closed her eyes, she saw Rose explaining how Antoinette's healing ability worked.

"She can control it," Rose had said. They were sitting on the porch swing with Antoinette between them. As Rose spoke, the tight lines around her mouth disappeared, as if talking about it removed a weight she had been carrying. "She doesn't help everyone, only people she *wants* to heal. And she can't heal herself. She touches the person, and then she hums. I don't know how she actually changes things."

"How does it feel?" Lily asked.

"It's like being turned inside out," Rose said. "Like your bones and muscles are stretching, and your skin can't contain them anymore. You want to burst apart and come together at the same time."

"Does it hurt?" Lily asked.

"Sometimes," she said.

Only three people knew about Antoinette's ability. Rose, Seth, and now Lily. Eli Cantwell suspected. Before they went inside, Rose made Lily promise not to tell anyone what Antoinette could do. "It's the only way to keep her safe," Rose said. "Healing everyone who needs help will kill her."

Despite her promise, Lily wanted to call Will, but how could she explain what had happened tonight? He wouldn't believe on faith alone.

Sleep was impossible. She kicked back the quilt and stood, putting on the jeans she'd worn earlier. She needed to see Seth. He had known about this from the beginning. What had he said in the truck her first day home? Antoinette was different.

What she'd learned earlier went way beyond different.

Before all of this, she had been afraid to be Antoinette's guardian. Now she was terrified.

She tiptoed out of the house and into the night, pausing to slip on the garden clogs she had left by the back door. She trembled as she hopped the white-plank fence between Eden Farms and Seth's property.

His farm bordered theirs. He owned twenty acres, but his house was only a short distance from the fence line. The moon was bright, but she didn't need its light to find her way. It was *his* home. Her feet knew the way.

The scent of honeysuckle drifted on the night breeze, and cornflowers bloomed around her feet. It was too early for them, and she wondered whether Antoinette had been here recently.

A page from her flower book came to her. Cornflowers meant "hope in love." Ridiculous. She didn't love Seth. At least, not anymore. She crushed a blue flower beneath her heel. "I don't love him," she said out loud. She was wading through flowers when his house came into view.

Before Seth's family bought the house, the front porch had sagged in on itself. The white paint was dirty and peeling. Seth's father restored the farmhouse. He shored up the porch, extending it until it wrapped around the first story. He sanded off the chipped white paint and repainted with a soft butter yellow. He removed the overgrown yew bushes that obscured the front of the house and planted pale pink Sharifa Asma roses in their place. He did everything except make the house a home. Given Seth's dark memories of childhood there, Lily was surprised he hadn't sold it long ago.

It was late, but the lights were on. She squared her shoulders as she climbed the porch stairs and knocked on the door. A full minute passed before Seth appeared to open it.

"Lily," he said, his eyes wide with surprise. "Is Rose okay?" He walked onto the porch and shut the door behind him. He wore a pair of faded jeans and nothing else. His stomach was taut. She could count each of his muscles. His brown hair was messy. It curled around his face, tousled by sleep.

"She's fine. Everything's fine. I need to talk to you." Lily couldn't stop moving. She tapped her fingers against her thigh as she paced back and forth on the porch.

"At midnight? Couldn't it wait till morning?" He leaned against the porch railing and yawned.

"No. It can't." She pointed at him. "Why didn't you tell me what Antoinette could do?" Her voice was loud.

"Would you have believed me?" he asked, infuriatingly calm.

"You should have told me." She poked him in the chest. "You said Antoinette was different. This is *way* beyond different."

He caught her hand before she could jab him again. "Does it matter?"

"I don't know," she said after a long pause. "Maybe." This close, she felt the heat from his skin. She could map the tiny lines at the corner of his eyes and around his mouth—could see all the ways his face had changed over the years.

He didn't let go of her hand.

"For what it's worth, I told Rose you needed to know, but even if she had listened to me you wouldn't have believed. I was with Antoinette every day for over a year. Strange things happened around her all the time, but I never thought she was *causing* them until I saw her heal Rose."

He made sense, but Lily was angry. For once, she didn't want logic. She wrenched her hand free.

"She's a little girl who's losing her mother," Seth said, still unruffled. "The rest of it doesn't matter."

His calm manner made her angry. Her face flushed as she turned away from him. "Of course it matters. I didn't know what I was doing before. Now . . ." She waved her hand in the air, searching for the right words, but they didn't exist. "I'm in over my head."

"No you're not. You can do this." He took her by the shoulders and turned her to face him.

A sense of betrayal washed over her, and she fought to hold back tears. "You should have told me," she said. "I thought I was your friend."

"You are," he said, and she thought she saw pain in his eyes.

"No. I meant something to you once. For that, if for no other reason, you should have told me." Frustration and fear overcame her. She turned and reached for the porch railing as tears spilled down her cheeks. "Coming here was a mistake." She hurried down the steps, unsure whether she meant coming to Seth's house or coming home.

Finally agitated, Seth reached for her, but he was too late. "Lily, wait!" he yelled. But she ran home without looking back.

LILY WAS ELEVEN years old when she realized she loved Seth. Before that, she hadn't understood why she smiled when she said his name. Or why her heart fluttered when his hand brushed hers.

They were walking through the fields one morning at the end of a long, hot summer. His right eye was purple and swollen. As usual, he pretended nothing was wrong, and she tried to make it easier for him. "He's drinking again?" Lily asked.

They trailed behind Rose, cutting through tall grass on their way to the creek. The sun was low, but soon it would be overhead, pulling pearls of sweat from their skin. Lily counted her footsteps from the house (forty-six) and plucked a piece of grass gone to seed. She stuck it between her teeth and chewed. It tasted both bitter and sweet.

"You could stay with us," she said, not the first time she made the suggestion. "Mom wouldn't care. We've got an extra bedroom."

Seth didn't say anything, but he never did. He was stuck. The best he could do was spend as much time as possible at their house, slipping home after dinner when his father passed out in the study. Most days he managed, but sometimes he made too much noise as he tiptoed into the house. Those were the nights he snuck out after midnight and ran across the field that separated their houses. Once there, he stood outside, throwing pebbles at the girls' bedroom window until either Lily or Rose woke and helped him inside.

As they walked, Lily held out her hand. He took it, and his hand swallowed hers. When had he grown so much bigger?

"What's holding y'all up?" Rose yelled, over her shoulder. She had draped her shorts over the low-hanging limbs of a river birch so they wouldn't get wet. Her legs were deep brown, and her hair was so long it reached the middle of her back. She looked more like a woman than a child, her body pushing into curves and softening in places where Lily was still narrow and flat.

Seth glanced at Rose, then dropped his eyes to the ground, but not before Lily saw a red flush creep up his neck. For the first time she was embarrassed for him to see her body.

"Come on!" Rose yelled again as she splashed through the creek.

Seth shoved his hands into his pockets and kicked at a rock on the trail. "You go ahead," he said, without looking at Lily.

Rose clambered up onto the flat rock that stood in the middle of the creek. Her white T-shirt was transparent. Earlier that summer, their mother had taken Rose to town and came back with two white cotton training bras. Jealousy twisted Lily's stomach when she saw the outline of Rose's bra through her wet shirt. She counted backward from one hundred, but it didn't help.

Seth kept his back to Rose. He shifted his weight from foot to foot. Every few seconds his gaze slid over to Rose.

Lily wished he would look at her like that, but she knew stripping down to her skivvies wouldn't accomplish anything. For one thing, she was wearing little-girl underwear with SATURDAY emblazoned across the back. For another, Rose outshone her in every way.

"Come! On!" Rose yelled again, sitting up on the rock, water glistening on her body.

"I don't want to," Lily said.

"Baby!" Rose called.

Lily clenched her teeth to keep from yelling. Instead, she turned to Seth. "Want to go pick some strawberries?"

He shook his head and mumbled something about forgetting to check the latch on the gate. Then he ran off toward his house, leaving Lily on the creek bank.

She wanted to dash after him, but her feet wouldn't move. A feeling of hate surged through her body. She splashed into the water without taking her shoes off. When she reached the center of the creek where Rose reclined on the rock, her long blonde hair splayed over her shoulders, Lily grabbed a fistful of hair and yanked as hard as she could.

"Ow!" Rose screamed as she toppled off the rock and into the water. "Why'd you do that?"

Lily jabbed a finger at Rose. "His dad hit him again." To her shame, she began to cry. She turned her back on Rose and sniffed hard while she clambered up onto the rock. She hitched up her knee and yanked her shoes off. Her mother was going to kill her for ruining another pair.

Rose stood in the middle of the creek, water rushing around her ankles. "I didn't know," she said.

"If you ever paid attention to anyone else, you would have noticed. It's not like it's invisible."

"Oh," Rose said as she stared at Lily. The anger disappeared from her face. "It's like that."

"Like what?" Lily asked, still mad. She tugged her socks off and wrung the water from them. If she laid them out on the rock, they might dry before she went home, at least enough that her mother wouldn't notice.

Rose shook her head. "Nothing," she said, but she cocked

her head to the side and looked at Lily as if witnessing something she had never seen before.

"Why are you staring at me?" Lily glared at her.

Rose hopped back up on the rock. Her feet dangled in the water. "You like him," she said.

"Of course I do. We're friends." It was true, but as she spoke, she suddenly realized it was more than that. It had happened so gradually, she wasn't aware of it until now. Seth made her feel lit from within, as if by a thousand fireflies.

Chapter Fourteen

L ily woke with sheets wrapped around her legs. The sun wasn't up, but she kicked back the covers and stood. An image from last night of Seth standing on his porch, yelling after her, flashed through her mind. She shoved it aside, ran her fingers through her snarled hair, and dressed in jeans and a green T-shirt.

Then she reached for her cell phone. She didn't care that it was six in the morning. After three rings, it went to voice mail.

"Will," she said after the beep. "It's me. I need to talk to you. Soon." She clicked off, then walked out of her room and down the hall.

Last night, she had to count backward from one thousand before she could fall asleep. Even then, she woke with knots in her shoulders. Farmwork might loosen her muscles; in the garden, she didn't need to count. Death statistics didn't roll through her mind. She was looser there, her mind not filled with numbers and calculations. With luck, she could harvest some tulips and figure out how to tell Rose that Seth would be a better guardian for Antoinette.

It had taken her most of the night to arrive at that decision, but once she had, it made sense. Seth had known Antoinette longer. He cared about her. Most of all, it didn't bother him that she was some kind of miracle worker.

The window at the end of the hall was open and a warbler's song drifted in. Lily started down the stairs, counting each one. There were nine, which she should have remembered. The odd number made her skin itch.

Eleven paces to the kitchen. Not good.

"You're up early." Rose sat at the large oak table, holding a cup of coffee. Early-morning sunlight streamed through the back door, painting her hair as white as her skin.

Lily stopped at the entrance. She couldn't talk to Rose yet. Not before she worked out everything she wanted to say. "I'll be back," she said, hurrying to the stairs.

"Are you okay?" Rose asked.

No. She wasn't okay. She pushed her heels back until they hit the bottom stair. She moved carefully, imagining herself as a teenager. She was on thirteen when she reached the kitchen.

She shook her head and turned around. Rose watched but didn't say anything.

This time Lily pretended she was a Chinese empress with bound feet, taking dainty, careful steps. It worked. She entered the kitchen on twenty-two, a safe number finally, and sank into the chair across from Rose. The room smelled like fresh coffee and cinnamon.

"Counting?" Rose asked. "Stay there. I'll get you a cup of coffee."

Lily let her. If she got up, she'd start counting again. "I didn't think you'd be awake," she said to fill the space between them.

Rose took a blue mug from the cabinet next to the stove.

"Still load it up with milk and sugar?" When Lily nodded, Rose put two heaping teaspoons of sugar and a large splash of milk into the cup. "Sleeping's hard for me. My lungs fill with fluid. I start coughing as soon as my head hits the pillow."

"I'm sorry. I didn't know."

Rose sat down. "It's been going on awhile. I'm used to it." She handed Lily her coffee.

Lily put the mug to her lips. The confused thoughts from last night came tumbling back. Agreeing to be Antoinette's guardian when she was just a kid with special needs had been hard enough, but adding this weird *ability* to the mix made Lily want to sit on the porch and count each blade of grass.

"About yesterday—we need to talk," Rose said.

No. They didn't. Lily's foot twitched. She took a large sip of coffee.

Rose ran a hand through her hair. "I didn't want to keep secrets from you. Seth told me not to."

He was right, Lily thought.

"It's just that I was afraid you'd leave once you found out about her," Rose said.

The remark hit dangerously close to home. She took another sip of coffee. "I noticed that the white tulips are budding. I thought I'd harvest some of them this morning before it gets too hot."

"You can't just pretend it didn't happen," Rose said, an undercurrent of vulnerability in her voice.

Lily had to look away. She stared out the window, noting that low-hanging fog sat over the fields. "The fog should keep everything cool." Cutting flowers was best done in the morning when it wouldn't stress the plant. She knew the routine by heart. Cut the buds right before they bloomed. Strip the leaves and put the stems in a clean bucket of water so the flowers didn't wilt.

They would store some in the commercial freezer in the barn for close to a month. They had a small greenhouse where they forced bulbs and other off-season flowers to bloom in order to supply the antiques shops and restaurants that formed the town center, but most of their flowers came from the fields or hoop houses.

"Lily," Rose said. "We need to talk about this."

Lily tapped her fingers against her thigh. "Do you still keep a spare pair of pruning shears in there?" She indicated the drawer next to the pantry where her mother used to store twine, bits of ribbon, and anything else that might be useful on a quick trip to the garden.

"Don't ignore me," Rose said. "This is important."

Rose reached out, but Lily stood and took her mug to the sink. It was still half full, but she dumped out the remaining coffee. Then she opened the drawer. It had been a mess when she was a child and it was still a mess now. "At least this hasn't changed," she said under her breath as she fished through metal plant labels, florist's wire, and mismatched garden gloves.

"What's that supposed to mean?" Rose walked over to stand beside Lily.

"Nothing. Things are different. That's all." Lily found a pair of garden shears and grabbed the first two garden gloves she saw. One was pink and the other green. They were both for the left hand. Exasperated, she tossed them onto the counter.

Rose reached around Lily's shoulder, grabbed a right-handed pink glove from the drawer, and handed it to her. "It's a house. Not a museum. If you wanted it to stay the same, you shouldn't have left."

"I didn't mean it that way," Lily said as she put the glove on.

"Then what did you mean?" Rose's cheeks were flushed. This was the healthiest she had looked since Lily arrived.

"Everything's different. It would've been nice if some things had stayed the same. That's all."

"From where I sit, nothing's changed," Rose said. "You're still running away."

"Give me a break, Rose." Anxiety made her short. "You can't spring something like this on me and expect everything to be fine. You should have told me *everything* about Antoinette when you asked me to come home."

"How could I have told you?" Rose's voice went up a notch in both pitch and volume. "You wouldn't have believed me until you saw it for yourself. Seth didn't even believe until he saw Antoinette heal me."

She was right, but Lily couldn't admit that. "You should have told me."

"And you shouldn't have left in the first place," Rose snapped.

Lily stepped back as if slapped. "I called you every day. You never answered. You didn't want me here."

"You're right. I didn't want you here; I *needed* you here. I was sick, and I had a special-needs kid. You think you were scared? You have no idea what fear feels like." Rose was yelling now. "Antoinette's special ability shouldn't change anything, but if you're leaving you might as well go now."

Lily wanted to say she wasn't running away, but wasn't that exactly what she had been planning all morning?

There was a sharp knock at the door. It was probably Seth—someone else Lily was angry with—but she yanked the door open, grateful for the diversion. "What?" she snapped, then stepped back in surprise.

Will stood on the porch, his dark hair meticulously combed and his blue oxford shirt wrinkle-free despite the two-hour drive to Redbud.

"Lily Martin," he said as he opened his arms. "Just the girl I'm looking for."

"What are you doing here?" she asked. In her shock, she was abrupt.

"Do I need a reason beyond missing you?" he asked. He grinned, but something in his eyes said it was more than that.

"To drive two hours south without telling me you were coming? Yes, you need a better reason than that."

"Who is it?" Rose asked. She came up behind Lily and opened the door wider.

"Will Grayson." He pushed past Lily and held out his hand. "Lily's friend. You must be Rose."

After a hesitation, Rose took his hand. "I'm sorry. I don't remember Lily mentioning you."

Will shrugged. "Keeping me all to yourself, hmm Lils?" He smiled at Rose. Then he leaned down as if confiding a secret. "Can't blame her. Women have trouble staying away from me."

Rose gave a shocked laugh. "I can see why."

Lily took his arm. "Why don't I show you around the farm?"

"Wait." Rose pulled Lily into the family room. As soon as

they were out of earshot, Rose said, "You can't tell him about Antoinette. The fewer people who know about her ability, the safer she is." She squeezed Lily's arm.

"You're hurting me," Lily said as she disentangled herself. She was angry, but a small voice in the back of her head said Rose was right. She closed her eyes and counted to ten. "Fine."

Rose didn't look convinced.

"I won't tell him," Lily said. "Besides, what am I going to say? 'Meet my niece, the miracle worker?'" She looked over her shoulder. Will stood in the middle of the kitchen, his hands still in his pockets, whistling. "I'm just showing him the garden."

A pained look flashed across Rose's face. "I would have told you. Eventually. I just wanted you to get to know Antoinette first."

There was a loud thump from upstairs. Rose glanced at the ceiling. "Antoinette's awake. I'd better get her." Before leaving, she said, "I know I'm asking a lot. But I need you. *We* need you. Please don't go."

She didn't wait for Lily to answer. Which was just as good, because Lily had no idea what to say.

Will was still standing in the middle of the kitchen. When he saw her, he smiled. "Surprised you, didn't I?"

"You could say that."

"Rose doesn't look scary," he said, continuing the conversation they had started several days ago on her deck. "No horns—not that I can see anyway. No cloven hooves. Just your average run-of-the-mill sister."

"You never answered me," she said as she held the back door open for him. "Why are you here?"

Will followed her onto the porch. "Simple. You sounded scared on the phone. I'm here to help you feel better." He leaned in to her. "Whatever it takes."

She shoved him.

"Hmm, into the rough stuff." He raised his eyebrows and rubbed his shoulder. "That's all right. I meant what I said. Whatever. It. Takes. I'm your man."

"Seriously, why are you here?"

"You want serious. Okay. I can do that." He stopped smiling. "When you called me and said you couldn't take care of Antoinette, I was afraid you'd leave. I've known you long enough to know that if you did you'd regret it for the rest of your life.

"It might seem easier to walk away, but one day you'd wake up and realize that abandoning your niece was the biggest mistake you'd ever made. I left Covington at five this morning and drove here to make sure that doesn't happen."

Was her fear that obvious? She stared at him, not sure whether she should be grateful, or angry, for his interference.

Will jogged down the porch steps. At the bottom, he said, "Well, aren't you going to show me around the farm?"

Lily counted to ten before joining him.

"So where are the pigs?" he asked.

"It's not a pig farm." She stopped at Will's sharp intake of breath. Without looking up, she knew what had captured his attention. The oak and birch trees had blocked his view of the land from the porch, but as they walked Eden Farms spread out in front of them.

Lilacs bloomed around the farmhouse. Daffodils nodded from beds framing the house. Beyond that, the commercial flower fields stretched. They were striped red, pink, and purple as flowers sprouted from the soil. Pink clematis, blooming a month early, grew over the drying barn.

"You grew up here?" Will rocked back on his heels. "Don't get me wrong, I'm city through and through, but how could you leave this?"

"No pigs," she said, and she smiled for the first time that day.

Chapter Fifteen

A strange man leaned against the kitchen sink. Antoinette tried studying his face, but when she did it fractured into pieces like the Picasso painting she'd seen, *Weeping Woman*. Focusing on faces was always difficult, but today was worse than normal. She cocked her head to the right and squinted at a spot on the wall above the man's left shoulder.

He was tall and had dark hair like Seth, but that was the only way they were alike. This man was thin and lanky. Seth was covered with a hard layer of muscle. Unlike Seth's warm brown hair, this man's hair was so dark it was almost black. But the biggest difference was the way they spoke.

Seth was quiet, his movements controlled. Sometimes Antoinette thought she heard him thinking before he acted. This man's gestures were big. His voice loud. He held a blue coffee mug and waved his hands as he talked.

"The air smells sweeter here," he was saying. He pointed at Lily with his cup. Antoinette waited for coffee to splash over the edge. "Why didn't you tell me? Trying to keep this place all to yourself? I want to see all of Redbud's finest establishments. The grand tour."

Lily laughed. "I'll give you a tour, but there's nothing grand about it." She sat at the table across from Antoinette's mother. The air between them felt tense; neither woman looked at the other one.

Antoinette stomped her feet. New people kept arriving at the house. First Lily and now this man. She tucked her hands in tight against her shoulders and paced in a tight circle. The house was too loud. The refrigerator hummed. The faucet dripped. The coffeemaker hissed.

"How long are you staying?" her mother asked the man. She seemed anxious. That morning, when she told Antoinette about the new man, she had said, "You can't touch him. Do you understand?" She wouldn't let Antoinette go downstairs until she bobbed her head yes.

"As long as you'll have me," he said. He crossed his legs at the ankles. His shoes were shiny and black, with no mud on them at all.

Her mother glanced at Lily and frowned slightly as if she didn't like his answer.

"Will's a doctor," Lily said. "He could help if Antoinette—"

"Lily told me she has seizures," he said. "Is there a trigger? If you isolate the trigger and remove it, the seizures might stop."

"That's what I'm trying to do," her mother said, but her voice was so soft Antoinette didn't think he heard.

He crouched in front of Antoinette. "I met you once before. You were a little thing. Only three?" He looked to Lily as if for confirmation. When she nodded, he continued. "Your mom rushed you home before we could be properly introduced. My name is Will." He inclined his head toward her in an odd little bow.

Antoinette was captivated. She stole a glance at his eyes. They were a paler blue than the sky at dawn. What would his song sound like? Bright and fast, she decided, like creek water bubbling downstream. She reached for his cheek, but Lily pulled her back.

Antoinette growled. Lily ruined everything. *Go home!*

Lily sighed. "She's never going to like me."

True. Antoinette stomped her foot. *Don't like Lily.*

Will walked over to Lily and kissed the top of her head. "Don't forget what I said. She's just like everyone else."

That wasn't true. Antoinette knew she was different and she didn't like it.

The kitchen door opened and Seth came in, not looking at anyone. He went straight to the coffeepot and poured a cup of coffee. With his back still to them, he said, "It's going to be hot today. I thought I'd get started early. Lily, I could use your help. And I'd like to talk to you about last night." His voice turned up at the end, as if he was asking a question instead of making a statement.

Antoinette stretched up on her toes and walked over to him. *Pick me up!* She tapped his back.

"Okay, okay. I'll pick you up." Seth set his mug down and finally turned to face the room. When he did, his body stiffened.

Antoinette turned to see what he was looking at. Will had his hands on Lily's shoulders, his mouth bent low to her ear.

Pick me up! Antoinette bounced on her toes. For the first time, Seth ignored her.

Lily shifted sideways, away from Will, but he moved with her, his fingers twitching slightly against her shoulders.

"This is Lily's neighbor, Will," Antoinette's mother said. Her voice seemed loud in the silence. "Will, this is Seth. He owns part of the farm. We all grew up together."

Antoinette patted Seth's hand. He always picked her up when he came over. *Up! Up, up, up.*

"Ah," Will said, "so you're Seth."

"You have company." Seth's words were precise and clipped. "Lily, forget I asked. I'm sure you'd like to spend time with your friend." Then he walked out the door, leaving Antoinette standing alone in the center of the kitchen.

WILL'S CAR WAS a black so shiny Antoinette could see her reflection in the door. She crawled into the back beside her mother. After Seth left, they had spent the day driving through Redbud. They stopped at the farmers' market and the library. Now they were headed for Teelia's to go over preparations for the garden show.

Will drove fast. Each time he rounded a curve, Antoinette listed sideways into her mother. Once, she tried to catch her mother's hand, but she pulled away.

"Time moves slower here," Will said. "I don't even need my watch. I stopped wearing it somewhere past Lexington. Tucked it into my suitcase." He held up his left wrist. A white band of skin showed where his watch used to be.

Maybe he drove fast to catch the time he lost, Antoinette thought.

"Lily tells me you're an artist," Will said to Antoinette's mother.

"I used to be," her mother said. "I gave it up after Antoinette was born and I took over the farm."

"Do you miss it?" he asked. "I've seen the paintings around

Lily's house. The Kentucky landscapes. The yellow lily on blue china. You're good."

"I miss it sometimes, but I have other compensations now." She smiled at Antoinette before turning to Lily. "You kept those old paintings?"

"They reminded me of home," Lily said. "And you."

"It's the only art she has in her house," Will said. "Aside from your paintings, the place is barren."

Antoinette's mother released some of the tension in her body. She leaned forward and tentatively squeezed Lily's shoulder.

Will rounded another bend. This time, Lily touched his leg. "Slow down."

Antoinette didn't want him to stop. She liked the sense of flying along the road, of being thrown suddenly against her mother.

"Turn here." Lily pointed to the string of refurbished houses that made up the Main Street shops. Art's Floral, Knitwits, and several small antiques and craft stores. The Bakery Barn was next to Teelia's. Antoinette bounced with excitement. If she saw MaryBeth again, she would fix her for good this time.

"Park here." Lily indicated an open spot in front of Teelia's shop. "Every grand tour of Redbud includes a stop at the local yarn store."

Will pulled the car in and cut the engine. He squinted as he looked out the front window. "It's just like Mayberry, R.F.D. I didn't think places like this still existed."

"It has its share of issues," Lily said as they left the car.

For once, Antoinette agreed with her aunt. She thought of the old ladies who stared at her in the grocery store, and the kids who teased her at the library playground.

"We won't stay long," her mother said. "I just need to know

when Teelia wants us to come out to her place to load up her stuff for the show."

Knitwits occupied the first floor of a redbrick house with a large white porch. Bradford pear trees lined the property, their branches heavy with puffy white flowers. Antoinette could detect a whisper of music, but she didn't try hard to capture it. Her mother had stopped her from healing MaryBeth, and Antoinette wanted to finish what she started.

MaryBeth's name went through her mind like a song. She started on a high note, then slid down, flapping her hands with each syllable: *MaryBeth. MaryBeth.*

"We're not going to the Bakery Barn today," her mother said as she steered Antoinette toward Knitwits.

This was a dilemma. Antoinette wanted to see MaryBeth, but she liked Teelia. Once, at the farmers' market, Teelia had handed Antoinette Frank's lead line. The alpaca had hummed softly, then nuzzled her cheek with his soft nose.

Thinking of Frank helped Antoinette decide. She would follow her mother into Knitwits. She could visit MaryBeth when they left.

Teelia bustled out from behind the counter. Bead bracelets and bamboo knitting needles hung from a metal counter display. "Who might this be?" She nodded at Will.

"Will Grayson. At your service." He executed a little bow.

Teelia bobbed her head. "A gentleman. We don't get much of that around here."

"Will's my neighbor," Lily said. "He's down here visiting for a few days."

"Days. Weeks. Months," Will said. "Who knows, maybe

longer. This place is growing on me." He looked at Lily as he spoke.

"I thought we'd drop by and finalize plans for the show," Antoinette's mother said.

"I have my yarn ready," Teelia said. "I just need Seth to transport some things to the farm."

While her mother and Teelia discussed details about the show, Antoinette wandered off. The shop was filled with cubbyholes holding yarn in every color imaginable. A group of women sat at a table in mismatched chairs, knitting and chatting. Their voices formed a soft hum.

"The shop hasn't changed since I was little."

Antoinette was surprised to look up and see Lily standing behind her. Anxiety rolled off of her aunt in waves.

"Teelia tried to teach me to knit once," Lily said, "but I kept dropping my stitches. Your mom was good. I think I still have a scarf she made when she was just about your age."

Antoinette didn't like standing so close to Lily, but she didn't walk away. She liked hearing stories about her mother.

"We used to come here after school when the growing season ended. Our mother would sit with Teelia while Rose and I picked through the yarn. In the time it took me to cast on a row of stitches, your mom would be halfway finished with a scarf or a hat."

To Antoinette's consternation, her anger toward her aunt softened. That couldn't happen, not if she wanted everything to go back to normal. She stomped to the corner of the room, as far away from Lily as she could get.

She would *not* like her aunt. She sat in the corner and twisted her hands in front of her face, letting the voices from the women sitting at the table wash over her. She didn't budge even when she realized they were talking about her.

"Is she okay?" a woman wearing an orange flowered shirt said.

"Does she need help?" another said.

Antoinette growled.

Then Lily was there. She stood in front of Antoinette, shielding her from the women. She counted to ten and then said, "Rose, it's time to go."

"I'll be right—" Her mother stopped abruptly as the shop door snapped shut.

"I thought I saw you come in here," Eli said. The scent of cinnamon floated through the air as he hurried over to them.

Antoinette flapped her hands. Eli would take her to MaryBeth. She pushed herself up and walked toward him, but her mother, with Will following, blocked her path.

"Can't stay to talk today," her mother said to Eli. Her voice was artificially bright. "We have to get Antoinette back to the farm. She's not herself right now."

That wasn't true. Antoinette was fine.

"Take Antoinette to the car," she whispered to Lily. Her mother was usually gentle, but this time she shoved Antoinette into Lily's arms.

No, no, no. Antoinette screamed and reached for Eli. She needed to see MaryBeth.

"It's not my place," Will started, "but maybe—"

"You're right," her mother said. "It's not your place."

"Will, why don't you help me?" Lily said. She grabbed Antoinette under the arms.

Antoinette bucked and kicked. Lily started counting, but she held on tight. *No, no, no!* Antoinette wanted MaryBeth. *Let go of me!*

"We don't mind if she's a little under the weather," Eli said. "The last time y'all were in town, MaryBeth felt so much better after seeing Antoinette. She had a couple of real good days, but now she's in a bad way again. Seeing Antoinette would help."

He peered at Antoinette, and she reached for him. "Why don't you let me take her? MaryBeth's having trouble breathing. The doctors say she'll need a ventilator soon. A visit from this little girl sure would cheer her up."

Antoinette went still. She knew that healings never lasted, but this one had faded too fast. Something was wrong.

Lily took advantage of Antoinette's momentary calm to head for the door.

"Next time," her mother said. She followed Lily but stopped just in front of the door, letting Lily carry Antoinette outside while keeping Eli inside the shop. "I'm so sorry about MaryBeth," her mother said.

And Antoinette realized it was the only true thing her mother had said since Eli entered the shop.

Chapter Sixteen

The garden show was in a little over a week. Music would be in the drying barn. Art would be in the house garden. Those two venues would be prepared later in the week. Tonight Lily and Will set up tables in the night garden for the food vendors. Rose directed them while Antoinette walked in circles.

As Lily worked, she thought of Eli. He was going to be a problem. Yesterday, at Knitwits, he had stared at Antoinette as if she were a science experiment. She might not be cut out to be Antoinette's guardian, but she didn't want harm to come to her.

She was surrounded by puzzles she couldn't solve. How to patch things up with Rose? How to get out of being Antoinette's guardian? How to keep Eli away from Antoinette? This was why she liked math—in math, there was always a set solution.

"How about here?" Will asked as he and Lily tugged a table away from the stone wall. He tapped the table twice. He should look out of place in his khakis and polo shirt, but he didn't.

"Back a little," Rose said. "Closer to the wall." She rested on a bench beside the fountain, her portable oxygen tank at her side. That afternoon, she had lost her breath walking from the kitchen to her room. She started carrying the tank after that.

They tugged the table into place and looked to Rose for approval. When she nodded, they moved on to the next table.

To Lily, the night garden felt magical. In addition to the bountiful flowers, concrete benches were scattered throughout the garden, and water trickled from a fountain. Plumes of astilbe swayed in front of the fountain. The plant had airy white flowers that sprouted above the dark green glossy foliage. Astilbe meant . . . Lily couldn't remember. How could she have forgotten?

Will grabbed one end of the table. "Ready?"

"Wait a minute," Lily said. "I have to get the Victorian flower book. I'll be right back."

By the time she returned, Will had maneuvered the table into place. Still holding the book, Lily moved to help him.

"Go sit down," Will said. He plucked the book from her hands and tossed it onto the nearest bench, one right next to Antoinette.

"I'll help," Lily said.

"And lose this chance to impress you with my manly prowess?" Will said. "No way."

"You're incorrigible. You know that?" Lily asked, but she sat down.

"God, I hope so. Where's the fun otherwise?"

Lily ignored him. She had known what quality astilbe represented years ago when she and her father planted the flowers. She could picture him tamping down dirt around the astilbe, see him scattering mulch over the ground. The flowers were still there; everything else, though, was gone.

"What are you doing?" Rose asked.

They hadn't had a chance to talk much since Will's arrival, and Lily hated the tension that had grown between them. Even more, she hated knowing that she would make everything worse when she told Rose she couldn't be Antoinette's guardian. "I can't remember what astilbe means," she said.

Antoinette started walking in tight circles around the bench where Lily sat, so she turned away. If she didn't see Antoinette, maybe she wouldn't start counting.

"Do you think Seth will join us?" Lily tried to sound casual, as if she was just making conversation, but she really did wonder. He hadn't been around much since Will showed up.

Rose glanced surreptitiously toward Will. "I don't think so."

Last night, after they had returned from town, Seth had turned to Will. "You're staying here, I suppose?" His words were careful, his face expressionless.

"If the ladies will have me," Will said with a half smile. "I'll earn my keep. Free physicals for all." His grin was infectious. Rose and Lily had laughed, but Seth left without saying a word.

A soft breeze ruffled the pages of the flower book. At the sound, Antoinette stopped pacing and moved closer. She seemed intrigued. The book was open to a picture of daisies, and she tapped it three times.

"She wants to know what they mean," Rose said.

"Innocence," Lily said, picking up the book but not looking at it.

Antoinette leaned forward and lost her balance. Lily automatically grabbed her before she hit the ground. "You okay?"

Antoinette growled and smacked Lily's hands.

"Are you sure you weren't a baby wrangler in a prior life?" Will asked as he pulled a table in place.

"No more than you were a priest," Lily said.

Antoinette resumed walking in tight circles. When she noticed Lily watching, she growled.

"A priest isn't out of the question." Will raised his eyebrows. "A dark confessional booth has possibilities."

"That's over the top, even for you."

Will grinned. "When will you learn, Lils? I'm a man of extremes."

Lily turned another page. There it was. "Astilbe. *I'll be waiting*," she read. "Can't believe I forgot it."

LILY DIDN'T RETURN to the house with everyone else but sat alone in the darkening garden, listening to the sounds around her. Most people thought it was quiet in the country, but they were wrong. Horses called to each other over their stalls. Cicadas buzzed in the trees. Creek water gurgled over rocks.

And now a violin sang in the distance.

Now was as good a time as any to talk to Seth about being Antoinette's guardian. She stood and followed the stone path to the drying barn. Pieces of a melody floated through the early-evening air, and she pictured Seth, eyes closed, violin under his chin, swaying as he skimmed the bow across the strings.

When she reached the barn, a faint beam of light shone beneath the door. Quietly, she eased it open.

He stood at the far end of the barn, his back to her, a single light shining down on him. Even if Lily had wanted to look elsewhere she couldn't. She had missed hearing him play, missed watching him transform into someone carefree.

Their first kiss had happened here in the drying barn, and she flashed back to that day. It was autumn, and they were both sixteen. Sunlight filtered through cracks in the old wood slats, and the air was crisp with the scent of wood smoke. Seth took off his jacket and spread it over a straw bale.

"I thought we were going hiking," Lily said as he pulled her down next to him.

He picked up a twig and scratched lines on the dirt floor. "I've been thinking," he said.

"About what?" She leaned against his shoulder.

"Do you think God has a reason for all of this?"

She was used to his odd questions. Last week they had been sitting on the rock that rose out of the middle of the creek when he said, "What if this is all a dream?"

"If it is," Lily had said, thinking of her need to number everything, "it's not a very good one."

Now she frowned at him. "All of what?"

"This." He waved the stick in the air, indicating her, the barn, everything. "I've been thinking that maybe my dad is . . . you know, the way he is, for a reason. Maybe something good will come from it." He drew three parallel lines in the dirt.

Lily thought for a moment. If God had a purpose, she didn't see it. "I don't know," she said, choosing her words carefully. "I think things are just the way they are—whether for bad or for good, there's no reason—and you learn to live with it."

Seth frowned and Lily could almost see him considering her words. He had always been serious, sometimes too much so. He tossed the stick aside and ran his foot across the dirt, smearing the lines.

"The whole town knows about my dad," he finally said. "That's what most people see when they look at me. At least the bad parts, anyway. No one talks about the person he is when he isn't drinking."

"That's not true—"

He laughed. "Really? Haven't you lived in Redbud long enough? When's the last time you heard anyone talk about his skill with the violin?" He rested his elbows on his knees and clasped his hands together. He had grown taller in the past year, and his hair was longer. When he leaned forward, it brushed the skin beneath his eyes.

Lily didn't want to admit that he was right. Cora and Teelia whispered about Seth in church, saying he was too serious for someone his age and that it was his father's fault. The kids at school snickered when he walked down the hall. It wasn't as bad as their treatment of her, but it was close.

"You're the only one who sees *me*. Not my messed-up family. Just me. Do you know what a gift that is? To be able to be myself around someone?"

The air was electric. She felt hot and cold at the same time. If she leaned forward just a bit, their lips would touch. "Being with you is easy," she said. It was true. She never needed to count when she was with him.

He wrapped his arm around her hip and pulled her close. He leaned his forehead against hers. "We fit together."

Lily closed her eyes when he tangled his hands in her hair. He smelled like autumn leaves and fresh tobacco. When he kissed her, it felt like coming home, and Lily realized that love grew in familiar places.

Now, as she watched him play, she thought of how much she missed the freedom to be completely herself with someone. She was close to Will, would even say she loved him, but she kept part of herself from him in a way she never had with Seth.

"I know you're there," Seth said as he finished the piece he'd been playing.

She walked deeper into the barn. It was fully dark outside now, and the cicadas sang. "I didn't mean to interrupt," she said. "I was on the way back to the house when I heard you playing. Haydn. Right?"

"You remembered." He took a well-worn chamois cloth from the case and wiped down the violin.

"Why didn't you join us in the night garden?" she asked.

"I didn't want to interfere with things between you and Will." He kept his back to her, but his shoulders tightened at Will's name.

Lily wanted to say there wasn't anything going on between her and Will, but of course that wasn't quite true. She watched as he put the violin in the case, then snapped it shut.

"I've been thinking," Seth said. He was standing so close that she felt the heat from his body. "About what you said the other night. You were right. I should have told you about Antoinette— her special abilities."

This was her chance. Seth loved Antoinette. He'd be a perfect guardian for her. "About Antoinette. I need to ask—"

But he wasn't paying attention. He kept talking. "You have to know that you did mean something to me. You still do."

Lily was too surprised to respond. All thoughts of asking him to be Antoinette's guardian left her.

"I won't interfere with your life," Seth said as he picked up his violin, "because I don't want to hurt you again. But I need you to know that breaking up with you is the biggest mistake I ever made. I *do* care about you, and if I thought that you would've believed what Antoinette can do, I'd have told you, no matter what Rose said." Then he turned and walked out of the barn, leaving Lily staring at the door as it shut behind him.

ROSE'S JOURNAL
August 2009

—+—

I HOIST ANTOINETTE over the fence between our house and Seth's. Since she healed me, everything is easier. I don't run out of breath, and it's been a year since I've had any chest pain. But I can't escape the guilt of knowing that my health comes at a price.

Over the past year, Seth and I have watched Antoinette carefully. We still don't know *exactly* how she works her miracles, but we do know that for the healing to work she must be touching the person or plant or animal.

I miss holding her hand, and I let my fingers linger against her shoulder for a moment before I slide the painting I'm carrying between the fence rails. I'm her mother; she's my child. I want to hold her, to pull her against me—but I can't. The cost is too great.

Once through the fence, I help her up the steps to Seth's house. My hands shake as I knock on the door. I'm not good at thank-yous.

As soon as he opens the door, I thrust out the painting. "For you," I say. It's a rendering of the creek that runs through the back of our properties, the spot where a large flat rock sits in the middle of the water. I haven't painted since leaving school and doing so felt good, but I'm unsure of myself in a way I never was when I was younger.

"Take it." I stumble over my words. "Without you, I would have had to sell the farm."

"The rock," he says as he accepts the painting. His smile is bittersweet. "I spent a lot of time there."

"We all did."

"It's still there." He looks sheepish. "I checked. The first night I was back."

This is a side of Seth I don't often see: shy, soft.

He stands back to let us in. His house is old, like ours. The wood floors are scratched in places, and the French doors leading into the living room sag slightly in the middle. The gray stone fireplace is flanked by a set of bookcases filled with books and photographs.

"Did you build these?" I ask. The wood is solid. I imagine them standing long after the house has fallen down around them.

Seth nods. "I made them for my mother. She loved this room."

It's strange hearing him talk about his parents. I know he spoke to Lily about them, but he rarely did so with me.

Antoinette plops down on the soft beige couch. Her legs stick out from her cutoffs like twin toothpicks. She bounces on the couch, shrieking as she does. I touch her shoulder to calm her, but it doesn't help.

"She's happy," he says. "Let her bounce."

I love the way Seth takes Antoinette in stride.

He holds the painting over the fireplace. "I think it should go here."

"It looks nice," I say. I feel a flush of pride.

"I need a hammer," Seth says. "Be right back."

When he leaves, I examine the bookcase. The wood is

beautiful. Oak stained a rich mahogany color. The streaks of red set off the wood grain. On the middle shelf, beside a stack of books about music therapy, is a picture of Seth and his mother. She has her arm looped around his waist.

When he returns, carrying a step ladder and tools, I nod at the photo. "Your mom was really pretty, especially when she smiled."

He pops open the ladder and climbs up. "Hand me the painting." I hand it to him and he says, "That was the problem. My dad liked to own things. Pretty things. She was just one more possession."

He nods at the painting. "Is it centered?"

I step back and look. "A little high."

He lowers it slightly. "Better?"

I nod and glance at Antoinette, who seems happy twisting her head from side to side and flicking her fingers.

Seth presses a nail into the wall to mark the spot where he'll hang the painting. "He wasn't all bad, my dad," he says. It seems important to him that I know this. "After all, he's the one who taught me to play the violin."

I pick up the photo of his mother. I wonder how she felt about Seth's father. "You don't need to explain," I say. I set the photo back on the shelf, causing some books to slide down. When they do, another picture falls out.

It's of Lily. She's sitting on the creek bank, her arms around her knees. Though the photo is black and white, the sun flashes in her dark hair.

I miss Lily as much as I miss holding Antoinette's hand.

Seth taps a nail into the wall and motions for me to hand him the painting. He hangs it and then sits down on the top ladder step. "I think we're programmed to love our families no matter how screwed up they are."

I look down at the picture of Lily and nod.

Seth follows my gaze. "Have you talked to her?"

I shake my head.

"She'd come home if you asked." He takes the picture from me, holding it gently, as if it's something precious.

Unlike me, Lily forgives easily. But I'm afraid. What if by ignoring her, I pushed her away? "She won't," I say. "Not after the way I treated her."

"Of course she will. She's your sister."

But I shake my head. "I can't call her." I'd rather live with the fantasy that one day Lily and I will reconcile than contact her and discover that I have succeeded in pushing her away forever.

Chapter Seventeen

A ntoinette concentrated on following her mother. The market was busy on Saturdays and getting lost would be easy. The people clumped around the booths could shift, engulf her mother, and then poof—it would be like she never existed at all.

The largest crowd surrounded the Eden Farms' booth; they had the biggest and brightest flowers at the market. People milled about under the green awning, examining black-eyed Susans and purple coneflowers that shouldn't bloom for another two months.

"There are too many people here," her mother said, frowning. She walked carefully, shielding Antoinette from the crowd. A knot of old ladies stood outside of their booth. "Excuse me," her mother said as she and Antoinette eased by them.

Antoinette took two big steps to stay close to her. Normally, she loved crowds—so many people to touch, so many songs to hear. Today was different.

Today it seemed like death sat on her mother's shoulder. She struggled to catch her breath, and she walked even more slowly than normal. As Antoinette followed her, a marigold pushed from the soil, and unaware, her mother stepped on it, flattening its orange petals and filling the air with a sharp scent. Antoinette stopped, mesmerized by the crumpled flower. She tried to move, but her feet tangled, and she pitched forward.

Right before she hit the ground, her mother caught her. "Are you okay?" she asked. She was breathing hard. The short walk from their van to the booth had worn her out.

Yes. The word was small and simple. Three letters. *Y-E-S.* Antoinette opened her mouth. A high-pitched squeal came out.

Her mother quickly squeezed Antoinette's hand. "Come on," she said. "You don't want to be late for delivery day."

Faintly, she heard her mother's song through their linked hands, but Antoinette needed all of her concentration to keep up. Healing would have to wait.

One of the old women gathered around the booth turned to Antoinette's mother. "Bless your heart," she said. "Stuck with that retarded girl. As if you don't have enough to deal with."

Retarded. The word was a slap across Antoinette's face. It was supposed to mean "slow." It really meant "worthless." *Worth. Less.* Antoinette groaned and curled forward.

"Come on, Antoinette." Her mother tugged her hand.

Antoinette couldn't straighten. The sun bit through her thin cotton T-shirt.

"Poor thing," the old woman said.

"Get out of my booth," her mother said, the words clipped and sharp.

With a sniff the woman shuffled off, and the pressure on Antoinette's shoulders eased.

"Crazy old woman," her mother said. She knelt in front of Antoinette and tapped her first two fingers against her nose. "Look at me."

Antoinette fixed her gaze on a gauzy cloud over her mother's left shoulder.

Long ago, her mother had brought home a prism. "Look, Antoinette," she had said before shining a flashlight through the glass triangle. "All these colors were hidden in the white light. The prism broke it open."

Antoinette's brain was like that prism. In her mind, faces shattered. It was confusing and disorienting, like looking at a puzzle with the pieces scattered over a table.

"Please, Antoinette. I need to know you're listening." Her mother tapped her nose again. The pain in her mother's voice was worse than looking at her dissembled face. Antoinette flicked her gaze from the cloud to her mother, then back again.

It was enough.

"Don't listen to that woman," her mother said. "Everyone's life is hard in some way. Yours just happens to be easier to see than most. Do you understand?"

Slowly, Antoinette looked into her mother's eyes, holding her gaze until her own eyes burned.

"Thank you," her mother said, and Antoinette could feel relief in her voice.

Her mother straightened and looked around the booth. "Where's Seth?" She guided Antoinette toward the back of the tent where they looked across the grassy square separating the market from the parking lot. Seth was at the van, unloading planters of early tulips and late daffodils. When he saw them, he jogged across the grass.

"Ready to go, Antoinette?" he asked as he tousled her hair.

She stretched up on her toes. Saturday was the day she helped Seth deliver flowers to stores and restaurants around town. She loved delivery day.

"Is Lily here yet?" her mother asked.

"I didn't know she was coming." He glanced over his shoulder, an odd look on his face. Antoinette recognized it at once: longing. She imagined she looked like that when she watched kids at the playground—she wanted to be like them.

"She and Will are meeting me here. I want Lily to handle the deliveries today," her mother said. "She and Antoinette need to get to know each other."

Antoinette stepped away from her mother. *No*, she thought. A low moan filled her throat. Seth did delivery day, not Lily. Everything was changing. Her knees buckled, and she dropped to the ground, screaming as she fell.

The concrete stung, but Antoinette didn't care. She screamed until her throat was raw.

"What's wrong?" Lily's voice cut through the noise of the crowd.

"You're late," her mother said.

No! No! No! Antoinette kicked the concrete. She did not want to go with Lily.

"Sorry," Lily said. "We lost track of time."

A crowd gathered around them. Someone said, "Would you look at that."

"What a shame," someone else said. The words whooshed through Antoinette's ears, and she screamed again.

"It's my fault," Will said. "I asked Lily to walk through the woods with me."

"All right," Seth said to the people who had gathered to watch. "Show's over."

No one left.

Then Antoinette heard Will. "At least back up," he said.

"It's delivery day," her mother said.

Antoinette stopped screaming and focused on her mother's voice.

"Doesn't Seth—" Lily started.

"I thought you could do it today." Her mother grabbed Antoinette's wrists and tugged. "With Antoinette."

No, Antoinette wanted to say. *I don't want things to change.*

"You mean the two of us? Alone?"

"That's exactly what I mean," her mother said.

"I'll get her," Seth said. Antoinette let herself go limp, but that didn't stop him from picking her up.

"Will, come with me," Lily said.

"You don't need me, Lils," Will said.

Antoinette banged her head against Seth's arm. *Not Lily. Not Lily. Not Lily.*

"She doesn't like me," Lily said.

Antoinette stiffened until her spine curved like a backward C. It didn't make a difference; Seth tightened his grip until she couldn't twist free.

"This is why I called you home, Lily," her mother said. "Did you think it would be easy?"

"Well, I didn't think it would be like this," Lily said quietly.

Will pulled her aside, but they were close enough for Antoinette to hear what he said. "When I was in the hospital, you told me stories about growing up here. Just from your voice I could tell how much you missed this place, how much you missed Rose, Antoinette. Don't let fear drive you away. You'll be fine, Lils."

They would *not* be fine. Antoinette kicked her feet, but Seth buckled her into the van's passenger's seat anyway.

Will held the driver's door for Lily. "You can do this."

"I can do this," Lily repeated, but she didn't sound sure of herself.

"We'll meet you at Cora's when you're finished," her mother said.

Antoinette shook her head. *No, no, no!*

Lily slid in behind the wheel. Antoinette sat at the very edge of her seat, as far from Lily as possible. Lily did likewise, leaning against the driver's-side door as she started the van.

As they pulled away, Antoinette forced herself to look directly into her mother's eyes. She didn't break eye contact until they turned out of the market and her mother disappeared.

ANTOINETTE STUCK HER hand out of the van window, letting the wind whistle through the spaces between her fingers.

"I can run into Art's Floral if you want to wait in the van," Lily said as she drove around back to the service entrance. Her voice was so soft Antoinette barely heard her.

Lily's hair swung down her back in a loose ponytail. Antoinette imagined grabbing a handful of it and yanking as hard as she could.

When they stopped, Antoinette bounced on the seat, making the springs squeak. She knocked her hand against the door. *Out.* She looped the word through her brain, attempting to push it past her lips, but the only sound that came out was a low groan.

Lily hopped out and opened the van's back door. Antoinette smacked her hands against the door. She *always* went into Art's. *Out. Out. Out.* She stamped her feet against the floor and flapped her hands.

"Okay, okay," Lily said. She opened the door and stood back. "Do you need help?"

Antoinette pressed her elbows against her sides and wiggled her fingers. *Out. Out. OUT!* She focused all of her energy into pushing the word past her lips. "Ouuu!"

Lily wiped her hands on her jeans. "Rose and Will are both crazy," she mumbled as she reached for Antoinette and unbuckled the seat belt. "I don't know what I'm doing."

Antoinette fell forward. Lily caught her and eased her to the ground. "You okay?" she asked. Without waiting for an answer, she headed toward the back of the van. "Five," she said. "Can't stop on five." She returned to Antoinette's side.

When she noticed Antoinette staring, Lily blushed. "I don't like odd numbers." She pressed herself against the passenger's door and started walking again. Her steps were smaller this time, and she counted out loud, ending on nine.

After three tries, she made it to the back of the van in six paces. "Thank God," she said. She grabbed two buckets of cosmos and set them down. Then she reached for a couple of pails of hoop-house zinnias.

"You want to carry some?" Lily asked.

Antoinette hopped up and down.

Lily held out a small metal pail, and Antoinette curled her fingers around its handle. She worked hard to smooth her gait so water didn't slosh from the pail as she walked. This time, she wasn't the only one with a problem. Lily had to retrace her path twice before she landed on an even number, and they finally walked through the service entrance.

Antoinette loved the back room of Art's Floral. A row of glass-front refrigerators filled with roses, irises, and lilies lined one wall. Spools of ribbon in every color imaginable hung above a worktable. Shelves of glass vases bounced light around the room. Most of the flowers were cut and dying, so there wasn't much music in the room, but as long as Antoinette kept her hands tight against her body the emptiness didn't overwhelm her.

The shop's owner was a thin woman named Ileen. She had dishwater-brown hair and never looked at Antoinette. Ileen was in the back room waiting for them. She flipped her hair over her shoulder and frowned when she saw Lily. "I'm surprised to see you, Lily. Where's Seth? He normally handles deliveries."

"He's taking a break. It's just us today," Lily said as she handed her an invoice.

Ileen accepted the paper, making sure not to touch Lily. "I'll get the check. Don't let her touch anything." She nodded toward Antoinette as she left.

"Don't worry," Lily whispered to Antoinette when they were alone. "She was a bitch in high school too, but don't tell your mother I said that. They used to be friends. Not anymore, I guess."

Lily fiddled with the flowers in one of the buckets. Her lips moved as she ran her fingers over the petals of a zinnia, and Antoinette heard her counting.

"Twenty-six petals," she said with a glance at Antoinette. "That's a good number. Even. I don't have to do anything to fix it. Sometimes if it's an odd number, I have to pinch off a petal to make it even."

Antoinette understood the need to bring order to things. Without thinking, she moved closer to Lily.

"It's like an itch that gets bigger unless I scratch it." Lily ran her fingers over the orange flower petals. "But this one's good."

A potted pothos plant sat on a shelf across the room, its leaves curly and brown around the edges. Antoinette bounced over to the plant. It was potted so there was no point in sticking her fingers into the soil. She couldn't pull water to the roots from anywhere else.

She flapped her hands to get Lily's attention, but her aunt was busy pinching the petals off of a fuchsia cosmos.

Antoinette stretched up on her toes and walked over to the sink. She smacked her palm against the stainless-steel basin. It made a ringing sound, but Lily didn't look up.

A green plastic watering can sat on the floor next to the sink. Antoinette tried to nudge it with her foot, but her muscles contracted, and she kicked the can, sending it across the room.

Lily jumped. "What in the world?"

Antoinette bounced and flapped her hands, bringing them down against the sink. Then she pointed at the dying plant.

Lily followed her direction. "Oh," she said, grasping Antoinette's intent. "You'd think a florist would know better." She picked up the watering can, filled it at the sink, and then watered the plant. "I never could stand to see them dying."

Antoinette wanted to say she couldn't either, but the words wouldn't come. Instead, she stood next to her aunt and flapped her hands, hoping it looked like *Thank you*.

Chapter Eighteen

Cora's Italian Restaurant was their last delivery stop. Lily parked the van and walked to the passenger's side, but this time when she leaned in, Antoinette didn't recoil. Instead, she climbed out and laid her cheek against Lily's hand. Her long blonde hair fell forward, covering her face.

Something inside Lily softened, and the need to count faded. "I missed you," she whispered. When Antoinette didn't move, she continued, "I have pictures of you when you were a baby. I stared at them every night before I went to sleep, wondering what you looked like now."

Antoinette cocked her head to the left. Slowly, she curved her arm around Lily's waist and tapped her back.

"The real you is better than anything I imagined." Lily brushed her hand through Antoinette's hair. It was as thin and fine as it had been when she was a baby. A seedling of hope sprouted in Lily's heart. Maybe she could be Antoinette's guardian after all. Maybe this time, she wouldn't disappoint Rose.

The restaurant door opened, and Seth walked out. "I thought you might need some help," he said. He turned to Antoinette. "Bet you were a big help today."

She stretched up on her toes, flapped her hands, and shrieked. Lily now knew that was her happy noise.

"Did she carry flowers into Art's?" he asked. "I forgot to tell you that's our routine." Lily couldn't help but notice that he was awkward with her, more like a stranger than someone with whom he shared a past.

"Antoinette told me," Lily said. "It's amazing how much she can communicate without words."

Seth walked to the back of the van. "If I've learned anything about Antoinette, it's not to underestimate her."

Antoinette walked in circles on her toes. "Don't think I've forgotten about you, kiddo," Seth said. "Brush up on your Brahms. I'll stump you yet."

For a moment, he was the boy Lily remembered. She forgot herself and touched his arm. "Thank you for being here when I wasn't."

He flinched and pulled away. "I'll unload the flowers," he said as he grabbed two buckets of hydrangea puffs. "Rose is inside waiting for you."

At the mention of her mother's name, Antoinette started across the parking lot to the restaurant entrance. She moved slowly. Several times her knees folded, and she almost fell, but each time she caught herself before hitting the ground.

"I didn't mean anything beyond 'thank you,'" Lily said, confused by his reaction. "I'll leave you alone if that's what you'd like." She hurried to catch up with Antoinette.

They were at the restaurant entrance when Seth called out, "You look comfortable with each other. Like you belong together."

Lily paused at the door. Her fear had vanished in the hours

she and Antoinette had spent together that afternoon. "You're right," she said. "We do." She put her hand on her niece's shoulder and helped her inside.

Cora's Italian Restaurant had changed. The black-and-white floor tile was the same, and the scents of garlic and oregano still hung in the air, but everything else was different.

Years ago, Cora's had looked like a thousand other small town restaurants: cheap, plastic, nothing breakable, and everything easy to hose down.

Now the walls were painted eggplant purple. The metal tables had been replaced with tall red booths sporting cushions covered in a hodgepodge of patterns: zebra stripes, cheetah prints, and splashy old florals. The drop ceiling had been removed, exposing stainless-steel air ducts. Thousands of white Christmas lights were laced through boxwood topiaries that dotted the restaurant.

Rose and Will were waiting for them. "You're both in one piece," Rose said. She seemed tired and had her portable oxygen tank with her, but she looked pleased with herself.

"Antoinette was a big help," Lily said. "We're getting to know each other."

Antoinette gave Rose the same half hug she had given Lily in the parking lot. Then she stuck her hands into a boxwood that had been shaped into a cat.

"What'd I tell you, Lils?" Will said. "Just like everyone else, right?"

"Don't get cocky. Just because you were right once—"

Will pressed a hand to his chest. "Once? You wound me."

"What do you think of the place?" Cora asked, appearing from behind the bar next to the hostess station. She had bundled her long dark hair into a knot. It was more gray than black now, but her face was smooth, as if time were afraid to touch her. "Rose redid the place a few years ago. Said she needed the extra money. I have no idea how she managed for so long without any family around."

Cora was a busybody, and while she never meant for her words to sting, they did.

"She's here now," Will said, nodding at Lily. He didn't touch her, but his presence steadied her.

"I managed just fine," Rose said as she tried to keep Antoinette's hands out of the boxwood.

Cora turned to Antoinette. "I've got something special for you. You want to come to the kitchen with me?"

Antoinette crossed over to Cora and took her hand.

Before they left, Cora narrowed her eyes at Lily. "Your mom and dad would be proud of you for coming home. Don't disappoint them." Without another word, she guided Antoinette through green double doors that led to the kitchen.

Lily was mute for several long seconds. When she found her voice, she said, "Will Antoinette be okay?" She was surprised by how protective she felt of her niece.

Rose threaded her way through the maze of booths and oak tables with ladder back chairs. "Cora's good with her. Besides, she's probably got chocolate back there. Antoinette will do anything for chocolate."

Waitresses dressed in black and white circled through the room, polishing empty tables and folding napkins. The clink of silverware and plates echoed through the room.

"Eccentric place," Will said, taking in the decor.

Rose picked a booth against the far wall and slid in.

Lily sat across from Rose with Will next to her. He leaned down and whispered to her. "It's like a date."

Lily elbowed him. He was so thin, she connected with his ribs more forcefully than she meant to, and he winced.

"You did a good job," Lily said to Rose. "I would have never thought to put all of this together." Separately, the purple, red, and green seemed too strong to ever stand together. Instead, it reminded Lily of the wildflowers in the field behind the farm—beautiful in an unexpected way.

The door to the back room opened and a waitress came in, arms loaded with boxes of flowers. Lily had wondered at Rose's choices when she had picked them: blue irises, green and white hydrangea puffs from the greenhouse, and bright purple hyacinths. As she looked around the dining room, the flowers made sense.

For the first time since arriving home, Lily felt at peace. She leaned into Will, grateful he was there.

There was a bang and a clatter of metal from the kitchen. Rose winced. "Antoinette."

They all turned toward the kitchen, just in time to see Antoinette wobble through the doors. Cora followed, a bright red splat across her white apron.

"Oh Cora," Rose said. "I'm sorry."

Cora held up her hand. "It wasn't her fault. The staff knows better than to leave a pan of Bolognese sauce on the counter where she can grab it."

Antoinette swiveled her face toward Rose and raised her hands.

Lily added another word to her growing lexicon of Antoinette-speak. Raised hands equals *up!*

Rose lifted Antoinette across her lap. The little girl wiggled against the cushions, rocking the booth with her motion.

"Seth finished unloading the flowers," Cora said. "Now he's helping me with a load of fresh tomatoes." She wiped her hands on her apron. "I'm going to check on him, and then I've got something special for you. Antoinette's already tried it, haven't you?" Cora tried to catch Antoinette's eyes, but Antoinette looked away. "Maybe next time," she said, walking away.

Rose shifted. "Switch seats with me for a minute? I've got to use the restroom."

As Lily took Rose's place, Antoinette whimpered. She stretched across Lily toward Rose. If Antoinette was a flower, Lily thought, she would be lavender heather: loneliness.

Lily ran her fingers through Antoinette's hair. "She'll be back. I promise." When she looked up, Will was staring at her.

"You're different here," he said. "Looser. More relaxed." This was Will the doctor speaking. Thoughtful, observant—with anyone else she would have felt uncomfortable.

Antoinette slapped her hands against the wall. Lily touched her shoulder to steady her. There were only a few families in the dining room. No one seemed to notice Antoinette's agitation.

"Some people just fit places. You fit here." His smile was bittersweet. "I wish I had known you when you were growing up."

Lily laughed. "No, you don't. I was the strange kid everyone avoided."

"I wouldn't have avoided you."

Lily knew he probably believed that, but everyone had avoided her when she was younger, everyone except Rose and Seth.

Rose returned before Lily could respond. She was grateful for the interruption; her feelings for Will were complicated.

"Diuretics," Rose said with a shrug. "I can't stay out of the bathroom for long." The bathroom was only a short walk away, but Rose was winded from the effort.

Antoinette shrieked.

"See, I told you she'd be back," Lily said as she slid out of the booth and tried to stand up. When she did, her feet tangled with Rose's and she fell. As she went down, she flung out her left hand.

She felt it snap when she landed.

Pain shot through her hand and up her arm. She curled her body into a ball, her hand cradled in her lap. The last two fingers on her left hand were bent backward.

"Lily!" Will knelt beside her.

"Are you okay?" Rose crouched on Lily's other side. "Your hand. I think it's broken."

Rose and Will hovered over Lily, shielding her from the view of others in the room, for which she was grateful. She felt light-headed. She sat up and put her head between her knees. There was a soft scuffle to her right. Then she felt a little hand on her shoulder.

"I'm okay," she said through the haze of pain. She looked at her hand. Her last two fingers were fixed at a ninety-degree angle against the back of her hand.

"I'm going to be sick," she whispered.

The little hand she felt on her shoulder inched down her arm to her hand. At the touch, electricity sparked through Lily's skin. She cried out and arched her back.

Antoinette was next to her, eyes closed, humming an odd little song.

"Antoinette, no!" Rose yelled, but it was too late.

The spark of pain fanned into a blaze.

Lily groaned as her bones repositioned themselves under her skin.

"Holy shit!" Will said.

Lily's hand burned until she couldn't stand it anymore.

Then, just as suddenly, the pain stopped. She opened her eyes, and when she looked down she gasped.

Her hand was perfectly whole.

"Lils, your hand." Will's blue eyes were wide.

Lily curled her fingers into a fist. "It doesn't hurt."

He grabbed her hand and turned it over. "It was broken. I saw it." He traced the bones from the tips of her fingers to the base of her hand.

"No," Rose said. She caught Lily's eye and slowly shook her head. *Don't tell*, she mouthed.

"It couldn't have been broken." Rose leaned forward, shielding her daughter. "I don't think anyone else saw," she whispered to Lily.

Antoinette moaned. Then her eyes rolled back, and she began to shake.

"She's seizing," Will said, taking charge. "Get her on her side."

A statistic popped into Lily's mind: two percent of people with epilepsy died suddenly from seizures. Quickly, she rolled Antoinette over.

Will grabbed a penlight from his shirt pocket, lifted Antoinette's eyelids, and shined the light in her eyes. "Does she seize like this often?"

"Yes," Lily said, without thinking. "She seizes after . . ." She stopped as she looked down at her hand.

Will followed her gaze. "I saw it. She touched your hand and the bones moved." His voice shook. "The bones *moved*! What the hell is going on?"

"Don't be silly," Lily said. "You're seeing things." She faked a laugh.

"Antoinette!" Seth suddenly appeared from the kitchen. "What happened?"

"I . . . I fell, on my hand. It's okay now." Lily held up her hand and flexed her fingers, horrified that healing her hand had caused Antoinette's seizure.

For the first time since realizing what Antoinette could do, she understood Rose. Lily would rather suffer a broken hand than watch, helpless, while Antoinette seized.

"The seizure's winding down," Will said. He tucked the penlight back in his pocket and sat back.

"We've got it from here," Seth said. He tried to take Will's place next to Lily, but Will wouldn't move.

Cora appeared, her face a mask of worry. "Do you want me to call 911?"

Rose shook her head and clenched her jaw. She glanced at Will. "She'll be fine. She just needs some rest."

As Antoinette stilled, quiet conversation resumed around them. Waiters moved through the charged atmosphere setting bread and wine on tables.

Lily looked up. Eli and MaryBeth Cantwell stood in the middle of the dining room, staring at them. A hostess had been leading them to a table. Eli's eyes were wide in stunned amazement.

Rose pulled Antoinette onto her lap. "She can't keep doing this."

"Eli's here," Lily whispered. She stepped behind Rose, hoping to block his view of Antoinette. "We need to leave."

"I'll carry her to the van," Seth said.

Rose pulled Antoinette closer to her chest. "I can't let go," she whispered. She wrapped her arms around Antoinette and tried to stand, but her knees buckled.

Lily caught her elbow. "Let me help." She slid her arms under her sister's, and together they carried Antoinette outside.

Chapter Nineteen

It didn't work. Antoinette knew.

She lay with her head in her mother's lap as Seth drove home. She was drowsy but not asleep. Soon she wouldn't be able to fight the fatigue, but she wasn't there yet.

She had hummed along with Lily's song, changing the notes that were wrong, but the seizure came before she could lock everything in place. Lily's bones wiggled like teeth ready to fall out. Healings never lasted, but this one would end sooner than most.

Antoinette twitched, her hand opening and closing on its own. Her mother smoothed her hair back from her face. The van bumped down the road, and Antoinette's eyes became heavier. The thought came again as she fell asleep.

It didn't work.

Chapter Twenty

Lily stared out the window as she and Will drove back to Eden Farms. Cherry blossoms decorated the trees along the road, but she didn't notice. She also didn't count. Furthermore, she didn't care that failure to wear a seat belt accounted for 51 percent of deaths in auto accidents, and Will was not wearing his.

Instead, she examined her hand, turning it over, looking for a clue that would explain how Antoinette fixed things. But there was nothing. Just her hand, perfectly whole. Her fingers bending. Her skin unbruised.

And yet, something wasn't right. She felt a small catch in her last two fingers. She curled her hand into a fist. As she straightened it, something shifted. Her bones felt loose. There was a sharp pinprick at the base of her little finger.

She dropped her hand and looked out the front window at the rear of Seth's truck, Rose and Antoinette riding with him. Will hummed distractedly and tapped the steering wheel. Lily stole a glance at him. He looked at home driving the Eden Farms' van. His black hair was slicked back making his face seem thinner and his cheekbones sharper.

Had he been this skinny back in Covington? she wondered.

"You keep doing that," he said, glancing at her hand and the way she was flexing her fingers. "How does it feel?"

He reached for her hand, but Lily pulled away. Everything felt fragile. "It's fine." She stretched her fingers as far apart as they could go. There it was again. A small needle prick. This time, she felt it in both fingers.

An image of Antoinette's head hitting the floor flared in her mind. It was one thing to be in pain yourself; it was quite another to cause someone else pain.

"I know what I saw," Will said. "I don't care what you say, your fingers were bent completely back. Then Antoinette touched you, and your bones moved. They *moved*, Lils."

She straightened her fingers again. "Do you hear yourself? What you're suggesting is impossible."

"The universe contains wonders," he said. "You can't be a doctor and not know that."

They were almost at the farm, but he pulled over on the shoulder of the road. "Talk to me," he said. "I was there. I saw what she did. I need to understand."

"I need to get home and help Rose." Lily's stomach twisted.

"Seth will help her. I'm not moving the van until you tell me what's going on."

Lily covered her left hand with her right. "She's a little girl. Nothing's going on."

Will stared at her intently, as if willing her to speak. When she didn't, he closed his eyes and dropped his head back against the seat. "I'd like to believe there's something beyond this," he said. "That the death of the body isn't the death of the soul."

"When did you become a philosopher?" Lily tried to laugh,

but the sound stuck in her throat. She wanted to believe her parents existed somewhere, believe that after Rose died she and her sister would find each other again.

He coughed slightly, then opened his eyes. "I've been rethinking my life. Time to grow up, I guess. Does Antoinette often seize like that?"

Lily pressed her lips together and nodded. She knew Will. He hadn't given up trying to find out about Antoinette's ability; he had just switched to a different puzzle.

"There has to be a way to stop the seizures," he said as he pulled the van back onto the road and drove to the house.

"How?" Lily asked.

"I don't know yet," he admitted.

In the driveway now, they watched as Seth lifted Antoinette from the backseat of his truck. Her skin seemed almost translucent. Then Rose climbed out of the truck. She walked slowly, as if each step was a struggle. Seth caught her arm, and she leaned into him.

"I'll figure it out," Will said as he got out and jogged toward them.

Lily counted to ten before following.

"Lily told me what Antoinette can do," Will was saying as Seth helped Rose up the porch steps. "It's amazing."

Seth glared at him. He had his hands full, Antoinette in one arm and Rose on the other. "I don't know what you're talking about."

Lily ran up the porch steps, only a few paces behind Will. "I didn't—" she said.

"Of course you didn't," Seth said.

Despite herself, Lily felt a warm rush at his words. Seth had always believed the best of her.

Rose stopped on the top step and grabbed Will's arm. "You can't tell anyone. I mean it." She shook him a little.

Will pulled free and raised his right hand. "The Hippocratic oath: first do no harm. I promise. I don't want any harm to come to Antoinette."

"I didn't say anything," Lily said. She needed Rose to believe her.

Rose sighed and closed her eyes. "It doesn't matter. He saw the whole thing." She studied Will for a moment before seeming to come to a decision. "Healing triggers seizures, and the seizures are getting worse. If word gets out about what she can do, I won't be able to keep her safe."

"What about Eli?" Lily asked. "I tried to block his view of what was happening, but I think he saw Antoinette fix my hand." There was no use hiding anything from Will now.

Rose looked worn as she opened the kitchen door. "Then we have to keep him and MaryBeth away from Antoinette."

When Rose went inside, Lily turned to Seth. "You saw Eli. Do you think he'll leave Antoinette alone?"

The little girl let out a contented sigh. She looked so small nestled in Seth's arms. He frowned, his eyes dark. "No," he said, as he followed Rose into the house. "I don't."

LILY AND WILL walked to the drying barn. "What she can do is amazing," he said. "Why didn't you tell me about her?"

"Would you have believed me?" Lily said, noting with irony that both Seth and Rose had asked her the same question.

Will ran his hand over hers. He pressed along her fingers, feeling each joint, then gently bending her wrist back and forth. "Is the size of the seizure related to anything? The difficulty of the healing, maybe?"

"Rose said the seizures aren't as bad when Antoinette does something like bring wilted flowers back to life." She flinched when Will bent her little finger. "Another thing: the healings don't last."

He frowned. "I can see that. She does this with flowers too?"

Lily pointed to a semicircle of dead pansies to the left of the barn entrance. "A few days ago, they were as brown as they are now. Then Antoinette touched them, hummed, and they turned bright yellow. That was the first time I saw her fix anything."

"Something must be taxing her system." Will frowned. "This isn't safe for her. The risk of brain damage grows as her seizures increase. You'll have to monitor her, Lils. She can't keep this up. Meanwhile, we need to get you to the ER. You need an x-ray of that hand."

Lily promised to go tomorrow. Then she knelt and started pulling out the dead pansies. Rose didn't need a tangible reminder that Antoinette was getting worse. It wasn't long before she had a pile of uprooted flowers by her feet. When she finished, she sat down and leaned against the barn.

"Do you ever feel like you have absolutely no idea what you're doing?" she asked. In less than a week, everything she believed about the world had changed. A black ant crawled up the side of the barn, making its way along the splintered wood. She traced its progress, wondering whether it knew where it was going.

Will crossed his arms. The late-afternoon sunlight slanted

across his face, but it didn't warm his skin. He looked tired. "Truthfully, no," he said. "But I have heard that others sometimes feel that way. For me the question isn't whether I know what I'm doing, but whether I'm making the best decision I can at the time. Nothing's perfect, Lils. No matter how much we want it to be." He smiled sadly.

He bent down to pick a yellow viola that sprouted through a crack in the stone path, and he handed the flower to Lily. "I always wonder how something so fragile can survive in such a rough place. But you see it all the time don't you?"

Lily twirled the flower between her fingers. Violas meant faithfulness. A few others bloomed in the cracks between the stones. "They're stronger than they appear," she said as she gathered a handful of blossoms. She needed all the strength she could get.

The ant had reached the top of the barn. It turned around and started down as if it realized it was going the wrong way.

The breeze picked up, ruffling Will's hair. He didn't bother to smooth it back. He looked at Lily as if she was the only thing he saw. "Like you," he said. "And Antoinette. If we can figure out what triggers the seizures, we can stop them. There's a solution for everything. We just have to find it."

Chapter Twenty-One

L ily woke to the staccato beat of rain on the slate roof. She pulled the quilt over her ears, but it didn't shut out the sound. *Get up*, the rain whispered.

"I don't want to," she said aloud. The light in her room was the pale gray that said the sun wasn't up yet. *Thirty minutes*, she thought. That's when the sun would be completely up. The rain sounded like it was lessening and probably would stop by then.

Across the hall, Antoinette shrieked. "Aey! Aey! Aey!" Then a loud thump, like a hand slapping against the wall.

Last night, Lily stole into Antoinette's room while she slept. The girl was sprawled on her back, and she looked younger, more like a child of five or six instead of ten.

An overstuffed blue chair sat across from Antoinette's bed. Lily was worried about Eli. What would he do if he knew beyond a doubt that Antoinette could heal?

Lily sank into the blue chair. "I'm here," she said. "I'll make sure you're safe." It was a promise she meant to keep.

She had stayed beside Antoinette's bed for most of the night, only sneaking back to her room when her eyes grew too heavy to keep open.

Antoinette shrieked again, and this time, Lily whispered along with her. "Aey! Aey! Aey!" She closed her eyes, shutting out everything except the sound of her voice blending with Antoinette's.

"Lily? Are you awake?" Rose opened the door. Light from the hall fell over her thin shoulders. "Can you help me get Antoinette ready this morning? I don't think I'm up to doing it alone today."

"Let me get dressed." Lily grabbed a clean pair of jean shorts from the dresser and slid them on without changing the T-shirt she'd slept in. She rubbed her eyes and detangled her hair by running her fingers through it.

"How's your hand?" Rose asked.

Lily held it up. A deep purple bruise had blossomed at the base of her fingers. It hadn't been there last night. "Will's taking me to the doctor today."

"I like him," Rose said with a sly smile. "He's nice. And he likes you."

"Will isn't nice," Lily said. He was arrogant and abrasive, she thought, charming if he tried, but not nice. "And he doesn't like me that way. We're friends. That's all." She tied her hair back.

"Maybe you're too close to see it, but he looks at you like you're the only person in the room."

"Will looks at anything female that way. Trust me."

Rose giggled, sounding startlingly healthy for someone who looked like she belonged in the hospital. "Might be worth it, even if only for a night."

Lily laughed along with her. It wasn't as if she hadn't thought about it. Sometimes Will looked at her as if he were hungry, and when he did her knees grew weak. Those were the times she made herself remember the nights after her parents' funeral. When she couldn't sleep, Will sat up with her, watching old movies. He was the one person who had never left her. They had become true friends. Sex would change that.

"I love Will," she said, "but not like that."

"Not like Seth, you mean," Rose said, suddenly serious.

Lily wished she could refute the words, but she could never hide anything from Rose. No matter how hard she had tried to push Seth out of her heart, she hadn't been able to. "No," she said softly, "not like Seth."

"You should tell him," Rose said. "He hasn't really dated since you two broke up. I think he still cares about you."

Lily's heart leapt at Rose's words, but it was dangerous to think that way. After he broke up with her, Lily would not leave her dorm room for hours. She counted lightbulbs, carpet threads, and wall cracks. A year had passed before she could leave the dorm without twisting the doorknob first left, then right, sixteen times.

She couldn't go through that again, and now she had Antoinette to think about. She wasn't going to let Rose down a second time.

"I can't," she said. "Not right now. Not with you and Antoinette . . . If things didn't work out with Seth a second time—" She broke off and started counting under her breath. She felt Rose watching but couldn't stop mouthing numbers.

"I want you to be happy," Rose said.

Her words made Lily stop counting. "I am happy," she said in surprise. "I'm home. I'm with you and Antoinette when I thought I'd never see you again. That's enough for me."

Rose hugged her gently. "But you could have so much more," she said softly.

With the door to her bedroom open, Antoinette's shrieks were louder. Lily pulled away and slipped on an old pair of flip-flops. "I don't need more," she said. And not wanting to discuss Seth further, she changed the subject. "I'm worried about Eli and what he saw."

"Maybe he didn't see anything," Rose said.

"He was looking right at me." Lily could still see Eli's eyes, wide and hopeful.

"He'll go away if we ignore him," Rose said. On the bureau was a teacup filled with the violas Lily had picked yesterday.

"For faithfulness, right?" Rose asked as she ran a finger around the rim of the cup.

Lily nodded. "Isn't that what sisters should be?" She looked at Rose, seeing two of her: the woman she was now, faded and diminished by her illness, and the girl she had been, beautiful and full of life. Lily closed her eyes, committing her sister's face to memory. "Faithful," she said. "In everything."

"We'll keep telling Eli he's imagining things," Rose said. "After a while, he'll believe us."

Lily didn't agree and said so.

"This has happened before," Rose said. "Once, Cora was here at the farm. It was September, and we were walking down the driveway. You know the tiger lilies by the front gate?"

Lily nodded. Every year in late summer, a profusion of the orange flowers framed the entrance to Eden Farms.

"Cora wanted to add the petals to a field green salad she was making. I told her she could pick as many as she wanted.

Antoinette followed us. On the way down the drive, every for-sythia was green.

"When Cora finished cutting the lilies, we turned around as Antoinette touched a bush, and it burst into bloom. Every other plant along the drive was already blooming. Yellow flowers were everywhere.

"Cora saw everything. Just like Eli, she thought it was a miracle. I told her she was imagining things. That the bushes had been blooming on our way down the drive. When that didn't work, I faked a heart episode."

"You didn't," Lily said.

Rose grinned. "You play the cards you're dealt. Cora forgot all about the forsythia bushes after that. It'll be the same with Eli."

Across the hall, Antoinette shrieked again. "Come on," Rose said. "Let's go get our little miracle worker."

"Wait." Lily grabbed Rose's hand. She didn't want to leave anything unsaid between them. "I need you to know I won't let you down. I'm not running away. I was scared before, but I'm not now. It's hard being different, and I thought that being around Antoinette would make my . . . my quirks more pronounced."

"But don't you see?" Rose asked. "That's why you're perfect for her. You know what it's like to be on the outside looking in. You know that 'different' doesn't mean broken. Antoinette needs someone who will tell her that."

She squeezed Lily's hand, then walked across the hall to Antoinette's room. When she opened the door, Antoinette shifted, and her eyes opened.

"Good morning, sleepyhead," Rose said. Antoinette reached for her, but Rose stepped aside. "Lily's helping us today."

Rose glanced over her shoulder at Lily. "I know I'm asking a lot, and I wanted to thank you. Having you home makes me feel young again."

Lily had been so long without a sister that she had forgotten the pleasure of being with someone who held your history in her heart. "Tell me what to do," she said. She was nervous, but she knew she could do this.

"Stand over here and let her see you," Rose said.

Lily crossed the room, but her stride was too big. One more step and she'd be at Rose's side, ending on five. She quickly halved her stride and stopped on six. "I heard you singing this morning," she said to Antoinette. "It was pretty."

Antoinette ignored Lily and stretched toward Rose.

"Sit on the bed and let her get used to you," Rose said.

Lily sat tentatively on the far edge of the bed.

"Tell her it's time to get up," Rose said.

"Okay. Hi Antoinette. I'm going to help you get ready this morning."

Antoinette bounced on the bed, and Lily's stomach dropped with the motion. "Let's try this again," Lily said, with a glance at Rose. "Are you ready to get up? We could go down and get some breakfast. What do you like to eat? I don't normally eat breakfast, but I will this morning."

Antoinette hummed.

"Did I do something wrong?" Lily asked.

"She's singing. It means she's happy. You're doing great. Keep going."

"Can you get up?" Lily stood. Antoinette flopped down and rolled to face the wall.

"You have to say it like you expect her to do it," Rose said.

With confidence that was ninety percent fake, Lily said, "Come on Antoinette, it's time to get up." She stood back and waited.

"Get up," she said again, feeling Rose's eyes on her back. Without warning, and much to her surprise, Antoinette sat up and scooted to the edge of the bed. Lily grinned. "Does she need help?"

Rose shook her head. "She knows what to do. You just need to keep her on track or she'll wander off."

Slowly, Lily moved toward the door. "Come on, let's get breakfast." When Antoinette took first one step and then another, Lily felt her world shift, and she wondered how she could have ever thought of abandoning her niece.

Chapter Twenty-Two

After eating breakfast with Lily, Antoinette stumbled down the back porch stairs, her body hurting everywhere. The happiness she had felt upon waking was gone, replaced by a constant low-level anxiety.

She wagged her head from side to side to loosen her neck muscles. When she stopped, she noticed a sparrow lying on the ground. The bird was on its side, its gray chest quivering. Antoinette hadn't known it was possible for something to breathe so fast.

She crouched down so that she was inches from the bird, so close she could ruffle its feathers with her fingers. The sparrow tried to turn its head toward her but couldn't. Its wing, the one it was lying on, was bent backward. Antoinette mirrored its position, twisting her right arm behind her back and turning her head the other direction.

It hurt.

"Antoinette," Lily called from the porch. "We have to go. Seth's waiting for you in the drying barn. Don't you want to help him get it ready for the show?"

Of course she did. But the bird distracted her. It kicked its legs, but it didn't go anywhere.

Antoinette leaned closer. The bird breathed faster.

Since healing Lily's fingers, Antoinette's arms rarely stayed at her side. She couldn't walk from the porch to the house garden without stopping to rest, and she was tired all the time.

Lily's feet made soft swishing sounds as she walked through the grass. "Come on, Antoinette. Let's go. I have to drop you off with Seth before Will takes me to the doctor."

Over and over Antoinette saw herself reaching for Lily's hand. The tiny bones rearranging themselves. The skin stretching. The muscles lengthening. Everything was almost locked in place. Then the seizure came.

Lily's hand looked normal, but things weren't always what they seemed. The bones weren't properly fused, and it wouldn't be long before they slid out of place again. Lily's hand would be just as broken as it was before.

The bird opened its beak; a tiny squeak escaped. Antoinette leaned forward until she was right over it. Slowly, she dropped her hand to its chest.

I'm not going to hurt you, she thought. The bird's heart skittered beneath her fingers. Antoinette closed her eyes, listening.

At first, she didn't hear anything, and her heart raced. The bird opened and closed its beak, but nothing came out.

Antoinette concentrated until a faint song emerged. It was the sound of a piccolo, high and fast, the notes bright.

She followed the melody until she found the spot where the notes were off-key, deep, pain-filled things. The wing was broken. She absorbed the wrong notes and hummed, welcoming the pain into her body, knitting the bird's bones back together.

It took longer than usual, but gradually the song corrected itself. When everything was right, the bird shuddered. It twisted upright, hopped once, and leapt into the sky.

Then Lily was there. "No!" She grabbed Antoinette, but she was too late.

Antoinette tracked the bird, even as she started to shake. She fell sideways but kept the sparrow in sight as it flew higher and higher.

Then, just before the seizure claimed her, the bird stuttered in midair. Its wing folded backward, and it tumbled to the ground.

SEVERAL HOURS LATER, Antoinette sat by her mother's knees, listening to Dvorak's *New World Symphony* on head-phones Lily bought for her. Her mother was at the kitchen table, going over her notes for the garden show. "Thirty-two vendors," she said under her breath. "That's up from last year."

Antoinette couldn't forget the bird. After seizing, she slept for a while and woke to the image of the sparrow falling from the sky. She shivered at the thought and pressed her cheek against her mother's knee. The day was hot for April, but she felt cold. She looked around the room, expecting to see icicles edging the table, but everything was normal.

Gold light shimmered through the window on the kitchen door. She wanted to be outside where the sun would warm her.

She stretched her arm up. It was heavy. Dvorak's symphony rolled through her headphones, helping her focus. When her arm was high enough, she let it fall against her mother's elbow. Tap. Tap. Then she pointed. *Outside.*

"Not now. I have to finish," her mother said, without look-ing up.

Sometimes Antoinette spoke in her dreams. Often she woke sure a word had made it past her lips, but she was always a second too late. The room was silent every time.

If she could speak, her mother wouldn't ignore her. Antoinette would say, "Outside," and they would go. She opened her mouth and tried to push the word out, but not even a whisper escaped.

She scooted across the floor on her rear. At the door, she stood and pressed her nose against the glass. Through the window, she saw Lily and Seth digging weeds in the kitchen garden. Lily worked a triangle of basil. Her back was to Seth so she didn't see him reach for her, as if wanting to stroke her skin.

Will was also outside. He sat on the porch swing, staring at Lily, but she didn't notice him either.

Lily had spent the morning in the emergency room, and she returned home with her hand bandaged. Looking at it made Antoinette's stomach feel hollow, so she shifted her gaze to the plants.

Dill, basil, and oregano grew in wedges bordered by lavender and salvia. Later, marigolds would poke from the soil in a neat circle around the bed. Cora was the only one who used the herbs now that Antoinette's mother no longer cooked. Their names ran through Antoinette's head like a song. *Dill, basil, oregano. Dill, basil, oregano.* She flapped her hands and hummed.

Over the headphones, a flutist began a solo. Antoinette swayed in time to the music. The notes were smooth and round, each one perfect, the sound of loneliness.

Sometimes Antoinette didn't mind being different. When she stood outside and felt the sun on her face—not only its heat, but its essence—when that slipped under her skin, she felt special.

But she didn't feel anything now, so what was she? A weird kid who couldn't control her body. She couldn't completely heal her mother or Lily. She couldn't hear the flowers sing. And now she couldn't even save the life of a sparrow.

She looked back at her mother, curled over her notebook, entering numbers in her neat, even handwriting. She made one last notation, then stood and removed Antoinette's headphones. "Will you come outside with me?" she asked.

Moving was difficult. Antoinette's legs popped most of the time, and when she tried to sit still her arms flew over her head. With her mother's help, she made it outside, but her legs telescoped as soon as her feet touched the porch. She fell, banging her knees on the wood floor.

Will helped her up. "You're going to have a bruise," he said as he brushed off her knees.

She could already feel the bruise forming as she walked to the edge of the porch.

Will stood beside her. "She's fascinating," he said.

The swing sighed as her mother sat down. "Do you mean Antoinette or Lily?"

What a silly question, Antoinette thought. Didn't her mother see the way Will looked at Lily?

"Antoinette, of course," Will said.

"If you say so," her mother said. "But I don't think Antoinette's the reason you drove all the way down here."

Will looked out over the fields. "The reason I came doesn't matter anymore." He looked like he wanted to say more but broke off, coughing.

Antoinette flapped her hands and walked to the edge of the porch. The mountain ash had bloomed. Its branches were a cotton-candy canopy of blooms. Anemones grew around its base, their foliage like thousands of little fingers.

She eased down the stairs and walked to the tree. She sat down and listened to the bees as they darted in and out of the tiny white blossoms.

Sit, she thought. *Stay still.*

For a moment, her body was quiet. Then a twitch started at the tips of her toes. She tried to pin her arms down, but the twitch burst out of her body, and her hands flapped over her head.

Disappointment filled her.

Everything was changing.

She looked at the anemones. One plant had leaves that were yellow, but the veins were neon green. That was not normal. The leaves should be a nice even green.

Antoinette wiggled her toes deep into the ground and listened, straining to hear. The flowers were silent.

She pushed her hands wrist-deep into the dirt and closed her eyes.

Nothing.

No, no, no! She whipped her head back and forth and slumped over, her face on the ground. Mulch scratched her cheeks and her forehead. She still couldn't hear the plants, couldn't *feel* them. The despair that had been building in her since she had failed to heal Lily's hand finally erupted, and she screamed.

Then Will was there. He slid his hands under Antoinette's arms and picked her up. "I'm taking you to your mother."

Antoinette stiffened until she was board flat, but Will was strong. He carried her to the swing and settled her into her mother's arms. Then he stared into her eyes. "Her pupils aren't fixed," he said. "It isn't a seizure."

Antoinette could have told him that. A seizure didn't fill her with emptiness. A seizure would mean there was still hope, a chance she could heal her mother.

Chapter Twenty-Three

"Y ou worked at the market *every* day?" Will asked Lily on the way to the commercial fields, Antoinette with them. "No running around the farm? No chasing boys? You know there are laws against child labor." He carried a pitchfork, leaning on it as he walked.

Farming was a never-ending battle against decay, even in winter, when everything was dormant. There were fences that needed mending, barns that needed painting, or glass panes in the greenhouse that needed to be replaced.

The garden show was on Sunday. Broadleaf weeds dotted the house garden. Overnight, wild onions had sprouted among the daffodils, and dandelions dotted the night garden. Lily added weeding to her long list of chores.

But first she would turn the compost heaps at the end of the peony rows. Instead of one big pile, her father had built several small white containers and placed them among the rows of flowers, where microbes would transform shredded paper, coffee grounds, and kitchen scraps into the gardener's version of black gold.

"It's wasn't as boring as it sounds," she said. "It was peaceful. Fun." She didn't add that Seth often joined her in her work.

Antoinette moved down the path in front of them. Since healing Lily, walking had been harder for her. Her knees frequently folded as if about to drop her in the dirt; yet today she stayed upright. Lily walked with her good hand out, ready to catch her if she fell.

"You have a peculiar idea of fun—" Will broke off and started coughing. Lily thumped him on the back, surprised she could feel his spine beneath her hands.

"That's enough. You can stop hitting me now." His face was pale and his chest heaved.

"Are you okay?" Lily asked. "*Really* okay, I mean." Remission didn't mean his lung cancer was cured, only that there was no evidence of the disease at the moment.

He grinned and gestured to the sky. "It's all this fresh air. My lungs aren't used to it."

She didn't believe him and was about to say so, when a sharp pain shot through her left hand. Yesterday she found out that it was indeed broken. An x-ray showed a fracture at the base of her fingers. The doctor wrapped her hand in an ACE bandage and told her to set up an appointment with an orthopedist in a few days.

Will noticed her massaging her hand. "It hurts?"

She nodded.

"Are you taking your pain meds?"

"They make me groggy. There's too much work to be done." She took the pitchfork from him and opened one of the compost bins. A rich earthy smell wafted out.

"Let me do that," Will said, reclaiming the pitchfork and jabbing it into the bin.

"Not like that," Lily said. She showed him how to dig down to the bottom of the bin and turn the compost over. "Rose and Seth will be here soon." Rose wanted to have a picnic. They didn't have time for it, but Lily couldn't say no to her.

"Your boyfriend doesn't like me, Lils," Will said as he worked. Over the past few days, he had relaxed. He no longer wore pressed khakis and starched shirts. Though his jeans were too expensive for farmwork, he almost looked like he belonged.

"He's not my boyfriend."

Will shrugged. "Could've fooled me. I've seen the way he looks at you. Not that I blame him."

Antoinette stomped her feet and flapped her hands. She turned in a slow circle. Her legs trembled, and her fingers flicked back and forth. The movements seemed random, like she couldn't control her body.

A stone formed in the pit of Lily's stomach as she watched her niece. "Antoinette's getting worse, isn't she?"

Will wouldn't look at her. That alone told her she was right.

She turned his face to hers. He hadn't shaved, his skin was rough. "You're my friend. I need to know."

"Friend?" He leaned into her hand.

"Why would you think you weren't?"

He turned his face a fraction of an inch. His lips grazed her palm.

Lily went still. She felt her face flush, and for once she couldn't find anything to count. "Will, I don't—"

"Are we interrupting?" Rose asked as she and Seth crested

the hill to the commercial fields. Seth carried a picnic basket with one hand and helped Rose walk with the other.

Antoinette shrieked when she saw her mother. She stumbled across the grass and held her hands up. It was eighty degrees out, but Rose wore a long-sleeved yellow cardigan.

Seth set the basket down and swung Antoinette into his arms. "Your mom's tired. You'll have to make do with me, kiddo." His voice was light, but he frowned at Lily's hand on Will's face.

Lily pulled away from Will. "We were just turning the compost piles." Without thinking, she grabbed the pitchfork in her left hand, then flinched when she squeezed her fingers shut.

Rose took the pitchfork. "The healing faded fast."

Lily turned to Will. "You didn't answer me. Is something wrong with An—"

"Antoinette and I are going for a walk," Seth interjected. He directed a sharp look at Lily.

She flushed, knowing he was right. This wasn't something Antoinette needed to hear.

"Come on, kiddo. Let's go find some fun." Seth tossed Antoinette into the air. She flung her head back and giggled, her face bright with joy.

"I don't know," Will said when Seth and Antoinette were out of earshot. He was calm, and Lily wondered if this was the way he delivered bad news to his patients. "This is all new for me. It's not like there's a medical category for child miracle workers."

"But if you had to guess?" Lily asked. "What does the doctor in you think?"

Will stared at the sky for so long she thought he wasn't going to answer. When he did, she saw resignation in his eyes. "How long do the healings normally last?" he asked.

"They used to last months," Rose said quietly. "But lately they've been fading faster and faster." She gestured toward Lily's hand. "This is the shortest I've seen."

Lily was still thinking. Antoinette's seizure after healing the bird hadn't been as large as it had been after healing her hand. Was the seizure larger because of the complexity involved? Maybe the difficulty overwhelmed Antoinette's small body until she seized.

Or maybe that wasn't it at all. Nature abhorred a vacuum. Maybe Antoinette pulled the illness or the pain from the injury into her own body. After all, it had to go somewhere. It couldn't just disappear.

She watched Seth and Antoinette. He held her under her arms as he spun with her—they were a picture of happiness. When they stopped, Seth pretended to stumble, but even as he fell he cradled Antoinette. Their laughter carried over the farm.

"Keep in mind this is just a guess," Will said. He looked like he wanted to be somewhere else. "I'm way out of my league here, but the worsening seizures, the diminished effect of the healings—it all says something is going wrong. How quickly things might get worse, though, I can't predict."

As he spoke, Seth returned with Antoinette on his shoulders. He swung her down but didn't set her on the ground. Instead, he held her in his arms.

"You don't know how strong she is," he said to Will. There was pain and anger in his voice. "You don't know a damn thing about her."

"Lily asked for my opinion," Will said, "and I gave it. I'm

not saying I'm right, but when the body is fatigued or under stress, it doesn't operate as well as it should. High blood pressure, the ability to fight off common colds, certain types of cancer . . ."

"He's right," Lily said. "Something's wrong." She unwrapped her ACE bandage to reveal the deep purple bruise at the base of her fingers.

"Damn," Seth said softly. He set Antoinette down and turned to Lily. "Can I look at that?"

When he took her hand, electricity skittered over her skin.

"Does it hurt?" he asked.

"Not as much as it did at Cora's when I fell, but more than it did last night or even earlier this morning."

He ran his thumb across her palm. "I want to *do* something. Anything. But I can't." He spoke softly, so that only she heard. "Things like this shouldn't happen to kids."

"No," she said. "They shouldn't."

THE KITCHEN LIGHT was on, illuminating the hallway with a soft yellow glow. "Will?" Lily said. "Are you still up?" It was past midnight.

The kitchen was empty. She was about to switch off the light and go to bed when she looked out the back door. In the starlight, she saw Will sitting on the porch swing. He tilted his head back, and every once in a while he'd raise a finger and drag it along the sky as if tracing the constellations. His dark hair blended into the night sky.

A bottle of beer sat on the small table next to him. He took a drink, then shoved his feet against the porch floor, making the swing rock.

Lily bit her lip as she studied his profile. He looked older than he had a week ago and weary.

A light flickered in the fields, drawing her attention away from Will. A thin beam shone beneath the drying barn door. She knew Seth must be out there preparing for the garden show. She should be helping him, but she didn't think he wanted company. Like the rest of them, he was upset at the downturn in Antoinette's health. She knew him well enough to know that at times like this, he wanted to be alone.

She opened the door to the porch and stepped out.

"I was wondering when you'd stop watching me and come out here." Will said. "How's Rose? I figured you'd call me if you needed help."

The past two nights, Lily had sat beside Rose as she fell asleep. They talked about their childhood, Antoinette, or nothing at all. "She's finally asleep."

"You're doing good, Lils." He held up the beer bottle. "Want a drink?"

When she shook her head, he lifted one shoulder. "Suit yourself. You know I'll do what I can to help, don't you?"

"I know." She sat down beside him and rested her head on his shoulder. "Rose is getting worse. It's taking longer for her to fall asleep, and when she does, she wakes a couple of times every night. I don't know what else to do for her."

Will took another swallow. "Do you remember when I was in the middle of chemo? I hated sitting in that open room, tethered to an IV, staring at the other cancer patients. We were all hooked to the same drug cocktail, but most of them had twenty or thirty years on me. Every time I looked at them I wondered whether I'd live to see forty or fifty.

"Then you started coming with me, and I had someone else to focus on. One time you counted the number of chairs in the room while the nurse was flushing my port. 'Twenty-two,' you said. 'That's a nice even number.' Then you counted the ceiling tiles, the nurses behind the desk, the number of patients in the room.

"I don't think you realized you were doing it. When you finished, you looked at me and said, 'Everything's even, so we're good.' You seemed so sure of yourself. So grounded. I held on to your belief that everything would get better when I couldn't believe for myself." Will squeezed her good hand. "That's what you can do for Rose. When she loses hope, hold on to it for her."

"But things aren't going to get better for Rose." Lily stared into the dark. Crickets sang and somewhere an owl hooted. The light in the drying barn flicked off. She squinted, trying to make out Seth as he left, but the night was too dark and she couldn't see anything.

"The point isn't whether she gets better," Will said. "The point is whether she goes through this alone or has someone with her who loves her, someone who tells her everything will be all right after she's gone. Love her enough to believe *that* for her. And if you can't believe it, fake it, because most of the time, things work out all right."

Lily looked at him. "How did you get to be so smart?"

He took another drink. "Perception, Lils. It's my gift and my curse. For example, I know you still have feelings for your farm boy."

"Seth?"

"The very one." Will saluted her with the bottle.

She straightened. Her cheeks flushed, and she was grateful for the dark. "I don't—"

"No sense trying to hide it. But he's not right for you." He grew serious. "Where was he these past six years? Where was he when your parents died? He could have found you, but he didn't. That has to mean something."

Will was silhouetted in the light from the kitchen. He drew a finger across her cheek. "I wouldn't have left you," he said.

He was right. He had never left her. And now, he was here again, right when she needed him. She was a tangle of emotion. Though the night was warm, she shivered. "Don't." She took his hand, willing him to stop talking.

"Having cancer taught me one thing," he said. "I want my life to count for something. For me, that means spending it with you. We're good together, Lils. You just have to let it happen."

Everything he said made sense. But still she couldn't forget Seth. "I wish it was that easy," she said.

Will took another swallow of beer. "It is. Life doesn't stand still. You have to move with it. Look at me. A few days ago I was at home in Covington. Today I'm here with you. Easy as wishing."

Even in the dark she could see his smile. It filled his face. "How long can you stay?" she asked.

He lowered the bottle and looked at her. "As long as you need me," he said, as if it was the simplest thing in the world.

Chapter Twenty-Four

The land was silent. Antoinette cocked her head to the left and listened. Cicadas buzzed. Crickets sang. Wind rustled the leaves on the birch trees. But the music was gone. For the first time, she did not want to be outside.

Her mother walked beside her. Lily and Will walked ahead of them. "It's a lot of work for a garden show, Lils," Will said.

Antoinette didn't hear Lily's reply.

If Seth were here, he would play for her, play until she forgot that she had become deaf to the land. But she hadn't seen him since yesterday when he twirled around with her in the flower field.

Her mother bent down. "Do you remember when you were a little girl?" she asked. "I'd catch fireflies in mason jars for you. Remember the time the whole barn was lit up with their glow? We must have had thirty jars."

Antoinette remembered. The barn had glimmered with their light. Her mother wove a crown of daisies for her. "You're my fairy princess," she had said, and Antoinette believed her—that night anything felt possible.

"You're still my princess," her mother said.

At the split in the drive where one path led to the house and the other to the drying barn, someone called Antoinette's name.

At first, she thought it was the crickets, but then it happened again. She stopped and looked up.

Eli Cantwell stood behind the iron gate at the end of their driveway. "Antoinette!" he yelled again.

Antoinette felt her mother stiffen. "Ignore it," she said. "He'll leave if we keep walking." Her mother motioned for her to move forward, but Antoinette planted her feet.

"Who is it?" Will asked, bringing a hand up to shade his eyes.

"It's Eli," Lily said. She put her good hand on Antoinette's back. "Come on, you need to keep walking."

Antoinette didn't budge.

"I know you're there," Eli yelled. "Please, Rose. MaryBeth's worse. Let her help us!"

"Wait here," her mother said. She walked down the drive to Eli.

The wind carried bits of their conversation to Antoinette.

"She's just a little girl," her mother said.

"I know what I saw!" Eli sounded angry.

"You're confused," her mother said. "You need to leave us alone."

"Please," Eli's voice cracked. "MaryBeth's all I've got."

Her mother wrapped her hand around Eli's. "If Antoinette could help you, don't you think I'd let her?"

"Please." Eli stared at Antoinette as if she were a savior or a saint.

But Antoinette had never been either of those. She looked

at Lily's injured hand. She remembered the sparrow falling from the sky.

This time when Lily gently pushed her forward, Antoinette turned from Eli and kept walking.

ANTOINETTE SHUFFLED THROUGH the cedar shavings and dried flower petals on the barn floor. Twice a year Seth spread shavings throughout the barn—their scent kept flies away. As she walked, she kicked up puffs of sawdust that drifted through the air like dandelion seeds.

At the other end of the barn, a plywood stage had been set up. On Sunday, Seth would stand there, playing bluegrass for the crowd. Bluegrass was happy music, and Antoinette wished he was playing it now. She needed something happy.

They had been in the barn for an hour, and though Eli was gone, she still heard him screaming her name. She balled her hand into a fist and smacked her forehead.

"Shouldn't you make her stop that?" Will asked as he lifted a folding table from the stack against the wall.

Lily looked up from where she stood at the other end of the barn. A can of white paint sat at her feet. She was almost finished painting the walls.

"She'll quit if it hurts," Antoinette's mother said. She sat on a straw bale, too tired to help. Her skin was paler than usual, and every few minutes she took a deep breath. When she did, she steepled her fingers over her heart and pushed.

Antoinette mirrored her movement, pressing her fingers into her heart as if she could tease the grief out. But when she dropped her hand, she hurt just as much as she had before.

Will ran a wet rag over the table, and sawdust slid to the

barn floor. "Won't most of the artists bring their own tables?" he asked. "Seems to me that you shouldn't be doing all of this work for them."

"Each year a few people forget something. Besides, we need tables for our flower arrangements and lavender bread." Her mother closed her eyes and leaned back against the wall. After talking with Eli at the gate, she had grown quiet. She seemed to be withdrawing inside herself.

Antoinette tucked her elbows tight against her side. She felt sluggish, the way she did after a seizure. Except she hadn't had a seizure today. She hit her head again.

"Why don't you go home, Rose," Lily said as she dipped her paintbrush into the can. "We've got this."

"I'm fine," her mother said.

Lily looked at Antoinette. "*You'd* listen to me, wouldn't you?" Her gaze was heavy, but Antoinette didn't mind. As her mother grew weaker, Lily seemed to grow stronger.

Antoinette stretched up on her toes and walked to the far end of the barn. She paced under the herbs hanging from the rafters. Basil, rosemary, oregano. And lavender. They always had lavender.

Her mother used to pick a basketful of the flowers. Then she'd spend the rest of the day baking lavender bread and lavender butter cookies.

The scent would spread through the house. On those nights, Antoinette would dream she was so full of words they popped from her mouth like soap bubbles. She'd wake with her lips buzzing, sure that if she had opened her eyes a second earlier, the room would have been ringing with words like home, love, safe.

And Mommy. Most of all, Mommy.

"What's the story behind this garden show?" Will asked. He popped the metal legs of a table open and righted it.

"It's a family tradition," her mother said.

Antoinette focused on her mother's face. It hurt to do so, but she didn't look away. She studied the sharp line of her mother's jaw, the curve of her cheek, the color of her skin—pale white, like the Honor roses Antoinette had pushed into bloom a week ago.

"Our parents' first year of farming was rough," she said. "Thirty years ago, there wasn't a big market for commercial flower farms. They lost most of their crop and thought they might have to sell the farm."

"Toss me that rag," Will said to Lily.

She threw it to him, her aim true. "They were tough," Lily said, picking up the story. "Mom decided to have a garden show. What did she say, Rose? She wanted to—"

"Spit in the eye of defeat." Antoinette's mother laughed. "Mom was stubborn."

Will wiped dust from his fingers. "Sounds like it runs in the family."

Lily threw another cloth at him. It hit him in the chest with a loud thwack.

Antoinette only vaguely remembered her grandparents—a woman with soft arms and a man with a big laugh.

"Cora and Teelia invited the entire town," Lily said. "To everyone's surprise, the show was a success. Mom and Dad made enough money to hold on for one more season. Since then, we've had the show every year."

That's what Antoinette needed to do—figure out how to help her mother hold on a little longer. She flapped her hands and cocked her head to the left. "Aauugh," she said as she walked over to her mother and tapped her side.

Her mother gently pushed her away. "No touching."

Antoinette didn't stop.

"Antoinette, I said *no*."

Bits of dried lavender fell from the rafters, dusting Antoinette's shoulders. She stomped and a puff of sawdust caught in her nose. Then she smacked her head. Hard. She had to save her mother.

Lily gently tugged Antoinette's hand away from her head. "Don't do that. You'll hurt yourself."

I don't care. Antoinette wrenched free and bared her teeth.

Her mother sighed. "Leave her alone. She'll stop when it hurts."

I hurt now. She didn't mean her head; her heart hurt more than her head ever could.

Lily whispered in Antoinette's ear. "It'll help your mom. She worries about you." She squeezed Antoinette's hand, then went back to painting the wall.

Antoinette wanted to curl up against her mother's side. They would hold hands. Antoinette would hear her mother's song again. Then she would fix everything.

She screamed and stamped her feet. Her mother was dying and she couldn't stop it.

"I wish you could tell me what's wrong," her mother said.

Me too, Antoinette thought. Someday the words would come; she would start talking and never stop. She paced in a tight circle. The rhythm of one foot falling after another was soothing. A minute passed where the only sound in the barn was the scuff of her feet through the sawdust.

Lily broke the silence. "Try counting."

Antoinette didn't realize Lily was speaking to her.

"Antoinette," Lily said again.

This time she stopped. She cocked her head to the right and curled her hands to her shoulders. Her heart beat faster, and her eyelids flickered.

"Try counting," Lily said as she walked toward Antoinette.

"What are you doing?" her mother asked.

"She needs help." Lily stopped just out of Antoinette's reach. "One. Two."

Antoinette's arms uncurled and dropped to her sides.

"Three. Four."

Her jaw unclenched, and her eyelids stilled.

"Five. Six."

Antoinette sighed, and her heart slid back into its normal rhythm.

"It's best to stop on an even number," Lily said. "At least it is for me. That way everything fits together."

Antoinette made herself look Lily directly in the eye. It hurt, but she didn't turn away.

"Counting will help you make sense of things," she said.

Peace settled deep in Antoinette's middle as she realized she wasn't alone. Lily understood.

ROSE'S JOURNAL
April 2013

—✠—

I DON'T REMEMBER the sound of my mother's voice, or the way it felt when she held me in her arms. Since she died, pieces of her have faded away. Sometimes it seems like she was never here at all.

Memory is like that. And one day soon it will be my turn. Pieces of me will start to fade away. Five months have passed since Dr. Teyler told me I was dying. But now that Lily is home, I'm not afraid anymore.

Tonight I sit in the van, watching as she cuts armloads of white Honor roses and Casa Blanca lilies from the night garden. We are going to visit our parents' graves. Her arms overflow as she walks toward the van. I whisper a prayer of thanks for Antoinette's ability to pull life from unexpected places.

I whisper another prayer for Will. He's watching Antoinette for me, and I hurt for him. I see the way he looks at Lily.

But I also see the way Lily looks at Seth. They still fit together.

The drive to the cemetery is short. When we arrive, Lily helps me from the van, then hands me a bundle of flowers. "We probably should have waited until tomorrow," she says as we start toward our parents' grave.

"We're here now." I need to be a family again. Mom, Dad,

Lily, and me. I put my nose in the flowers and inhale. The night is warm as we start up the hill. Lily walks backward, as if not being able to see what lies in front of her makes it easier to face.

"What's it like?" she asks. "Dying, I mean."

I watch my feet. The path is smooth, but lately I fall easily.

"You always did get right to the heart of things, didn't you?"

"I did it again, didn't I?" Lily says. The ground changes from flat to a slight upward slope.

"Subtlety was never your strong point."

Lily laughs, and I am young again. "I'll answer your question, but I need you to promise me something." I wait until she agrees before continuing. "Keep Antoinette safe and tell her how much I love her." I shift the flowers to my left hand. "I've got to stop for a minute to catch my breath."

My lungs strain and white dots float before my eyes. I sit on a stone bench next to a grave, shut my eyes, and explain what's happening. Then I say, "Tell me it's snowing." It's a bad joke, but Lily laughs anyway.

"It's a miracle," she says. "A snowstorm in April."

Stranger things have happened.

I catch my breath and open my eyes. Lily has stripped the petals from several roses. She scatters them over my head. "I told you. It's snowing."

She takes my bundle of flowers and adds them to hers. "Maybe we should go home," she says.

"No," I say, "It'll pass." I should have brought my oxygen tank. I take a nitro pill from my pocket and slip it under my tongue. "Do you remember that hollow feeling when Mom and Dad died? The impossibility of it?" Some mornings I still wake expecting to find Mom cutting flower stems at the kitchen sink. When I remember she's dead, I experience that feeling of loss all over again.

"You don't have to talk about it," Lily whispers. "I shouldn't have asked."

"It's okay. Telling someone makes it less lonely." I loop my arm through hers, careful of her broken hand. "Help me walk."

She shifts the flowers to her other arm so she can take my weight.

"Dying feels like that," I say. "Except you're losing everyone you've ever loved at once. There's this panic. You try to hold on because you feel yourself slipping away, but you can't control your body. The weird thing is, you don't think about dying yourself. You think about the people you're leaving behind. It feels like they're the ones dying. Not you."

Mist twirls around us. It's normal here, but tonight it feels like the dead rising up to greet me.

"After panic, resignation sets in. There's nothing you can do to stop it. No one beats death. Not even Antoinette." I wave my hand in air, dispelling the mist. "It's not bad. Make sure you tell Antoinette. Tell her it's not bad."

This day has been coming since the first time I held Antoinette. So much of mothering is about fear. Fear that your child will be hurt. That she will get lost. That no one will ever love her with the same all-consuming intensity that I do.

But most of all, I fear the day I will have to say good-bye to her, because no matter when that day comes, it will be too soon.

We buried our parents side by side, under a shared headstone.

Lily stops shy of the gray stone carved with their names. Then she kneels and I see her lips moving. She's counting, her version of prayer. She rests the flowers beneath the stone, and when she turns to me, I see my past in her eyes. "I promise. Antoinette will *never* forget you," she says.

Chapter Twenty-Five

L ily had worked harder in the past week than she had in
the past six years. Her muscles were knotted in places she
couldn't reach, and no matter how much she coughed she
still felt sawdust in the back of her throat.

She needed a drink of water. It was early—not even six in
the morning—when she padded into the kitchen and flipped on
the light.

A low groan filled the room.

"What in the world?" She turned in a slow circle. The room
was empty.

There it was again. A moan, like a tree creaking in the wind.

She knelt and peered under the table. Antoinette sat under
the farthest end, her knees folded to her chest.

"I thought I heard someone in here," Lily said. She held out
her hand. "Why don't you come out here with me? I'll make you
something to eat."

Antoinette dropped her head to her knees and started rocking. She had been agitated at the drying barn last night. Apparently, she still was.

"Your mom's asleep, but I don't think she'd mind if we woke her. I know she wouldn't want you to sit out here alone."

Yellow butterflies dotted Antoinette's pajamas. The print was light and happy; the exact opposite of Antoinette's demeanor.

"What about Will? We could wake him up."

Antoinette groaned. If grief had a sound, this was it.

"Well, you can't sit under there alone." Lily crawled under the table and sat next to her niece. Their hips touched, and Antoinette leaned into her.

Lily rested her cheek against the top of Antoinette's head. "I know it's hard watching your mom get sicker. When my parents died, I felt . . . lost. Everything just stopped. Like the world forgot how to spin. I always felt like I moved to a different tune than everyone else, and that feeling got worse after they died. I was so lonely."

She wrapped her arm around the little girl and pulled her close. "I won't let it be like that for you. You'll never be alone. I'll be right here with you."

The planks in the wood floor were old. With time and temperature changes they had shifted slightly, creating tiny cracks between the boards. Lily ran her fingers along the spaces, counting each one.

"Count with me?" She took Antoinette's hand and placed it on the floor. She guided it along a split in the floor by their feet. "One."

Where that crack joined another, Lily shifted Antoinette's fingers. They followed the new line. "Two."

When Lily reached twelve, Antoinette stopped groaning.

On twenty-two, she stopped rocking.

On thirty, she crawled out from under the table and pointed to the back door.

THE DAFFODILS WERE starting to brown, only the tips of the leaves so far, but they'd need to harvest the remaining flowers soon. Tomorrow, or the next day, Lily thought.

She and Antoinette sat in the grass at the head of a row. Antoinette was still in her pj's, and Lily still wore the T-shirt and shorts she slept in. Yellow and white flowers stretched into the distance. If they stored half of them in the commercial freezer, they'd be selling daffodils into May.

Antoinette grabbed a browning flower, but Lily pulled her back. "Leave it alone," she said.

Antoinette struggled for a moment, then sighed and rested her head in the crook of Lily's arm.

"I don't like it when they turn brown either," Lily said. "It's messy, but it's part of the process. They'll come back next year."

Lily sensed someone standing behind them, and she turned.

"You're out early," Seth said.

Lily was unsettled by his sudden appearance but tried not to let it show. They would be working together. To make that possible, she'd have to ignore the heat in her cheeks and the twinge in her heart she felt every time she saw Seth.

"Trouble sleeping." She raised her eyebrows and nodded toward Antoinette who shrieked and flapped her hands when she noticed Seth. "This is the first time she's smiled all morning."

"Well, we go back a ways, don't we?" He sat on Antoinette's other side. She shrieked again and pointed to the daffodils.

Lily and Seth went back even further, but she didn't say so. She kept the conversation safe: "I hate watching them die." She indicated the daffodils. Some people braided the leaves or cut them back before they browned. It was cleaner, but those same people were always surprised when their plants didn't flower the following season. As the leaves browned, they absorbed nutrients the plant needed for the next year.

Seth stretched out his legs and crossed them at the ankle. "After the leaves brown, we'll divide the bulbs. We should more than triple the crop next year." He looked past Lily to Antoinette. "She's happy with you."

He had always known what to say to make her feel better. Lily stroked Antoinette's shoulder. "I hope so."

"I'm going to Teelia's this morning to pick up her stuff for the show. Why don't you two tag along?"

His invitation surprised her, but she tried not to let it show. Antoinette flapped her hands and kicked her feet. She made a happy shriek.

"I guess that's a yes," Lily said, her relief at seeing Antoinette happy outweighing her discomfort at being with Seth. "Let me change and leave a note for Rose."

TEELIA WAS WAITING when they parked in front of her old barn. As they got out of the truck, she ran over, carrying a faded red toolbox. "I'd stay and help, but one of the fences in the back field is down."

Several alpacas stood at the fence by the barn. A brown one nudged Teelia's elbow. "You already ate," she said, pushing it away.

Alpacas hummed. It was a strange upturned sound, as if they were asking a question. *Hmm? Hmm?* Several of them clamored for Teelia's attention.

"Hush up," she said before turning to Seth. "The wheel's just inside the barn, and the yarn's in the blue milk crates. I also need the metal portable pen for Frank."

Seth disappeared into the barn while Lily helped Antoinette from the truck. The little girl tumbled down and headed over to a circle of dead grass by the front paddock. There she sat and pressed her fingers to the ground.

"He smiles more when he's with you," Teelia said, nodding in the direction Seth had gone. She stood at Lily's shoulder, and they both watched Antoinette. "You're good for him. And unless I'm wrong, he's good for you. You're lighter around him."

"I thought you had to go fix a fence," Lily said. She was trying to suppress her feelings for Seth. The last thing she needed was Teelia stirring them up.

"What's a fence compared to true love?" She grinned.

"Teelia, you're hopeless," Lily said, glancing over her shoulder to make sure Seth hadn't overheard. Then she dropped the truck's tailgate and hopped up.

"I know what I see," Teelia said. "He's changed since you came home. He's smiled more in the past week than he has all year."

"I'm here for Rose," she said, pitching her voice low. "And Antoinette. I have to focus on them, not on reviving my love life."

At the sound of her name, Antoinette cocked her head. She looked like she was listening for something.

"Who says you can't do both?"

"*I* do," Lily said. She had never been good at dividing her focus. With her good hand, she opened the long silver toolbox attached to the truck bed and fished out several bungee cords which they'd use to tie down the metal pen.

The alpacas stretched toward Antoinette. One with a particularly long neck leaned down and nibbled her hair. Antoinette hunched her shoulders and giggled.

"Shoo!" Teelia waved her hands, and the alpacas drew back. "Seth needs someone who knows his burdens. I warrant he doesn't talk much to anyone."

"Not my business," Lily said, though she figured Teelia was right. She looped one of the bungee cords through an eye hook in the pickup bed. It was hard doing things one-handed. The cord slipped out of the hook several times before she was able to secure it.

"Maybe it should be," Teelia said. She smiled as she turned and started to walk away. "I'll be out to the farm later to set up. Think about what I said."

Lily watched Teelia until she became a small blue smudge on the horizon. It wasn't as if Lily hadn't thought about resuming her relationship with Seth. Of course she had. But there were other people to think about too, like Rose and Antoinette . . . and Will.

"This thing is awkward." Seth startled her, and Lily dropped her head, hoping her thoughts didn't show on her face.

He heaved the collapsed pen into the truck, then grabbed the bottom of his T-shirt and used it to wipe the sweat from his forehead, revealing his taut brown stomach. Lily quickly looked away.

She threaded the cord through the metal pen, then secured it back to the eye hook so it wouldn't fall out on their drive back to the farm. Using her good hand, she tugged on the cord until she was sure it wouldn't tumble out.

"You and Will seem close," Seth said as he sat down on the tail gate. He lifted one shoulder and let it drop as if he didn't care. But that was the thing about growing up together: even after being apart for so long, Lily knew what each twitch of his eyes or shrug of his shoulders meant. He feigned indifference when he was afraid of getting hurt, something he had done when they were kids.

"We're friends," she said, then hopped down from the truck and walked to the fence. Antoinette flapped her hands as Lily passed, thin strands of hair floating around her head like a halo. Four alpacas nosed at Antoinette over the white-plank fence.

Lily rested her elbows on the top rail and watched the animals. They had giraffelike necks and stocky bodies covered in thick fleece. A brown alpaca stretched its neck across the fence and nuzzled her hand.

"That's an awfully *good* friend to drive all the way down here to help you out." Seth plucked a piece of grass and moved to stand beside her. He twisted the grass tight around his finger.

"He is," she said, all the while thinking, *But he's not you.*

She shoved the thought aside. It didn't matter that she felt like she was falling when she stood next to Seth. Or that a deep ache opened up inside of her when she pictured him lying next to another woman. She was here for Rose and Antoinette. Nothing else.

Seth stretched his arm out toward a little white alpaca. It head-butted his hand, then closed its eyes as he scratched behind its ears. "You wouldn't expect something so strange-looking to be so gentle."

Lily felt him watching her, and her blood roared in her ears.

"Seminary was a mistake," he finally said. "I knew that within weeks of arriving."

"What was the first clue?" Lily asked, eager to keep their conversation *away* from their past relationship.

He sighed and uncurled the piece of grass from his finger. "It wasn't just one thing. It was several little things . . ." He pressed his lips together and looked up at the sky as if searching for the right words. Finally, he shook his head. "I was there for the wrong reasons. I didn't want to study the laws in Leviticus or learn how to lead a congregation or counsel newlyweds. I wanted to know why life is so messed up. Why good people get hurt."

Lily didn't have an answer. She suspected no one did.

In the middle of the herd, a baby alpaca rested its long neck over its mother's back. Mother and baby were both white, making it impossible to tell where one stopped and the other began.

Antoinette rocked back and forth on the ground beside Lily. She made an odd buzzing sound and poked at the dead grass. Then she waved her hands in front of her eyes and screamed, "Aey! Aey! Aey!"

Automatically, Lily said, "End on four, remember? Do things in even numbers." Antoinette gave four loud shrieks and calmed a bit. She pounded the ground again, but this time she looked forlorn, not angry.

"Did you find the answers you were looking for?" she finally asked.

"No," Seth said, "but I've learned to live without knowing. 'He makes his sun rise on the evil and the good, and sends rain on the just and unjust.' I could've just read the Gospel of Matthew and saved myself a lot of heartache." He laughed, a sharp, brittle sound.

"It wouldn't have been enough for you." Lily knew him well enough to know that. There had been a restlessness about Seth when he was younger. A need to understand the *whys* of life that mirrored her need for order and control.

He rested his hand on the fence next to hers. "I used to worry about my dad—that I'd turn out just like him. I think that's what started everything. I wanted to know *why* he was so short-tempered. I needed there to be a reason, because if there wasn't one, it meant he didn't love me—or Mom—enough to stop hitting us. It also meant I wouldn't know how *not* to be like him."

He shrugged. "Now I know it's random. Sometimes bad things just happen. Sometimes people make bad choices, but that fact doesn't negate the great good in the world."

He smiled, and his arm brushed hers. Lily couldn't tell where he stopped and she began. "A wise woman I know once told me that. I should have listened to her all those years ago."

"You're nothing like your father," she said.

He smiled, but it was a small, sad thing. "I wish I had realized that before I let you go. Maybe if I had, you'd be leaning on me instead of Will." He cupped her cheek and tilted her face toward his. "I tried to forget you."

Lily wanted to close her eyes and lose herself in the kiss she felt coming. She wanted to run her fingers across his back until the electricity tingling along her skin exploded, but she remembered losing him the first time. The urge to count had overwhelmed her. She couldn't step outside without first counting one hundred twenty-two heartbeats. She couldn't bear to get stuck like that again, and now she had Antoinette to think about too. She couldn't let Rose down a second time.

"I can't," she said. It hurt as she placed her hand on his chest and pushed. "Not unless I know it's real. Not unless I know you won't leave again." She turned away and walked to the truck without looking back.

ROSE'S JOURNAL
April 2013

—+—

TIME IS SLIPPING away from me. This morning I woke to a note from Lily saying that she and Antoinette were at Teelia's with Seth. Lily and Antoinette have made their peace with each other. It's what I wanted, so I'm surprised that when I think of them together, I feel hollow inside.

"You okay?" Will asks. He pushes a wheelbarrow loaded with steel pails, pruners, and gardening gloves.

I have stopped in the middle of the path leading to the fields. I shake myself and start walking again. "Sorry. My mind was elsewhere for a moment."

His smile is too kind. "You should try music. An iPod? Put the little buds in your ears and the world fades away. At least for a little while."

I appreciate his thought, but that's the problem. I don't want the world to fade away.

Will looks uncomfortable with the wheelbarrow. The land dips, and the wheelbarrow lists left. The steel pails clang together.

"There's an art to it," I say. "You have to distribute the weight evenly in your hands. It'll tip if it's unbalanced."

"Now you tell me," he says as he wipes his hands on his pants. "I thought working the ER was hard. It's nothing compared to farming."

I hear birds call from the woods, and I'm glad of their voices. Without Antoinette, everything is too quiet.

"Can I ask you something," I say, "as a doctor?"

"You can ask," he says. "I might not have an answer."

"Is this my fault? Did I make Antoinette this way?" My words come out in a rush. "If my heart had been stronger. If she hadn't been born so early . . ."

Will sets the wheelbarrow down and takes me by the shoulders. "It wasn't your fault. Millions of babies are premature. Some have trouble. Some don't. You couldn't have done anything to prevent this. You have a beautiful daughter, and a sister who loves you. I'd say you're one of the lucky ones."

"I don't feel lucky."

"You're surrounded by people who love you. There's not much more you can ask from life."

"More time would be nice." I laugh and wipe the corner of my eyes. My cheeks are wet. When did I start crying?

"No matter how much time you have, it won't be enough," he says.

I feel a catch in my chest, and I know he's right. "The tulips are at the edge of this field."

Will follows my lead, sensing that I need to change the subject. "Tell me again what we're doing," he says as we resume walking.

"You know Lily's obsession with the language of flowers?"

"It's kind of hard to miss."

I laugh. He's good at helping me forget.

"Lily used to leave bouquets around the house for me," I explain. "Ivy for friendship. Sweet basil for good wishes. I had to guess what she was saying. I want to do the same for her."

He bumps my shoulder. "She thought about you all the time. She had boxes under her bed filled with pictures of the two of you as girls. One box held baby pictures of Antoinette."

"How do you know what she kept under her bed?"

"I have my ways." He grins.

I laugh. It's been a long time since anyone has made me feel this good. Will has only been here a week, but I feel like I've known him much longer. "I bet you do."

We stop at the edge of the tulip row. The green buds have split open to reveal a flash of white petals. Will rubs his hands together. "Now I know how Lily got so tough. Farmwork isn't easy."

"She's softer than you think," I say as I take a pail from the wheelbarrow. I hook it over the spigot at the end of the row and turn on the water.

"I know. I sat with her when she cried because she missed home. After your parents died, she didn't sleep for a month. And when she finally did, it was only because I slipped Ambien into her hot chocolate."

Regret sits heavy on me. "She did that? Cried that much, I mean?" The pail is full. I try to pick it up, but the weight jerks my hands to the ground.

He takes it from me. "Where do you want it?"

"Just there, at the top of the row."

He sets the pail down among the tulips. "She missed your parents—and you—a lot."

"I shouldn't have been so stubborn," I say as I kneel in the dirt.

"Maybe you should tell her that." Will hands me a pair of pruners.

"That's what I'm trying to do." I run my hand down a tulip stalk and clip it near the base. I put it in the pail and cut another. "I was mad. Not just at her. At everything. Mom and Dad dying. Me being sick. Antoinette."

I sit back on my heels. "Not asking her to come home sooner is my biggest regret."

Will shoves his hands in his pockets and looks out over the fields. "You can't hold on to the past," he says. "Life continues whether you want it to or not."

A car door slams in the distance. I look up to see Lily helping Antoinette from the truck. Seth walks to the back of the truck and drops the tailgate.

"Speaking of regret," I say, "does she know how you feel?" I nod toward Lily.

"What?" He sounds surprised and embarrassed at the same time.

"I'm dying, not blind," I say. "If she doesn't know, you should tell her." I cut another tulip. The bucket is half full. Some flowers stand straight up and some drape over the sides. I'm already breathing hard from just this small amount of effort. I had planned to give Lily the flowers today, but I'm too tired. I'll have to store the tulips in the commercial freezer and fashion the bouquet tomorrow.

"I'm not the one she wants."

"Sometimes we don't know what we want until we're about to lose it," I say. "I used to feel trapped on the farm. Now I can't bear the thought of leaving."

As I did earlier, he changes the subject. "So why white tulips? What do they mean?"

I look down at the bucket. "Forgiveness. Something I should have given Lily a long time ago." I don't mention the other meaning. *Until we meet again.* This is also my way of saying good-bye.

Will takes the pruners from me. "Let me help." He kneels among the tulips, cutting flowers until the pail overflows.

Chapter Twenty-Six

Thursday afternoon, the kitchen in Cora's restaurant smelled like garlic, oregano, sweet basil, and thyme. Cooks clanged metal spoons against copper-bottomed pots and speed-chopped onions and tomatoes. Antoinette used to love the room, but not today.

Today she wanted to go home.

She had tried screaming, but Cora ignored her. Now she stood in the middle of the kitchen and spun like a top. The room blurred into a whirl of color and scent. When she stopped, her knees bobbled and the walls shimmied.

"Slow down," Cora said, without looking up from a pot of marinara sauce. "You're going to hurt yourself."

Antoinette didn't care if she hurt herself. She didn't want to be here. She wanted to go home and lie down next to her mother. She'd curl into a ball and push herself into her mother's side. They'd sit together all day, Antoinette memorizing her mother's heartbeat until it was so much a part of her, she'd never forget it.

She needed to find Lily—she would understand. Antoinette looked around the kitchen, but aside from Cora there was no one else she knew.

Lily had already delivered the fresh lavender Cora needed to make bread and cookies for the garden show on Sunday. That meant Lily was probably in the dining room setting out extra flower arrangements. And wherever Lily was, Will was sure to be close by. He wasn't as good at deciphering her desires, but he usually figured things out. Between the two of them, they would realize that she needed to go home.

Antoinette tugged Cora toward the door that led into the dining room.

"Wait a minute, I need to check this." Cora left her pot and turned to a plump man searching for something in the walk-in freezer. Cora stared at food the way Antoinette stared at flowers. She would be a while.

Antoinette didn't want to wait. When Cora's back was turned, she headed for the dining room. The restaurant wasn't open yet, and the room was empty.

Antoinette started toward the hostess stand. Maybe Lily was out front in the parking lot.

She had her hand on the door when Cora ran into the room. She pulled Antoinette back. "Don't you ever do that again! You scared me, running off like that!"

Antoinette yanked free. She scanned the room but didn't see any sign of Lily or Will. *I want to go home!*

"Let's go back to the kitchen. I should have chocolate cake in there for you."

Antoinette didn't want chocolate cake. When Cora reached for her hand, she growled.

Cora held her hands up. "We don't have to hold hands, but you need to come with me. I promised your aunt I'd look out for you. I can't have you wandering off."

Antoinette stomped her feet. *No, no, no.* She was not going back to the kitchen. She would find Lily; then they would go home, and she would sit with her mother for the rest of the day.

She whipped her head back and forth, then she screamed as loudly as she could.

"What's going on?" Lily ran into the dining room with Will. "We heard her screaming from the back room."

Cora blew out a breath. "I don't know. She wandered out here and wouldn't go back to the kitchen with me."

Even though Lily was here now, Antoinette couldn't stop screaming.

Lily knelt in front of her. "What's wrong?"

Home, Antoinette thought. *I need to go home.* She balled her hands into fists and hit her head. *Home, home, home!*

"Antoinette." Will touched her arm. "You need to stop."

No. She *needed* to go home. She shook her head and stomped her feet. Then she pointed to the door.

"Home?" Lily asked. "You want to go home?"

Antoinette flapped her hands. *Yes, yes, yes!* She knew Lily would understand.

"Will and I haven't finished the arrangements yet," Lily said. "It'll just be a little longer."

Antoinette wanted to leave *now*. Not in a few minutes. She slumped to the floor. She needed to be with her mother.

"Count with me," Lily said. She grasped Antoinette's hand, her skin warm and soft. "One. Two. Three. Four."

Antoinette had heard Lily's song before, so she should be able to hear it now. She closed her eyes and concentrated for several long seconds.

When she didn't hear anything, her last bit of hope drained

away. Without hearing the music, she would never be able to heal her mother. She started to cry.

"Why don't y'all take her home," Cora said. "I'll set up the flowers. I'll keep that chocolate cake for you, Antoinette." Cora blew her a kiss as she hurried back to the kitchen.

Antoinette was ten years old. She knew she was too big to be lying on a restaurant floor, crying, but she couldn't stop.

"I'll carry her," Will said. "You can't do it with your bad hand."

Lily kept holding Antoinette's hand. "We'll go home and see your mom. You'll feel better then."

Antoinette melted into Will when he picked her up. She wrapped her free arm around his neck and rested her head on his shoulder. She hiccuped sobs.

"Hey now," Will said. "It can't be that bad."

But it was. Her mother would never get better. Lily still held one of her hands. Anxiety made the fingers on Antoinette's other hand open and close. Without meaning to, she pinched Will's neck.

He flinched and took her hand, pulling it away.

At his touch, power jolted Antoinette. Two songs—Will's and Lily's—raced through her body. It was as if she had been wearing earplugs until now. She arched her back and tightened her fingers around both of their hands.

She could hear *everything*.

Most of Lily's song was steady and precise, but in one spot the notes were flat and the tempo a count behind.

Antoinette knew she could fix this.

She was sure of it.

She hummed, correcting the flat notes and increasing the

tempo. As she did, a current sparked up one arm and down the other. She was a vacuum, sucking up the wrong notes in Lily's song and sending everything bad into Will.

She didn't mean to, but when they touched her, everything sparked to life, and she couldn't stop.

Lily groaned and tried to twist free, but Antoinette held on tight. In seconds, Lily's song was fixed. Only then did Antoinette let go. Lily's bones were solidly in place, and this time, they wouldn't shift and pop free. Antoinette shrieked with joy.

Will dropped to his knees. "What happened?" He put Antoinette down, staring at her as if he had never seen her before.

At the same time, Lily unwrapped her ace bandage and wiggled her fingers. The bruise was gone. "It doesn't hurt."

The room was turning gray and Antoinette's eyes rolled back. "She's seizing," Will said. He sounded tired.

"Help me get her on her side," Lily said.

Their voices merged until Antoinette could no longer make out the words, but she didn't care.

Lily's hand was fixed. Antoinette didn't know what had been different this time, but it didn't matter. She giggled as the room went black.

If she could do this, if she could mend Lily's broken hand, she could save her mother.

Chapter Twenty-Seven

L ily burst through the kitchen door, waving her hand in the air. "It worked," she shouted, but no one was there. She ran down the hall and shoved Rose's bedroom door open. "Rose, something was different this time."

Rose wasn't there either. Her bed was made, the white quilt tucked in around the edges. Lily deflated as she looked around. She wanted to tell Rose what had happened at Cora's. Something had changed, but she didn't know what. She curled her fingers into a fist. Not even a twinge. The bruises and swelling were gone.

She went back out onto the porch where Will sat on the swing with Antoinette. "She's not inside."

A light rain had started to fall when they got back to the farm, but that didn't stop artists from trickling in to get ready for the garden show. Several people wandered about the garden, setting up white tents and unloading tables and chairs.

Antoinette slept in the crook of Will's arm. "You're a natural," Lily whispered.

He looked exhausted. On the way back from Cora's, he had slumped against the van door with his eyes closed.

"Are you okay?" she asked.

Will smoothed Antoinette's hair from her forehead. She shifted in her sleep but didn't open her eyes. "No worse than before."

He was lying. Lily could see it in the way he avoided her eyes. The porch boards creaked as she knelt by his knees. "Tell me the truth, Will. What's wrong?"

The rain fell in a soft patter against the porch roof. The show was on Sunday, and she hoped it would be dry by then.

Will raised his eyes to hers. Flecks of purple mixed in with the deep blue. "Nothing's wrong," he said.

"I know you well enough to know that you're lying."

"Would I do that to you?" He caught her hand and examined it, pressing his fingers along the bones that had been broken. "Does it hurt?"

She wiggled her fingers. "Not at all. Last time, it started hurting as soon as Antoinette let go."

Antoinette sighed. It sounded like a word. "Mmmmaaa."

A tickle of guilt began somewhere below Lily's stomach, and intensified when she looked at Antoinette. The seizure had been smaller this time. That had to mean something. "Is she okay?"

Will kissed Lily's forehead. "She's fine. I'm fine. Go find Rose."

Lily hesitated. She looked from Antoinette to Will and back again.

"Go," he said, shooing her away. "Before the rain gets worse. We're fine."

She took one last look at them, then ran down the porch and into the rain.

LILY FOUND ROSE and Seth as they left the drying barn. Seth carried a basket of white tulips in one arm and steadied Rose with the other.

"Lily," Rose said. She stopped under the barn eave. Seth stood in front of her, shielding her from the rain, which was falling harder now. "I didn't think you'd be home so soon."

Lily's hair was wet and it stuck to her face. The air smelled like ozone. "You won't believe what Antoinette did." The words tumbled out as she recounted what had happened at Cora's. When she finished, she held up her hand. "The seizure was smaller than before. Less than a minute. Something's different this time. I don't have any pain. And Antoinette's okay. Will's with her now. He promised she's okay."

The rain was now a downpour, and Lily raised her voice to be heard. "My hand is fixed, Rose. Completely. If she can do this for me, there has to be a way she can heal you." In her eagerness, the words tumbled out.

Seth set the basket down. "Can I see?" he asked. She held out her hand. "It doesn't hurt?" He ran his fingers over hers.

Lily shook her head. By now they were both soaked, but neither of them noticed.

"She's right," Seth said. There was a trace of excitement in his voice. He held her hand a moment longer. "There's not a mark here."

"What if we're missing something?" Lily asked. "What if there's a solution?"

Rose's eyes were sad as she shook her head. "It's never been about whether she can heal me. It's about the price she pays. It's too high." Rose took Lily's hand and laced her fingers through hers.

"But the seizure was small." Lily squeezed her sister's hand; it felt cold. "What if you both can live? What if it's not a choice between you or her?" She started to tremble.

Seth placed his hand on the small of Rose's back and pressed. "Maybe she's right," he said. "If there's a chance, and we give up—"

"I'm not giving up," Rose said. "I'm making a choice."

Rain now fell in sheets from the barn eaves. It splashed over their feet, turning the ground to mud. "But I can't lose you," Lily said. "Not again." Rivulets of water ran down her nose, but she didn't wipe them away. She knew Rose was right, but it hurt to admit it.

Gently, Rose released Lily's hand. Despite their best efforts to shield her from the rain, she was soaking wet. "Sometimes the best love means letting go." She pointed at the basket of flowers on the ground. "Seth, give them to her."

He took the bunch of tulips and handed them to Lily.

"Forgiveness," Rose said. "That's what white tulips mean—right?"

Lily couldn't stop shaking. White tulips were also a symbol of heaven and remembrance, but she didn't say that.

"I need you to forgive me," Rose said. She raised her voice to be heard over the rain. "For staying mad so long. For taking things out on you that weren't your fault. I can't leave things unsaid between us."

"I abandoned you. If anyone needs forgiveness, it's me." Lily dropped the flowers and gripped Rose's hands.

"We're sisters. There's nothing to forgive."

The rain kept falling. It mixed with Lily's tears as she said what she should have said the morning of their parents' funeral. Unlike then, the words came easily now: "I promise I'll keep Antoinette safe."

ROSE'S JOURNAL
April 2013

—✦—

I USED TO believe life was easy. You walked in the direction of your dreams, and abracadabra, they appeared in front of you. You only needed to scoop them up and tuck them in your pocket or press them, like a flower, between the pages of an old book.

Now I know the best parts of my life have been the moments I didn't dream. Like Antoinette.

Life is not a straight line. It's a spiderweb that twists and tangles. We crawl along our strands until we touch the people who are meant to be in our lives. The strands can knot, as mine did with Lily's, but they don't break, and the unexpected paths are often the best ones.

The life I planned bears little resemblance to the life I have lived, but I don't mind. Not even a little.

Still, I dream.

In a corner of my heart, the one I don't allow myself to examine too often, I hope for a happy ending. Who doesn't?

Some mornings, when the light is pink and the air is sweet with lavender, I wake believing this is it. This is the morning the room won't spin when I sit up. I'll fill my lungs with air, and hold my breath until I feel like I'll explode. When I let the air out, I won't cough, I won't pass out, my heart won't throw itself against my ribs. I'll run to Antoinette's room, legs steady, heart strong.

Then the best part: she'll be sitting on the edge of her bed, waiting for me. She'll look into my eyes, and I'll find myself reflected there. She'll smile, and it will be more beautiful than any sunset I've ever seen.

"Mommy," she'll say in a bright silver voice.

This is my fairy tale. No prince. No castles or spinning wheels to turn straw into gold. Only my daughter and me, both of us whole, both of us here together.

That's my idea of happily ever after, and it's enough for me.

Chapter Twenty-Eight

Saturday night, Lily stood on a stepladder threading strings of white lights through the wisteria that grew over the gazebo. She stretched her fingers wide, waiting to feel the bones catch. Nothing.

Rose sat on the gazebo stairs, directing a flashlight beam toward the area where Lily worked. Antoinette was inside napping.

"Still good?" Will asked as he handed her another bunch of coiled lights. He had a faraway look in his eyes, as if preoccupied by a complex math equation.

"Perfect," she said as she wound the lights through the garland of hydrangeas and roses she had made earlier and twined around the gazebo posts. Wreaths of apple blossoms and lilies draped over the rails. The crabapple trees in the house garden had burst into bloom that morning. The night was magic.

She imagined what the garden would look like tomorrow. People would mill about, stopping by Cora's booth, or buying skeins of Teelia's yarn. Seth would stand on the stage they had set up in the drying barn, playing his violin, switching smoothly between Vivaldi and bluegrass.

White tents sprouted throughout the garden, and despite the

rain, the setup was successful. The only issue had been with Teelia's set up and even that was minor.

That morning, Lily had closed the kitchen door and set the alarm before setting out to work. Only seconds later Teelia burst through the door, tripping the alarm.

"My tent ripped," she yelled over the blaring noise. "I need to patch it. A garbage bag or something. The wool can't get wet if it rains."

Teelia ran through the kitchen, opening and closing cabinets, until Lily located the garbage bags for her. Lily wanted to remind her that rain wasn't predicted for Sunday, but given Teelia's agitated state she decided she probably wouldn't pay attention anyway.

After that, the alarm had stayed off.

It was evening now, and most of the vendors were gone. Earlier in the day, the farm had been swarming with artists setting up tables for tomorrow's show, but the majority had finished quickly. A few quilters remained, and Eli Cantwell had just arrived, but other than that the farm was empty.

Until now, Lily had never realized how many artists lived in Redbud. Among others, there was a woman selling handmade soaps and lotions, a silversmith who shaped wire into wrist cuffs, and a man with mounted butterflies in glass frames. Then there were the quilters—five women would have tables with quilts for sale at the show.

Lily grew up sleeping under thick covers her mother made, but her mother's work was utilitarian, more for keeping the cold out than for displaying. But as Lily looked at the women unfolding appliquéd and embroidered quilts, she imagined her mother here.

"Mom would have loved the show this year," Rose said as she aimed a flashlight beam at the tables.

"Shine it over here." Lily gestured to the left where Seth had taped an extension cord up the side of the gazebo.

Rose shifted the flashlight beam, and Lily plugged in the lights. Then she sat back, squinted, and examined her work. It looked beautiful and romantic, like the stars had left heaven and taken up residence under the gazebo.

"Uh-oh," Will said. He nodded at the stone path that led out of the house garden.

Eli Cantwell walked toward them. His face was skeletal, and the lights reflected off his pale skin.

"Want me to handle him?" Will asked.

"No, I'll take care of this." Rose's voice was light, but she pressed a hand to her chest.

Will held out his hand to help her stand and walk down the gazebo steps.

"It's a good thing the rain stopped," Rose said when Eli was a few feet away. Her words sounded forced. "Do you have everything you need to set up?"

"MaryBeth is worse," Eli said. He stopped a hand's length from Rose. He was close enough for Lily to see his knuckles whiten as he clenched his hands into fists.

"I'm sorry to hear that," Rose said, grief in her voice. "Is she here?" She looked past Eli's shoulder, as if hoping MaryBeth was behind him.

It was strange seeing Eli without MaryBeth, Lily thought. They were always together.

Eli shook his head. What little hair he had stuck out in wild tufts. "She's shaking so bad she can't hold a cup of water. Spills it all over herself."

"I'm sorry," Rose said. "I know how hard this must be for you."

"No, you don't," Eli said. He poked a finger at her. "If you did, you'd help us."

"That's enough," Will said, but Eli didn't stop.

"You look awfully healthy for someone with a heart condition," he said. "You're still here—what? Ten years later?"

Lily started counting. She had never felt nervous around Eli before, but he was different now. Angry. Scared.

Rose held out her hand. "You don't understand—"

Eli shoved her hand aside. "I know what your girl can do. It's not right to keep her all to yourself."

Lily stopped counting and scrambled down the ladder. No one touched her sister like that.

"I think you should go," Will said. He stepped in front of Rose.

"You *know* us." Eli stared at Rose, his eyes pleading. "Mary-Beth loves your little girl. How can you let her die?" On the word *die* his voice cracked.

"You don't understand," Rose repeated quietly.

"I understand perfectly. You're letting my wife die!"

Lily took Will's place in front of Rose. "Eli, stop," she said. "You know we love MaryBeth. If we could help her, we would."

"I know what I saw." He nodded at Lily's hand. "It was broken. I saw it. Then Antoinette touched you and it was fine."

Rose was shaking. "I'm sorry," she whispered.

Eli took a step toward Rose.

"You need to stop this," Will said, iron in his voice.

Eli didn't listen. He stepped around Will and reached for Rose. "Help us. *Please.*"

"Leave." This time, Will put his hand on Eli's chest and pushed until the older man backed away, then turned, and disappeared into the night.

Lily touched Rose's shoulder. "Are you okay?" she asked.

Rose's eyes glistened. "ALS is complicated. Healing MaryBeth could kill Antoinette. I can't let her do that."

"Of course not," Lily said, although she couldn't help but wish that it were otherwise.

Rose rubbed her eyes. "I need to check on Antoinette. I'll also ask Seth to make sure Eli's gone."

"I'll come with you," Lily said.

Rose shook her head and pressed her lips into a tight smile. Lily thought it was meant to be reassuring, but Rose's eyes were bright with tears. "I need some time alone," she said, and walked away.

Lily watched Rose until she faded from sight. "Do you think she'll be okay?" she asked Will.

"She's keeping her daughter safe. She'll be fine."

Lily wasn't sure. "What about Eli? If he won't leave—"

"Have you seen Seth? The guy's got arms like tree trunks. Eli might be upset, but he's no fool."

"I hope you're right," Lily said. She squinted into the darkness, straining to see whether Eli was still there.

Will sat down on the gazebo steps and patted the spot next to him. "The stars aren't this bright in the city. In thirty-five years I don't think I noticed them. Thirty-five years, and I never looked up. How sad is that?"

"You're looking now," Lily said, grateful for Will's attempt to distract her. He was right. Eli was upset, but he wasn't a real threat.

"Too little, too late, Lils." He flipped his hair out of his eyes. "Did you know that when a star goes supernova and explodes, a new star is born? The force of the explosion shoves clouds of hydrogen and helium molecules together. Gravity makes the clouds collapse and rotate. Once the heat and pressure reach a certain point, a new star is created from the old one.

"It's a transfer of energy from one place to another—ashes to ashes, and dust to dust, just on a much larger stage. One star dies. Another is born. Energy can't be created or destroyed, but it can be transformed."

He grew thoughtful. "What if it's something like that?"

"What?" Lily frowned, not following him.

"Antoinette's ability . . ." He shook his head as if to clear it. "I had the thread of a thought, but I lost it."

Lily sat down and leaned her head against his shoulder. "I'm glad you're here," she said.

"I am too." He stared at her for several long moments, and for the first time since she had known him he looked nervous. "Does he tell you you're beautiful?" he finally asked.

"Who?" Her answer was reflexive, but immediately she understood.

"Seth. Does he know how soft your skin is?" He traced his finger across her cheek.

Despite the tingle of electricity skipping across her skin, she caught his hand. "Don't." She saw expectation in his eyes, and her heart ached knowing she was about to hurt him. "I love Seth. I always have. And I love you too—just not in the same way."

Giving voice to her feelings unlocked something inside of her, and she finally realized how foolish she had been to push Seth away. All because she was afraid of getting hurt. It was the same thing she did the first time Rose had asked for her help with Antoinette.

No more. Fear had already occupied too much of her life.

Will tucked a loose strand of hair behind her ear, then ran his fingers down her neck to the hollow of her throat. His movements were small and tentative.

She froze, unsure whether to lean into him or turn away. "I'm not like the girls you bring back to your house."

He leaned forward until their foreheads were almost touching. "I know. Why do you think I've wanted to do this from the first time I saw you?"

"Will, don't." She put her hands on his chest. "It won't be real. It's not fair to you."

"Let me decide what's fair to me. Just once, Lils. Give me one moment when everything is perfect."

The wind began to blow, picking up a swirl of apple blossom petals and dusting them across his shoulders. Lily lightly brushed them off, leaving her hand on his shoulder. "It won't be true," she repeated. "I'm sorry. I love Seth."

"Ah Lils, haven't you learned? There's more than one version of truth. Let me have my version. Besides, I've been told I'm a pretty good kisser."

She believed him, but that wasn't why she let him press his lips to hers. It was because she remembered his fingers on her cheek, catching her tears after Rose called that first time. She remembered the nights he held her as she cried when her parents died. And she remembered sitting with him through his chemo treatments, when his fear was so heavy she could almost touch it.

She could give him this. She let him hold her close. He slid one hand around her hip and ran the other up her back. He was right. He *was* good at this.

The kiss was long and slow and held all the words they would never say to each other.

THE MOON HUNG in the sky when Lily left Will sitting at the gazebo. It rose above the treetops, speaking of second chances and hope. But it also spoke of regret.

Will had kissed her. It was beautiful and bittersweet, nothing at all like Seth's kisses, which were aggressive and passionate. When she pulled away from Will, she had pressed her hand against his lips and whispered, "I'm sorry."

She loved Will. Through the years of silence from Rose, he had been her only friend. But when she pictured herself sitting on the porch swing at eighty, it was Seth who sat beside her, not Will.

Lily had loved Seth from the beginning, when they were still children. He tied her life together—the good parts and the bad—and that, she realized, was worth risking everything for.

With Will's kiss still on her lips, she started down the flagstone path. A thin beam of light shone beneath the drying barn door. Seth must be in there, raking the cedar shavings and hanging fresh lavender from the rafters for the show tomorrow.

"Seth?" she called as she opened the door. No one answered. She walked deeper into the barn.

Everything was in place: the stage was set up; flowers hung

from the rafters; white cloths covered the tables. But the barn was empty.

Lily sighed. Seth probably forgot to turn out the light. She flipped the switch, plunging the barn into darkness. Once outside again, she decided to go to the creek. She was too restless to go back to the house.

Trees overtook the fields, but moonlight flickered through their canopy, lighting her way. Still, it was dark, and she was cautious, stretching her feet in front of her, searching for the stone path to the creek.

Reaching the water, she rolled her jeans to her knees, then waded in. The creek was stinging cold, and she gasped. The water was lower here than farther down the stream, but with the recent rains even here the creek was deep.

She waded out to the flat rock that jutted from the middle of the creek. When they were kids, Seth, Lily, and Rose would lie on the rock, their heads touching as they watched the sky, calling out shapes they found in the clouds above them.

Tonight the moon draped everything in blue-white light. Lily lay back and put her arm over her eyes. She was almost asleep when a splash to her left startled her. "Who's there?" she asked as she lurched upright.

"Lily?"

Instead of slowing, her heart sped at the sound of Seth's voice. "What are you doing here?" she asked.

"Same as you, I suppose." He crossed the creek and stood at the base of the rock. "Mind if I come up?"

"Suit yourself," she said, scooting over to make room for him.

He pulled himself up in one fluid motion. Moonlight outlined his profile, painting him black and silver.

"I saw the light in the barn," she said. "I stopped in, but you weren't there." She pressed her knees into her chest and wrapped her arms around them. If she touched him now, she knew she would never let go.

"I must have forgotten to turn it out." In the dim light she could trace the planes of his face, the small wrinkles around his mouth, at the corners of his eyes, and across his forehead.

"Rose told me what happened with Eli," he said, placing his elbows on his knees. "I was walking the farm to make sure he's gone when I saw you walk past."

"Is he?"

"He's gone. I checked everywhere."

Lily relaxed. The night was warm, more fit for August than April. She plunged her hand into the cold water, opening and closing her fingers, concentrating on the feel of the water.

Seth ran his hand through his hair, making it wave around his face. "I didn't expect it to be so difficult to see you again."

Lily raised her eyebrows. Whatever she had been expecting him to say, it wasn't that. She curled her hand in the water. The shock of the cold kept her in the present, preventing her mind from slipping back to the summer nights they had spent here. "It hasn't been easy for me either."

"I thought I could forget the past," he said, "but I was wrong. I've missed you. I don't want to interfere with your life. If you and Will are—"

"We're not," she said, the words coming out faster than she meant for them to. She took a breath, deliberately slowing her thoughts. "Do you remember when we used to come here and watch the clouds? You and Rose found shapes, but I couldn't see anything other than the two of you. I wanted to stay like that forever. How did everything end up so differently than I planned?" It was the question she had been asking herself since coming home. She didn't expect him to answer, and was surprised when he did.

"I don't know," he said. "For a long time, I never thought I'd be back here. Now I can't imagine being anywhere else. I believe there are places that get to you. They slip under your skin and won't let you go. Redbud's like that for me."

Lily shook the water from her fingers. Tiny droplets sprayed over her face, cooling her skin where they touched. "What about people?" she asked.

He shifted until their fingers touched. When he looked down at her, she shivered. "Some," he said. "I think it's like that for some people."

"What about for us?" The question was easier to ask in the dark, when the rustle of the trees and the buzz of cicadas covered her words as soon as they were out.

"When I left for seminary," Seth said, "I thought I could forget everything—it wasn't easy for me here. Dad made sure of that.

"But there, no one knew my family. People didn't stare when I walked across campus. No one whispered behind my back. No one pitied me. I felt like I could leave my past in Redbud and just be me, not the boy whose drunk father beat him. For the first time in my life, I was just Seth Hastings.

"It wasn't until I came back for Mom's funeral that I realized leaving didn't free me. Instead, it gave the past that much more power over me. I could never be myself because I was always hiding part of my life.

"I've tried," he said, "but I can't stay away from you. You're the only person I can be myself with. I don't have to hide from you." He moved closer.

"I bought into Eden Farms because I wanted to come home, but I stayed because I saw you everywhere. In the fields, I saw us running through the sunflowers down to the creek. In the barn, while hanging flowers to dry from the rafters, I would see you standing in a halo of sunlight. Sometimes it was so real I thought I could touch you. I'd sit on this rock at night and feel you beneath me."

Seth pressed his forehead against hers. "The best parts of my life have been with you. You see all of me and you love me anyway. Or at least you did."

She watched his lips as he spoke, wondering whether they would feel the same after all these years. She brushed his hair back. The thick strands slid through her fingers. Then she ran her hands over the broad planes of his back and down his arms.

"I still do," she said. "I never stopped."

It felt as if they had been slowly bending toward each other since that first day at the farmers' market. Instead of beating faster, her heart slowed as if trying to stretch this moment into an eternity.

His breath was hot when he lowered his mouth to hers. His lips were as soft as she remembered. He wrapped his arms around her, laid her back on the rock, and covered her body with his.

Chapter Twenty-Nine

ntoinette was talking in her sleep. She woke from a
dream where she rode the wind to the edge of the creek
and knelt in the mud. As in real life, ferns grew along
the bank, but in her dream the fronds were made of words instead of leaves. She searched until she found a word that calmed
her body and made her feel whole. She plucked it and placed
it on her tongue. The word tasted like blueberries, sweet and
tart at the same time. "Mommy," she said as it slid down her
throat.

Dream-talking wasn't unusual. Everything happened in
dreams, even the impossible, but this time was different. This
time, her lips hummed when she woke as if the actual word had
just left her mouth. A breeze blew through the open window,
billowing the sheers and sending goose bumps along her arms.

She tried again. "Mmmm," she said. She closed her eyes, trying to remember the ease with which she spoke while dreaming,
but it was too late. The word was gone.

It was the evening before the garden show, but the farm was
quiet now. Earlier that day, Antoinette had been so tired she fell

asleep with her head against her mother's knee. Vaguely, she remembered Lily carrying her to her room.

Outside her window, crickets chirped and an owl hooted. Everything had a voice except her. Even the wind whistled as it swept through the window. She balled her hand into a fist and hit the wall. If she could speak, she could make her mother listen.

"Let me help you," she would say, and for once her mother would be the silent one. Antoinette would hold her mother's hand and sing until everything was fixed. Until her heart was so strong it would never stop beating.

Antoinette's arms were stiff, but she shoved her covers back and concentrated on untangling her legs from the quilt. Some dreams came true. She had fixed Lily's hand after thinking she would never heal again. Why couldn't this dream come true too?

The wood floor was cool under her feet. Her knees wobbled as she stood, but she was calm, still under the thrall of her dream. She didn't twitch or flap as she walked downstairs into the kitchen, and she wondered, *Is this how other people feel?*

In her dream, the words grew on ferns by the creek bank, so that's where she'd go. She would sit there, eating leaves, singing under the moon until her throat was raw. Then she'd run home, wake her mother, and fix everything. Words had power.

Dark shadows sat in the kitchen corners, but Antoinette didn't care. It was easier to see without all the colors getting in the way. As she crossed the kitchen to the back door, her skin prickled in anticipation. What would it feel like to open her mouth and say anything she wanted? She flapped her hands and reached for the doorknob. Everything would change tonight.

She stopped when her fingertips brushed the flaked paint on the door. She had forgotten the red light. If she opened the door, it would squeal. Her mother would wake, and everything would be ruined.

Before looking up, she squeezed her eyes shut. *Please*, she prayed. *Let the light be off.* She flapped her hands twice for good measure, then opened her eyes one at a time. She let her head fall back and looked up.

The light was off.

She blinked hard and looked again. Nothing. The space above the door was beautifully blank. Her heart quickened, and she shrieked twice before she could stop herself. Her voice filled the empty room and echoed through the house, louder than the alarm ever was.

She didn't wait to find out if anyone heard her. She shoved her arm straight out and pushed the door open. It smacked into the wall with a loud crack. She stumbled through, her bones loose under her skin, her knees wobbling.

Antoinette was at the top of the porch steps when she heard a voice from inside the house. "Antoinette? Is that you?"

Her mother.

In a rush, Antoinette tumbled down the porch steps, cutting her leg in the fall. Blood dripped down her shin, but she didn't stop.

The sky was dark and the land silent. No music rolled through her mind, but that didn't matter. Everything would be better soon. Heat shimmered up from the ground. She easily made it to the stone path that led to the woods.

She was at the edge of the field when the kitchen door slammed, and her mother yelled, "Antoinette? Are you out there?"

Hurry, hurry, hurry. Antoinette walked as fast as she could. *This must be how birds feel,* she thought. She spread her arms wide to catch the wind.

"I can see you Antoinette!" her mother yelled. "Come back here!"

The woods marking the end of the fields had filled out. The trees' branches twined together to form a thick screen.

Antoinette shoved through. She lost her footing but locked her knees and didn't fall, even when twigs pierced the soles of her feet.

It was cooler and darker under the branches. Instead of following the well-worn path to the creek, she turned off onto a narrow deer trail. It would be easier to hide that way. She wasn't going home until she found the ferns from her dream.

A branch from a birch tree flicked back against her cheek. She felt blood welling along the cut, and she put her hand to her face, willing the edges of her skin back together, but she had never been able to heal herself, and this time was no different.

"Antoinette!" Her mother's voice floated behind her, to her right, so she went left, moving deeper into the woods, toward the sound of creek water.

In the distance her mother called again, closer this time. Antoinette imagined her mother's distress, and she almost turned back, but then she remembered the way her body had felt after speaking. She had to know whether it was possible.

By the time she emerged from the tree cover and onto the creek bank, her face was covered with tiny scratches. Blood trickled from her cheek to the corner of her mouth. It was warm and salty when she touched her tongue to it.

The creek was swollen with rain. Water rose halfway up the

muddy hill. Exposed tree roots hung over the thin lip of dirt separating the woods from the water. She was farther downstream than usual, far from the flat rock that jutted from the center of the creek. She wasn't familiar with this part of the woods, but that didn't matter. Ferns grew all along the water's edge; she could find them anywhere.

Though the moon was out, its light was blocked by the trees, and she could barely see. She found moss and twisted tree roots, but no ferns. She shifted to her left, brushing her fingers along the ground, searching. She was concentrating so hard, she missed the footfalls behind her.

"I thought I heard someone," a man said, startling her. "God must be smiling on me. I went for a walk in the woods to sort some things out and here you are."

Antoinette turned. Eli stood behind her. For a moment, she was happy to see him, but almost immediately she sensed that something was wrong. He stood too close to her, and he whispered as if he didn't want anyone to overhear him.

"I need you to do me a favor," he said. "Then I'll bring you back to your mama. A little girl like you shouldn't be out in the woods by herself."

Normally, Antoinette would be happy to help Eli, but he was different tonight. She tried to scoot backward to put some distance between them but she was at the edge of the creek bank.

"Antoinette!" her mother yelled, her voice closer. She must have followed the flagstone path to the creek, coming out downstream, across from the flat rock.

"Antoinette!" It was Will's voice this time. "Your mom needs you to come home." Her mother must have asked for his help.

Antoinette opened her mouth, but no sound came out. Her dream seemed foolish now. She should have known nothing could fix her.

There was nowhere to go except down the hill. It took all of her concentration to put one foot in front of the other without sliding down to the creek.

"Come on now," Eli said. "I'm not going to hurt you. I want to take you back to your mama. But first MaryBeth needs your help. You love MaryBeth, don't you? You want to help her."

His words made her stop inching toward the creek. She *did* love MaryBeth.

"Be a good girl," Eli said, holding his hand out to her. "That's right. Take my hand. The Lord works in mysterious ways. He must have known I needed your help and sent me out here to find you." Eli turned toward the woods, and this time, Antoinette allowed him to pull her along with him.

"We'll go see MaryBeth, and you'll fix her," Eli said. "Then I'll bring you back to your mom. You'll be home before she misses you."

"Antoinette!" her mother called again. "Where are you? Please make a noise, a sound. *Anything.*"

The panic in her mother's voice made Antoinette stop. She loved MaryBeth, but she loved her mother more.

"Come on," Eli said, tightening his hold on her hand. Though they were skin to skin, Antoinette couldn't hear his song. "We've got to keep going. Hurry."

But Antoinette didn't want to go with Eli anymore. She wanted her mother. *Mommy!* she thought over and over again, and she managed a small shriek.

"Hush," he said, and he gripped her tighter, his fingers pressing into her flesh until she felt the bone bruise. "I'm just taking you to MaryBeth. You like MaryBeth, don't you?"

She did, but Eli was scaring her. She wanted her mother. She shook her head hard. *No!* she thought. *I want my mommy!*

Eli pulled her into the woods, pushing aside tree branches. He was too strong. She struggled, but she couldn't break free. "I know what you can do. Your mama won't admit it, but I saw it. You healed MaryBeth, but she's sick again. I need you to fix her for good this time."

Eli was moving so fast she couldn't keep up with him. Her feet tangled, and she stumbled. She went down hard, scraping her knees on exposed tree roots. She cried out in pain.

"Antoinette?" her mother yelled. "Is that you? Are you okay?"

"I think she's over here," Will said, sounding much closer now.

"We're coming," her mother yelled. "Just stay there!"

Eli pulled her up. "Please," he said, his eyes wet with tears. "I can't lose MaryBeth. She's all I have. Help us."

There was a rustling in the trees on the creek bank. Antoinette strained toward the sound, her mother's face filling her mind.

"Come on." Eli tugged, but she couldn't get to her feet.

Then someone crashed through the trees and grabbed her free hand. At the touch, electricity shot through her, and two songs roared to life in her ears. The first was sad and dissonant, the notes in a minor key. The second was familiar.

Will's.

"Let go of her!" Will said, pulling her hand.

But Eli held on to her hand. "I need her help. Just for a little bit. Please. Let her come with me. I'll bring her right back."

Black spots dotted Antoinette's vision, and her hands were scalding where Will and Eli touched her. She couldn't think with both songs in her head. The discordant music competed for her attention, commanding that she do something.

She concentrated on the spot where Eli's hand gripped her. As when she had touched Lily's hand at Cora's, his song became louder.

Then she turned her focus to Will's hand, and his song flared to life. In one spot, the notes were off. Surprised, Antoinette realized that Will was sick. Very sick. In fact, he was almost as sick as her mother. Almost as a reflex, she grabbed Will's wrong notes—not all of them, there were too many—and pushed them into Eli.

At the same time, Seth crashed through the woods, Lily following right behind. "Get off her, Eli," Seth said. He grabbed Antoinette, pulling her free from both Eli and Will. Her connection to both men broke and the songs faded.

Then her mother was there. She touched Antoinette's face, her arms, her hands. "Are you okay? Did he hurt you?"

Antoinette tried to answer, but the world blinked black and white. Her mother's face disappeared and reappeared in quick flashes.

"Why couldn't you leave her alone?" her mother cried.

Antoinette's vision was fading and she was starting to shake, but she could still make out her mother's voice.

"She's not strong enough to do this. If she keeps seizing like this, she'll die. You could have killed her!"

"I didn't know . . . I would never." Eli sounded shocked. "I just thought . . . MaryBeth is dying—"

"And now Antoinette might be," her mother said. "Put her down, Seth. Roll her onto her side."

Antoinette felt the earth beneath her and hands on her side, rolling her over. She was shaking, but she was still conscious.

"Eli," Lily said softly. "You know we love MaryBeth. If we could help her, we would. But Antoinette can't keep doing this. The seizures are getting worse. Soon one of them might kill her."

"I didn't know," Eli said, his voice tight. "I swear, I didn't know. I would never hurt Antoinette."

Will knelt beside her, examining her. All of a sudden, he frowned; then his eyes widened in surprise as if something had just clicked into place.

"You're a conduit," he said, only loud enough for her to hear. "The sickness doesn't disappear, you just move it from one person to another. Matter can't be destroyed, only transformed. That's what you're doing. Transforming the illness by moving it."

Antoinette's last sight, before the world went black, was of Lily, appearing over Will's shoulder. He turned to face her. "I figured it out," he said.

Chapter Thirty

O n Sunday evening, white lights winked among the hydrangea vines growing up the sides of the gazebo. To
Lily, the garden felt alive. Anticipation buzzed through
the crowd gathered for the show. Every once in a while a person looked up, as if expecting the plants to grow legs and walk
among them.

Who knew? Lily thought. Given what had been happening
there lately, maybe they would.

Strangers and locals milled about the garden, stopping every
few feet to stare at one of Rose's paintings or run their fingers
through Teelia's hand-dyed alpaca yarn. Lily's favorite booth was
the glass blower's.

Earlier that evening, she stood in the shadows with her head
on Seth's chest, watching as a man twirled liquid fire at the end
of a long metal stick. Somehow the orange blaze at the end of
the pole transformed into a glass bowl with bright green streaks
running up the sides.

Seth bought it for her. "So you'll remember this night."

As if she could forget.

He was in the drying barn now, playing for a full crowd.

Tonight he eschewed the classics and chose old-time fiddling, some traditional tunes, but mostly bluegrass. She looked toward the barn and felt her face glow.

"He'll be beside you soon enough," Will said. He sat on the bench that ran the length of the gazebo.

Antoinette stretched up on her tippy-toes. She didn't wear shoes, and her skin was so pale her feet gleamed in the reflected light. Lily looked from Antoinette to Will.

Deliberately changing the subject, she gestured toward the people crowding the garden. "I didn't realize it would be as nice as this," she said. "No wonder Rose insisted on having the show." Right now, Rose was back at the house, resting and recovering from the effort involved with hosting the party.

Will watched Antoinette tiptoe around the gazebo. "Your sister's smart. I'd make a lot of the same decisions she has."

High praise from Will.

Lily cut a piece of lavender bread from the loaf on the stairs next to her and popped it in her mouth. It was sweet and a little lemony. Rose was right; it tasted like love.

She held out a piece to Will, but he shook his head.

Lavender was an herb like basil or oregano, but most people didn't think to cook with it. She turned to Antoinette. "Want some?"

Antoinette flapped her hands and took the bread. That morning, as she walked through the farm, marigolds had bloomed in her footsteps.

Marigolds meant grief.

Except for a light bruise circling Antoinette's wrist, she seemed untouched by her encounter the night before with Eli, but Lily wasn't. Eli's horror upon realizing the price Antoinette paid for healing was matched by his grief when he realized that nothing could help MaryBeth.

Antoinette closed her eyes while she chewed the lavender bread, as if shutting off her other senses helped her enjoy it more.

"It's good, isn't it?" Lily said. Antoinette flapped her hands.

Lily thought back to her conversation with Will last night, when he tried to explain how Antoinette's ability worked. "No wonder the seizures were getting worse," she said. "One little girl can't hold all of that sickness."

Will nodded, picking up on her thought. "It was overloading her system." He paused for a moment, thoughtful. "When she's the only one touching a sick person, she absorbs the illness. But when she's touching *two* people, she pulls the sickness out of one person and deposits it in the other. It's still a strain on her, though. That's why she seizes."

"I should have known you'd figure it out," Lily said, smiling up at him.

He didn't return her smile, though. Instead, he reached for her hand. "I'm better for you than he is. I mean really, choosing a farm boy over a doctor? How does that happen?" He twisted his mouth into a tight grin.

"I don't want to hurt you." She put both her hands around his.

"Can't help the way you feel, Lils, and neither can I. But maybe you could kiss me and make it better?" A string of lights over him winked out, covering them both in sudden shadows.

She kissed him on the cheek. Then she rested her forehead against his. "I'm sorry."

Will brushed his fingers down her face, then dropped his hand to his side. "You're not coming home, are you?"

She shook her head and swallowed. She hadn't wanted to tell him until later. "This is home. It always has been; I just didn't realize it until now. I've already called work and told them I'm not coming back."

"What will I tell our neighbor, Soup Can Artist? He'll be distraught."

She looked into his eyes, and for a moment she was lost. "Tell him I'll miss him every single day." She laid her head on his chest. His heartbeat was strong and reassuring.

The sky seemed darker than it had a few minutes ago, and she wondered whether a storm was coming. The air felt electric.

Antoinette came up behind her. She tapped Lily's shoulder and then pointed to the house. "Mmmm," she said. "Mmmm." She jabbed the air again and again.

"You want to go home?" Lily asked. "You miss your mom?"

Antoinette stumbled down from the gazebo steps. She pointed to the house again.

"Okay," Lily said. "Let's go see your mom." Will followed them.

The night air grew thick. The crowd sounded louder. Antoinette threaded her fingers through Lily's hand. In a moment the house came into view.

Rose sat on the porch swing, but something was off. She was too still. "Oh God," Lily said, "something's wrong."

Will was already halfway up the steps. Lily swung Antoinette up into her arms and ran after him. *Please*, she prayed. *Please. Please. Please.*

They were too late. Rose was unconscious. Her cheeks were pale and her lips blue. Lily set Antoinette down and knelt beside her sister. "Rose? Rose?" Lily shook her hand. This wasn't real. It couldn't be.

Will pressed his fingers against Rose's neck, searching for a pulse. "It's there, but barely."

Antoinette stretched past Lily and took her mother's hand. "No, Antoinette." Lily tried to pull her away, but Antoinette wouldn't let go. When they touched, Lily felt a strange buzzing beneath her skin. "I can't let you do that. I promised to keep you safe."

Antoinette growled and bit Lily on the wrist.

Lily tightened her grip, and the buzzing grew louder. "No, Antoinette. I promised her. I won't let you do this."

"Let her try." Will pulled Lily away from Antoinette.

Lily struggled. "No! I can't let her do this. I promised Rose I'd keep her safe." She didn't realize she was crying until she looked up and couldn't see Will through her tears.

"And you will," he said. He kissed the top of her head. "Don't forget I love you, Lils." He took Antoinette's free hand. Instead of pulling her away from Rose, he leaned down and said, "Send it to me."

"No!" Lily yelled as she realized what he was doing. She dug her fingers into his shoulders, but he shook her loose.

"Death always wins in the end, Lils," he said. "Somebody's got to lose." He locked eyes with Antoinette. "Send it to me. All of it."

Chapter Thirty-One

Wind skittered over Antoinette's skin, but she didn't twitch or flap. She kept her arms at her sides, even when the breeze lifted the hem of her white dress, and it fluttered around her knees. Around her, the land sang of new beginnings and old friends.

She closed her eyes so that she could hear every note. Today it sounded like the violins in Pachelbel's Canon in D. She swayed and raised her hands to the sun, letting the song flow through her and back to the land.

When she opened her eyes, the green hills were brighter, and the wild roses growing along the white-plank fence encircling the cemetery were sunset pink. Normally, the roses wouldn't flower for another month, but last year, after the funeral, Antoinette had pushed her hands into the dirt and they sprang to life. They hadn't stopped blooming since. Even bowed under a blanket of December snow, the pink petals shone like the spots on a butterfly's wing.

"Come on, Antoinette. Your mom's waiting." Lily caught

her hand and led her up the hill. It wasn't steep, but Antoinette slipped on a patch of dew-soaked clover.

"I've got you," Lily said, catching Antoinette by the elbow and steadying her. "I won't let you fall. Lean into me as you walk."

Antoinette was safe with Lily. She nodded, bobbing her head once up and once down. She still wasn't used to the new ease with which she moved. It wasn't perfect, and if she sat too long, her legs popped and her arms flew up over her head, but when she wanted to stand she thought, *Stand*, and she stood. Easy as that.

She bounced once, not because she had to but because bouncing made her happy.

"Maybe I should have brought roses," Lily said. "They have a longer bloom time."

Seth looked at the snowdrops Lily carried, and then across the cemetery to the Martin family plot. Behind the new gravestone black-eyed Susans, red double pinks, and lavender bloomed, all of them out of season. "I think they'll be fine," he said. "Will you?"

Lily blinked as if struggling not to cry.

Antoinette still couldn't look at faces for long periods of time, but she could hold eye contact for three whole seconds before needing to avert her eyes.

"It's been a year. I didn't expect it to still hurt this much," Lily said. Cherry blossoms floating on the wind caught on her hair.

Seth brushed the flowers from her hair. "I know." He wrapped his arms around Lily's waist and kissed her as sunlight

322 | STEPHANIE KNIPPER

glittered over the grass. They kissed a lot. It filled the air with warmth and made Antoinette feel as if love was something she could touch.

She wished she could tell Lily that death no longer felt hollow. Since that day a year ago, when she had held her mother's hand, death had not felt empty. Instead, it felt like waiting for something special, and its taste was unexpected, almost like chocolate, rich and slightly bitter.

A white cherry blossom landed on her shoulder, and Antoinette reached for it. Her arm moved slowly and surely, like someone else's arm.

It was strange thinking *move*, and then having her body respond. She overcompensated, starting too soon, still thinking she needed extra time to reach for a glass of milk or walk down the driveway. That morning she had followed Lily down to the creek. They went everywhere together now. The trip only took five minutes. Antoinette didn't stumble, and Lily didn't stop to count.

They were both almost normal.

Antoinette, though, kept waiting to change back into the girl who couldn't walk a straight line, the girl who bumped into walls or stumbled down the porch steps. Everyone was broken—she knew that. She didn't believe her change was forever; someday she would go back to that girl. But for now, she was free.

In the twelve months since Lily had taken over Eden Farms, everything had been quiet. The land sang with joy, and Antoinette didn't seize when she fixed things. Healings still took energy from her, and she grew sleepy, but for now at least, she didn't seize.

Lily walked forward, holding Antoinette's hand. The wind picked up, and petals danced around Antoinette's feet.

"You look like a snow princess," Lily said.

A snow princess—Antoinette liked the sound of that. She flapped her hands because she was happy, not because she had to.

"Come on. Let's go see your mom." Lily led Antoinette over a small hill, toward the back corner of the cemetery where Antoinette's grandparents were buried. Antoinette didn't remember them, but she could feel them here.

MaryBeth was also buried in this cemetery. After her death eight months ago, Eli sold the bakery and moved away. Antoinette hadn't seen him since.

A new marker stood next to her grandparents' graves. It was gray granite, the name carved in black: WILLIAM GRAYSON. There was one word under the dates that bracketed his life: FRIEND.

Grass didn't grow over his grave. Instead, there were forget-me-nots and blue violas. Lily looked at the flowers covering Will's grave. "Don't worry," she said as she ran her hand over the marker, "we won't forget."

Antoinette's mother knelt in front of the stone. Seeing them approach, she stood up and brushed the dirt from her knees. "You're a little late," she said.

Antoinette grabbed her mother's hand. Her skin was soft and warm. Sometimes her mother pressed her cheek against Antoinette's just because she could. Those were the times Antoinette put her palms flat against her mother's face and hummed. Not because she needed to fix anything but just for the joy of it.

"Do you need help?" Lily asked.

Her mother shook her head and bent to pick up the shovel she had dropped when she stood to greet them. "The lilies were easy." On either side of Will's marker, she had planted six lilies-of-the-valley. "It's the only way I know to say thank you."

The sisters hugged. Lily's dark hair mixed with Rose's blonde hair, and despite their coloring they looked more alike than different.

Seth took the snowdrops from Lily. "Do you also want these on either side of the marker?"

"No," Lily said. She placed the plants in the middle of the marker so that the white flowers stood below FRIEND.

Rose handed him the shovel, and he dug a hole. Lily gently settled the plants into the ground. Antoinette knelt in the dirt and pushed her hands into the soil until she heard the plants sing. The song was perfect, each note in the right place. She hummed along, and when she stopped the buds opened. They would bloom all year.

Her eyelids fluttered. She grew tired suddenly and closed her eyes for a minute. When the fatigue passed, she rocked back on her heels. *Thank you*, she thought.

She couldn't push the words past her lips, but it didn't matter. She looked at the snowdrops, bright white, blooming out of season. There were many ways to communicate; words were only one of them.

"Beautiful, Antoinette," her mother said, lifting her easily. Her mother's cheeks blushed pink, and her skin was firm and smooth.

Antoinette rested her ear against her mother's chest. Her mother's heart beat a steady thump-thump, and to her the sound was more beautiful than any music she knew. The doctors said the heart disease would come back but not for a long time. And when it did, Antoinette wouldn't have to deal with it alone. Lily would be there.

Thank you, she thought again.

Lily touched Will's marker and whispered, "You were wrong, Will. Death doesn't always win. Sometimes love does." Then she stood and wiped the dirt from her hands.

"Let's go home," Seth said. He took Lily's hand and walked toward the truck.

Antoinette closed her eyes and settled her head against her mother's shoulder, humming as they started down the hill toward home.

ACKNOWLEDGMENTS

———✦———

THIS BOOK WOULD not have been possible without help from several people.

First of all, my agent, Dan Lazar. When I started researching agents, you were at the top of the list—my dream agent if you will. I couldn't believe my luck when you offered to represent me. After working with you, I realize I'm even luckier. Your guidance and advice has made this a better book and me a better writer.

My editor, Chuck Adams. Your kindness and generous insight helped bring Antoinette to life. It's wonderful working with someone who "gets" what you're trying to do and who pushes you to be even better.

My copy editor, Jude Grant. You work fast and have a great eye. Thanks for catching my embarrassing mistakes!

The entire Algonquin team—you all are the best. Most publishing people are passionate about the books they sell, but I think you all got an extra dose of book love!

To my critique partners, Amber Whitley, Ann Keller, and Doug Clifton, thank you for your patience and comments on early drafts. I'm lucky to count you as friends. (Doug, you can finally find out how the book ends!)

To everyone at Northern Kentucky University Master of Arts

in English program, but especially Andy Miller, Stephen Leigh, Donelle Dreese, and Kelly Moffett. You are the heart of NKU's creative writing program. Your love and dedication to the craft of writing and to NKU's students shows in everything you do.

To the family and friends who put up with me during this long, crazy process: yes, the book really does exist!

To my husband, Steve, and my children Sarah, Zach, Grace, Caleb, Jonathan, and Gabrielle, thank you for understanding my crazy need to put words on paper and for the never-ending supply of coffee, dark chocolate, and hugs. You all are the best part of my life. None of this means anything without you.

Finally, to Marjorie Braman, thank you for taking a chance on me. I wish you were here to share this with us.

The Peculiar Miracles of Antoinette Martin

The Magic of Ordinary Lives
A Note from the Author

Questions for Discussion

The Magic of Ordinary Lives
A NOTE FROM THE AUTHOR

I was at a social function, mopping drool from my eleven-year-old daughter's mouth, when a woman interrupted me. "She's lucky to have you," she said.

I had heard this before, and as always the words made me uncomfortable. My daughter Grace is disabled. She has autism, developmental delays, and seizures. Grace can't speak, but she understands everything. While I know the woman meant well, I always imagine how Grace might interpret comments like this. To her, the words probably translated as: *Most people wouldn't want you.*

I hugged Grace and gave my standard reply: "I'm the lucky one. I get to be her mom." It wasn't just a line. I have six children and feel like I've won the parenting lottery with them. Even—no, strike that—*especially* with Grace.

I didn't feel that way initially. My husband and I adopted Grace from China following a particularly difficult time in our lives. After years of infertility, I had finally become pregnant only to go into preterm labor and deliver our son ten weeks early. Luckily, he was little but healthy. I wasn't so fortunate. I spent six weeks in the hospital and was diagnosed with Crohn's disease, an autoimmune disease that causes your body to attack itself. Crohn's is manageable, but as I learned during my pregnancy, it can become life-threatening.

I slowly recovered, but living with Crohn's taught me how fragile our bodies are. However, I wasn't going to let the disease control my life. When my husband and I wanted to enlarge our family, we focused on special needs adoption from China. After all, we were pros at navigating the medical world. Grace's special need was listed as a small heart condition that had already been surgically corrected. This was a need we thought we could handle, and we traveled to China excited to meet our little girl. But upon meeting Grace in Nanjing, we realized that something was very wrong. She was twenty-two months old and couldn't hold her head up. She couldn't walk or talk, and scars covered the backs of her legs.

This was not the child we had imagined. We had two options, leave her in China where she would be labeled "unadoptable" and left to die, or let go of our dreams for the child we *thought* we were adopting and bring Grace home.

Our first year was difficult. We spent hours in physical, occupational, and speech therapy. Grace was cast for AFOs (ankle braces), and I learned how to administer Diastat to stop prolonged seizures. I was more nurse than mother, and most days ended with me in tears.

To survive I had to throw out my expectations for Grace and see the world through her eyes. She was extremely tactile, so I filled our garden with lamb's ears. She loved Broadway tunes and old Gospel songs, so I learned the lyrics to "Goodnight My

Someone" and "Amazing Grace." She giggled when I brushed her cheek with lamb's ears and sat in my lap for hours, her ear pressed against my chest, feeling the vibrations as I sang.

Slowly, I stopped trying to pull her into my world and joined her in hers. I began to realize that the only thing *different* about Grace was the way she looked on the outside. She wanted the same things I did. To be loved. To belong. To laugh.

The title character in *The Peculiar Miracles of Antoinette Martin* is modeled after Grace. While writing, I thought about the ways we separate ourselves. Race, gender, physical ability, and all the other categories by which we define ourselves mask the fact that we are more alike than different. We are all broken people living in the shadow of death. When life is viewed that way, the things that divide us cease to matter and everyday tasks become exceedingly brave. That thought can either be terrifying or liberating. I choose to see it as liberating. Before being diagnosed with Crohn's and parenting Grace, I limited myself. I wouldn't have thought I was capable of parenting a disabled child or surviving multiple surgeries and hospitalizations with no real end in sight. My view of the world was too small. The truth is, when thrust into difficult situations, most of us not only handle them but thrive.

Through Grace, my book became a story about the ways in which love enlarges our lives, enabling us to do things we never dreamed possible. It became the story of a woman learning to love a girl who isn't her daughter and a mother who realizes that sometimes love means letting go. It became the story of a child with the ability to heal broken bodies—which is the *least* miraculous thing about her.

At its heart, *The Peculiar Miracles of Antoinette Martin* is about the ways in which we are more alike than different. It's about ordinary people stepping beyond their self-imposed limitations and changing the world around them. It is about the magic of ordinary lives and the impact that one person can have, even if that person is a little "different."

Questions for Discussion

1. In the beginning of the novel, Antoinette and Lily have a strained relationship. Antoinette feels that Lily is trying to take her mother's place, and Lily fears that she won't be able to care for Antoinette properly. In what ways are these two characters similar? In what ways are they different? How do they begin to bridge the gap between them?

2. On page 210, Rose says to Antoinette, "Everyone's life is hard in some way. Yours just happens to be easier to see than most." Do you think society views physical illness differently from emotional and/or mental struggles?

3. After leaving seminary and reconnecting with Lily, Seth concludes, "Sometimes people make bad choices, but that fact doesn't negate the great good in the world." Do you agree with Seth? Why or why not?

4. In one way or another, all the characters forego their own wants and needs in order to help someone else. Discuss the sacrifices

336 | QUESTIONS FOR DISCUSSION

that each character makes. Are the sacrifices reasonable? Do you
believe that love requires sacrifice? Why or why not?

5. As a child, Lily was fascinated with the Victorian language
of flowers. She and Rose made a game of leaving bouquets for
the other to guess the meaning. What do you think drew Lily to
the language of flowers? How does she rely on that language to
communicate? Is it a helpful tool or a crutch?

6. Much of the novel centers on the different ways we communicate. Antoinette is physically unable to speak, but she is very
capable of making her wishes known. Discuss the different ways
that Antoinette communicates. How does her lack of speech impact the way people view her? Is their view accurate? Why or
why not?

7. When Lily discovers that Antoinette can heal people, she is
overwhelmed. When Lily confronts Seth about this, he responds,
"She's a little girl who's losing her mother. The rest of it doesn't
matter." Is Seth right? Is Antoinette *just* a little girl who's losing
her mother? Do either her ability or disability change who she
is as a person?

8. In Rose's last journal entry, she writes, "This is my fairy tale.
No prince. No castles or spinning wheels to turn straw into gold.
Only my daughter and me, both of us whole, both of us here
together. That's my idea of happily ever after, and it's enough for
me." Rose's comment suggests that our true desires are simple:
a healthy life spent with our loved ones. Do you agree? Why or

why not? If you agree, why do you think it is so difficult to live with this in mind?

9. Will, a doctor, has spent his life fighting death. Near the end of the novel he says, "Death always wins in the end, Lils." Later, Lily counters with, "Death doesn't always win. Sometimes love does." With whom do you agree, and why?

10. Rose's point of view is presented in journal entries, which are written in first person, present tense. This contrasts with Lily and Antoinette's chapters, which are written in third person, past tense. Why do you think the author chose to present Rose's point of view in journal entries? How would the story have changed if Rose's chapters were written in third person, past tense like Lily's and Antoinette's?

11. Antoinette has the ability to temporarily heal people, but that ability comes with a price. In addition, she can't heal herself. What role does Antoinette's healing ability play in the novel? Why do you think the healing is only temporary? Why do you think she can't heal herself?

12. At the end of the novel, Will makes a difficult choice. Why do you think he made that decision? Was it the right decision? What impact does his choice have on the novel? Was there another way he could have achieved the same outcome without such a sacrifice?